LETHBRIDGE-STEWART

BEAST OF FANG ROCK

Based on the BBC television serials by
Mervyn Haisman & Henry Lincoln

Andy Frankham-Allen
Based on a story by
Terrance Dicks

Foreword by Louise Jameson
Afterword by Ralph Watson

CANDY JAR BOOKS · CARDIFF
A Russell & Frankham-Allen Series
2015

I guess I've got everything I need
I wouldn't ask for more
And there's no one I'd rather be
– *Man of the World* by Fleetwood Mac

This book is dedicated to all those pioneers who gave their lives in building the lighthouses of the British Isles. Providing security and protection to so many others from the sheer, ferocious power of our planet. The lanterns stand as a testament to your bravery.

The Gift That Keeps on Giving

Well, isn't *Doctor Who* the gift that just keeps giving? I'm delighted and flattered to have been asked to write this foreword.

That said, *Horror of Fang Rock* was not one of my favourites. Forgive the Blasphemy. The working atmosphere was tricky. The dynamics between Paddy Russell (the first female director at the BBC), Tom Baker and I needed to be negotiated. We were forced to record at the Pebble Mill studios due to industrial action taking place in London, and the script had originally been written for a different companion. When it arrived, as I recall, it had several '*Leela screams*' stage directions before/during/after various lines, but Leela's only scream ever was in the previous story (*The Talons of Weng-Chiang*) when she was being eaten by a giant rat. So there were some (albeit small) changes to be debated with the text and attitude of Leela. We were originally scheduled to do an adventure about vampires (later filmed with Lalla Ward called *State of Decay*) but the BBC in their wisdom were also doing a production of *Dracula* with Louis Jourdan and Frank Finlay around the same time and thought one would detract from the other, so poor Graham Williams (our new producer delivering his first story) was forced to find another gripping tale in a hurry. Where's a TARDIS when you need one?

Horror of Fang Rock has always been a favourite with the fans however, and I think its atmospheric setting, dramatic location and obvious sci-fi elements create a very powerful audience experience. Part of the 'recipe' for a frightening yarn is to create something claustrophobic... and that feeling of climbing the stairs at night taps in to almost everyone's personal childhood terror. Add the fog, the fear of being 'jumped' and you're left with the stuff of nightmares.

I worked with some amazing actors during my time in *Doctor Who* and Colin Douglas as the lighthouse keeper (turning Rutan) was amongst the best. It's a beautifully placed performance, subtle and touching with daringly slow but perfect timing.

The story managed to kill just about everyone off – shocking, when the Doctor usually manages to save at least some of the inhabitants of the adventure he's in, but not at Fang Rock!

...and of course I got my blue eyes back in a scene especially added by Robert Holmes at Graham's request.

Tom and I returned from Birmingham better friends than when we arrived. There's something about going on location, with a company, that irons out the creases. You are thrown together in a way you aren't when commuting. And to this day, as we reprise our time travel regularly with Big Finish audio dramas, we remain extremely fond of each other.

You'll find no spoilers in this foreword, but the pages will keep turning for you I know. This book is hard to put down, and it's marvellous, and very touching, that so many people are still connected to the classic series in a way I could never have predicted, even though I had the privilege of travelling through time.

Enjoy!

Louise Jameson, October 2015

— PROLOGUE—

*J*ames *sits on the edge of the chopper's rear door, and nods.
'Perhaps I have more intel than you know. Such as the results
of blood tests that Henrietta carried out.'*

*'Which are doubtless supposed to convince me that we're
brothers,' Lethbridge-Stewart says, his tone making it clear what
he thinks of the idea.*

*'No, they're meant to convince me. In any case, you're the one
with incomplete memories; how can you be so sure of anything?'
James sighs, sits back, and stretches out his legs, turning the ankles
to undo the tensions and incipient cramps in them. 'The logical
thing for you to believe is that I'm simply a foreign agent
maintaining my cover identity, and/or that I'm still trying to
convince you, in the hope that there's still a concentration of SB-117
in your bloodstream. Which, incidentally, there undoubtedly is.'*

*'So I believe you and tell myself it's the drugs that make me that
way?'*

*'If it helps you feel better. Though I must also point out that, of
course, I have not been subject to Henrietta's chemical ministrations
– as far as I know, which is always a matter of faith – and so have
no such excuse.'*

*James stands and reaches into a compartment in the chopper.
He pulls out a rucksack, ration packs, water bottles, and a few other
bits and pieces of gear suitable for hours of hiking.*

1

'*My brother had an imaginary friend,*' Lethbridge-Stewart says suddenly, testing.

'*Maha,*' James says quietly. *Lethbridge-Stewart can feel the colour drain from his face. How can the man before him possibly know that? He is not James Gordon Lethbridge-Stewart. James, his brother, died over thirty years ago.*

'*How could you know that?*' Lethbridge-Stewart asks.

'*How do you think, Old Man? And why ask, otherwise?*'

Lethbridge-Stewart blinked away the memory. He was loath to admit it, but as he drove back from his wild goose chase in Llandudno, he knew he had been grasping at straws since Deepdene. He still wasn't sure what had happened to him, but it had thrown up many doubts in his mind. For reasons he didn't really want to think about, he knew he was throwing himself at whatever crossed his desk, anything that hinted at alien involvement. He needed something tangible, not confusion produced by the psychoactives that Henrietta Beswick had administered. His memory still felt like Swiss cheese; it seemed people were intent on playing with it. First the Great Intelligence when he was only a boy, not that he had known about that until a couple of months ago, and more recently agents of the Eastern Bloc.

His history was important; it was something drummed into him at an early age, by his grandparents, by his parents. History defined the man you became, in Lethbridge-Stewart's view, and the man he was today was a direct result of his proud lineage, of his experiences, his memories... Mess with those and what became of the man?

He shook his head, feeling his thoughts drifting once again. He needed something solid to deal with.

It had all started almost three weeks back when General

Hamilton told him to look into Ed Hill, one-time lead singer of Kathmandu. The investigation had led to the strange goings on at Hill's free concert in Wembley Stadium five days ago, his so-called come back. But despite questioning several people, it seemed Lethbridge-Stewart was too late. Someone had got there before him and cleaned up rather nicely; someone with more clout and resources than he. Which left him with only the story of the Grinning Man that had crossed his desk. He had to get the evidence he and Hamilton required, to prove to himself that he wasn't going mad.

He reached out and opened the glove box, and pulled out the Embassy packet Sally had left behind. He wasn't a smoker, but he had to admit he was sorely tempted right now. He removed one, pressed the lighter on the dashboard and hoped that the nicotine would relax him.

Sally swore by it. And he owed it to her to give her the benefit of the doubt. Especially after all that business with Marianne Kyle.

Lethbridge-Stewart is looking at Marianne Kyle across the desk of his – what used to be his – office at the Joint Warfare Establishment in Wiltshire. Her expression is carefully impassive, but he can sense the tension in her poise. James and the provost are outside, doubtless with hands on their weapons.

'You wanted to see me... Colonel?'

'I wanted to know... How long have we really known each other? If at all.'

'About four months,' she says at last.

'And how much of our... good terms, are real?'

'Where they don't conflict with my duty...? All of them.'

'Did you know there was… someone else, back home?'

'I knew your cover said so, but I also knew it was a fiction.'

'Except it's not a fiction. Not a cover.'

'Then who is she?'

'I've no idea.'

Silence, then Kyle speaks again. 'Sometimes, no matter what stage of… processing you'd been through, you'd talk in your sleep – I could play you recordings – sometimes you say a name: Sally.'

Sally… He recalls a woman in a corporal's uniform. Sally… Wright. His fiancée. He wonders if she is worried about his absence, or whether, if he has already been declared dead, she was all right at the memorial service. There must have been a memorial service, surely?

The alarm awoke him again at zero-six-hundred, after only a few hours' sleep. For a moment he remained in his bed, groggy and aching. He stared at the clock, watching the second-hand tick… tick… tick.

The same dream again. No, a memory… Or at least he thought it was. But how much could be relied on? That was the question he kept returning to. The doubt. How many of his experiences were real, how many hallucinations? When he returned from *wherever*, three weeks had passed, not the four months Kyle insisted on. There had been no memorial, no declaration of death, just a missing man. Hamilton still waited on his report, but Lethbridge-Stewart had yet to deliver it. He'd started many times over, of course, but each time he found himself doubting the words he wrote.

No, this wouldn't do at all.

He dragged himself out of his bed and into the bathroom. Once shaved, careful to clip his moustache precisely, and in full uniform, he stood by the window of his Pimlico flat on Buonaparte Mews, and looked out towards the Thames. He sipped his strong tea. Outside it was the Spring Bank Holiday weekend; most Londoners would be off work for the weekend, only a few shops open, and those mostly the corner shops run by old men with nothing better to do, and immigrants who helped to keep London fed and watered in times when those native to the country preferred to waste their days watching football and drinking in the streets. And still, despite the valuable service such people provided to cities like London, they were assaulted and verbally abused almost daily. Sometimes Lethbridge-Stewart despaired of people.

Ten minutes later he was in his little silver Mercedes 280SL Pagoda convertible, the roof up, driving casually through the quiet streets of London to Chelsea Bridge Road; a journey that took him just over five minutes. He probably could have walked, but that was twenty minutes he didn't want to wait for his next morning cuppa. Would that he could stay in bed like most of London, but while he was stationed at Chelsea Barracks he had duties to perform, to maintain his *official* position while he continued to work in secret on behalf of Hamilton and seek more evidence of alien threats...

Lethbridge-Stewart laughed bitterly.

It had been almost two months since he had agreed to Hamilton's conditions, and in all that time what evidence had he found? Wild goose chases, false leads, and whatever it was the Eastern Bloc had done to him.

He pulled into the officers' car park behind the Barracks, the shadows of the two ugly tower blocks that accommodated the Guards blocking out most of the sun, and forced himself to switch to official mode. He was Colonel Alistair Lethbridge-Stewart of the Scots Guards F Company; that was how the men at the Barracks knew him, and that was the image he had to maintain.

The truth was something else, of course, something else entirely. He only wished he knew what it was. One thing was for sure, to him at least, Alistair Lethbridge-Stewart was no longer the man he once believed himself to be.

— CHAPTER ONE —

Summons

Official duties performed, Lethbridge-Stewart returned to his office. He was due his new adjutant today – sent to him on the orders of Hamilton, to assist Lethbridge-Stewart in finding the evidence the general needed. Lethbridge-Stewart was not new to the idea of having an assistant; Corporal Bell had performed the role admirably during the clean-up after the London Event, but this would be the first time he'd had his own official adjutant. Perhaps he really was going up in the world, after all?

He had barely sat down and placed his cap on the table, when there was a knock at the door. He glanced at the clock on the wall just above his Sandhurst passing-out photograph. Bang on time. Lethbridge-Stewart called out 'Enter'.

The door opened and a familiar figure walked into the room. Tall, at just over six-foot, with brown hair which had once been ginger, evidenced by the copper-ish tint to his thick eyebrows, under which sat unusually blue eyes, wide and with more than a hint of perpetual humour in them. A couple of things had changed since Lethbridge-Stewart had last seen the young man in Bledoe. First there was his uniform, which showed a transfer had taken place. No longer a Green Jacket, but now one of the Royal Scots

Guards. Lethbridge-Stewart couldn't help but smile at this, still amazed after all these years at the clout Hamilton held. Second was his rank insignia. When last seen, he had born no insignia as was befitting a rifleman, but now he wore on his sleeve the single chevron of a lance corporal.

'Congratulations on your promotion, Lance Corporal Bishop.'

The man smiled and saluted. 'Thank you, sir. Reporting as ordered.'

Of course, usually such an adjutant would be a junior officer, or under special circumstances a SNCO like a sergeant, but Hamilton had pulled some strings and assigned Bishop to Lethbridge-Stewart, complete with promotion. Already Hamilton had set Bishop on the fast track at Sandhurst. Bishop would be a junior commissioned officer, and just the man Lethbridge-Stewart needed. In the meantime…

'I take it that General Hamilton fully briefed you on my assignment, and the role you play in that?'

Bishop nodded. 'Sir. He also expressed the importance of not discussing it with anybody outside this office.'

'Quite so. It is vitally important that we, ah, play this close to our chests. The safety of the United Kingdom rests on our shoulders, and I can assure you, it's quite a weight. Officially I am here to support Lieutenant Colonel Grierson in orchestrating the smooth running of the shop window for the country, unofficially, however…'

'Understood, sir.'

Lethbridge-Stewart invited Bishop to take a seat and outlined the current state of his assignment. Judging by the look on Bishop's face, it was less exciting than he had hoped.

The young man would soon learn their assignment was heavy on administrative duties, with very little actual action and much pouring over reports of potential alien activity. But that would change, given time. Lethbridge-Stewart still believed he was right despite the most recent goose chase. He had seen enough in London and Bledoe to be convinced. Besides which, there was the obvious cover-up at Wembley Stadium last Sunday; the latest suspicious instance in the past month. Several times now Hamilton had hinted to knowing more than he was in a position to let on about. For now. Sometimes it was a long game of patience that needed to be played.

Three weeks earlier a black cab pulled up outside no.18 St James' Gardens, and Anne Travers reflected on the way her life had jumped to such a different track in such a short time. Returning to England back in February had never been the plan. For the last five years she'd been travelling the world, learning everything she could – not only about new and revolutionary scientific principles, but also about other cultures and the way they saw the world. There was so much to learn out there, so much to see and experience, she loathed the idea of being tied to one place. Her thirst for knowledge couldn't abide stagnation. She had settled for a short time in America, becoming involved in a think-tank there, but she'd been dragged back by an important telegram from her father.

She couldn't deny that what she found in London had been extraordinary, and her research into everything the Great Intelligence had brought to Earth had pushed her knowledge into new areas of discovery. Just studying the nature of the web that had surrounded London opened up all kinds of possibilities about networking information without the need for wires and radio transmissions. Nonetheless, she wasn't keen that her job now meant her being mostly secluded in the secret Vault, which had been founded by the Ministry of Technology, all part of Harold Wilson's mandate of 'stimulating a major national effort to bring advanced technology and new processes into industry'. Somehow Anne doubted, though, that the goings-on in the Vault were what the MPs had in mind when they passed its formation in the House of Commons. Her role in such a place was certainly not what she had planned on when returning to the UK. Not to say that she didn't find the work at the Vault rewarding, but it was nice to go outside once in a while. Which is why upon receiving the summons to London from her family solicitors, she had jumped at the chance.

Of course such a visit was also the perfect chance for her to check up on her father. She had heard nothing from him since he'd left the Joint Warfare Establishment. And so, after a brief detour at Fugglestone to deliver her report to Hamilton first hand, she had gone straight on to London.

She climbed out of the black cab, after paying the driver. She looked up at the terraced house her father owned – inherited from his own father, Lyndon Travers, some thirty years previously. She smiled to herself. So many good memories in the house before her. And some not so good, she considered sadly, thinking momentarily of her deceased mother.

It seemed like her maternal family ties were haunting her what with the unexpected letter from the Goff family solicitors and their mystery summons to discuss her 'inheritance'. She still didn't know what had gone wrong, but her father and the Goffs had once been very close, until a huge falling out.

She lifted her overnight bag and climbed the steps to the front door. She'd discover the truth one day, but right now she had her father to deal with. She pulled out her key and opened the door.

She called out but there was no answer. She closed the door behind her and stood there, listening for any sound of her father tinkering around upstairs. There was nothing. She walked towards the living room, and paused at the sight of the writing on the wall. Literally. Somebody had written down a phone number just below the light switch.

Anne chewed her lip. That could only mean one thing. Her father was out of town and he was letting his old colleague, Professor Watkins, stay there. And Watkins had brought with him his teenage niece, who had a bad habit of writing notes on walls as you 'can't lose a wall'. Anne remembered many *discussions* with Isobel about that! They had fallen on deaf ears, clearly.

Anne quickly looked around the house, just in case her father was in and asleep somewhere, but all she found was more evidence of Izzy. Photography equipment stored untidily in Anne's old bedroom. Feeling a bubbling righteous anger, Anne turned and left the house, but not before leaving a note (on the jotter beside the phone!) for Professor Watkins asking him to call her when he returned and to let her know where her father was.

She always worried about him when he disappeared like this. *Went on his travels*, her mother used to call it. Travels or adventures – either way, they often ended in some kind of trouble.

It was the first time Anne had visited *Morecombe & Slant Solicitors,* on Mason Avenue, slap bang in the middle of the Square Mile, but the elderly Mr Slant treated her like an old friend. She had read too many books about law firms to treat this with anything other than suspicion. She sat in his spacious office, in an ornately carved chair before an ornately carved oak desk with leather finish. Wall to wall there were shelves containing, no doubt dusty, volumes of law and legalese, and, unless she was much mistaken, a very well-thumbed original edition of *The Road to Oz*. She smiled to herself. Mr Slant looked old enough to have been an old man when it was first published in 1909.

'You are familiar with the *Oz* books?' he asked, as he returned with a silver tea tray, loaded with china teapot and cups.

'My father used to read them to me when I was a little girl,' Anne said, thinking of getting out of her chair to help Mr Slant. But she changed her mind. There was something about him, an aura of dignity, which told her he'd be offended if she treated him like a frail old man. Even though he looked like one.

'Then you should have this.' He placed the tray on his desk, before removing the book in question from the shelf.

Anne found herself accepting the book, even though she told herself that she really couldn't accept such a gift. She was here on business, after all, not a social visit.

'I'll be mother,' Mr Slant said, and started pouring out the tea.

While he did so, Anne flicked through the book, careful not to damage it. She blinked. Surely not. She read the inscription once again. *To my dearest Margaret, may you ever find Oz in yourself. Frank.* Surely that was impossible. She looked up at Mr Slant. He smiled at her, raising a sugar cube.

'One lump or two, my dear?'

'One, please. Did you know my mother?'

'Dearest Margaret, born in 1894 to my old friend Matthew Goff? Of course I've been your family's solicitor for a *very* long time.'

Anne considered. If what he was saying was correct… then just how old was he? Surely much older than he looked. Which was ridiculous. There was no way he was that much older than her parents. Carefully Anne placed the book on the table and accepted the cup and saucer, unable to help but look at Mr Slant with some suspicion, and sympathy. The poor man was clearly losing his marbles.

'Now, to business.' Mr Slant opened a small drawer and removed a sealed envelope, while Anne carefully placed the book in her handbag. 'This has been in our possession since 1839, given to us by Archibald Goff with the express instructions that we hand it over to you on this exact date. The second day of May, in the year of our Lord nineteen-hundred and sixty-nine, I believe the instructions say.'

'To me? You mean to his descendent, surely?'

'One would think so,' Mr Slant said, and peered closely at the envelope. 'But it quite clearly says here, *For the attention of Doctor Anne Travers.* Here, see for yourself.'

Anne took the envelope and examined it. The words were just as Mr Slant had read, written in ink, although very clearly not with a modern biro. The envelope had yellowed with age. She sniffed it. Musty. Old. She turned it over and noticed that it had been sealed with wax, and stamped with a date. September 24th 1839.

'This is impossible,' Anne said. She laughed at herself. 'What a silly thing to say, of course it's impossible.'

Mr Slant raised an eyebrow. 'And yet, here you are.'

'Yes, here *we* are.' Anne was stumped for an explanation. She knew she had to open the envelope, see what was inside, but she held back her curiosity for the moment. 'I do not even know of Archibald Goff. An ancestor of mine, I imagine.'

'I believe he was your great-great-*great* grandfather, on your mother's side, of course. Died in... well, 1839, only three years after the birth of his first grandson.'

Anne did a quick mental count. 'That would be my great-grandfather, John Goff. Yes, I have heard of him.' She shook her head. 'Very well, I suspect you're almost as curious about this as I am, Mr Slant.'

'Rupert, please. And yes, almost. The letter within should explain the item.'

'Item? What item?'

'Oh, sorry, I forgot.' Mr Slant (*Rupert*, Anne reminded herself) laughed at his own forgetfulness. 'I do rather get caught up in the mystery. Much more interesting than the usual boring litigation one deals with.' He stood. 'Come with me.'

Anne followed with caution. This whole situation was becoming more and more dumbfounding.

She shouldn't have been surprised to discover the small

building had a cellar. Despite the obvious care taken over the keep of the offices above, it was very clearly an old and well-used building. Anne suspected that Rupert Slant was the one after whom the solicitors were named – not his father, or grandfather, but the original Slant. She knew she was being silly – after all *Morecombe & Slant* had been established in 1830 – yet something told her she was right. She couldn't place her fingers on it, precisely, but there was an air about the place, and especially Rupert, that reeked of real age.

She smiled to herself as she followed the old man deeper into the bowels of the building, blaming the last couple of months at the Vault for her somewhat blasé attitude to the whole situation. Her father would approve.

'Here we are,' Rupert said, and lit a candle as he led her into a dark room.

She looked around. It was how she imagined a bank vault would look – not that she'd actually been in any. Rows and rows of small lockers lined the three walls beyond the doorway. Rupert reached into his coat pocket with his free hand and pulled out an impossibly large ring of keys. Anne blinked.

He walked directly to a particular locker and opened it with a key. Anne stepped closer. An object, carefully wrapped, rested inside. Rupert looked sideways at her, and nodded.

She removed the mysterious item and turned to the small table in the centre of the room. Placing the item gently on the table, she removed the wrapping. Rupert raised the candle so they could both see the item clearly as it was, finally, revealed.

At first Anne wasn't quite sure what to make of it. It looked like an oblong block of metal, with odd crystal-like protuberances emerging at irregular angles.

'Touch it,' Rupert said.

Anne wasn't sure she wanted to. There was a daring tone to Rupert's voice, like an adult goading a child into doing something that was wrong. She shook off the feeling and gently reached out with her fingers. It was an odd tingling sensation, like a pulse was surging along her nervous system. She looked at Rupert enquiringly.

'We believe it's alive,' he said.

'Alive? But it's a manufactured... thing. Look at it.' Anne pointed at the joins around the edges. 'This has been built. But...' She shook her head, only too aware of how mad she sounded. 'This is unlike anything built on Earth.'

Now Rupert nodded. 'Yes. I believe Archie found it on a place called Fang Rock. I remember him saying that he believed it to be... *supernatural*.'

'He left another note?'

'Oh no. Those were his words. To me.' Rupert smiled at her, once again daring her.

Anne chose to not take the bait. Instead she picked up the sealed envelope, which she had placed on the table beside the alien box.

It was time to find out some truths. She had lived with her family secrets for long enough, it would be a nice change to have some answers finally. She opened the seal and removed the aged-paper from within. As she read it she was conscious of Rupert leaning in by her elbow, peering to get as good a look at the letter as his old eyes were afforded in the candle-light.

September 23rd, the year of our Lord 1839

My dearest Anne,

I'm sure you have many questions, but I'm afraid I will be long dead by the time you get this letter, and so you will have to find the answers yourself. No doubt you're wondering how it is possible that I know you will exist in one hundred and thirty years' time – again, this is something you will need to discover yourself. You must take this crystal machine and find a way to make it work once again. I believe it was damaged in the crash.

What crash you ask? Check your history books and look up Fang Rock. A fallen star landed in 1822, and brought with it something from the heavens. A supernatural being! I saw it, Anne, in 1823. People have already begun talking about it these last sixteen years, exaggerating the truth. They call it the Beast of Fang Rock.

Your help is needed to solve this mystery, Anne, my dear. Our future, my past, is in your hands. Take the crystal machine, keep it safe, and find a way to make it work again. A vital piece is missing… I somehow lost it, although I suspect I know who has it. I trust that he will find a way to get it to you. In fact, I know he will. Everything that has happened, will happen.

Your great-great-great grandfather, Archie.

Anne looked up from the letter, her hands trembling. Rupert let out an 'hmm', and caught her eye. 'Well, my dear, it would seem the few answers you have been given only lead to more questions. A mystery indeed.'

He wasn't wrong. A thousand questions were running through Anne's mind. Quietly she folded the letter and returned it to the envelope. She handed it to Rupert.

'I feel you should keep this. You have had it for so long

now, it belongs more to you than to me. But I will take this crystal machine with me.'

'And the missing piece?'

Anne shrugged. What could she say? 'I honestly have no idea. I don't even know what it is. But it seems Archibald Goff believes it will find its way to me...' She shook her head. 'This is all madness. Quite impossible.'

Rupert smiled softly. 'I find that often the most interesting parts of life have a little bit of madness in them.'

Anne reflected on that for a moment, and considered growing up with her father, and all the stories he'd told her. Yes, she decided, perhaps Rupert was right. Her life had rarely been dull, and she had seen more than her fair share of madness along the way.

CHAPTER TWO

The Legend of Fang Rock

Lethbridge-Stewart needed something to distract himself. His regular duties at the Barracks simply weren't enough. His mind kept returning to whatever it was the Eastern Bloc had done to him in Deepdene.

He still felt a strange disconnect deep down.

His office telephone was one of those modern 'trimphones' with its narrow body and thin, angular receiver that rested along the length of it. It rang just as he reached for it. 'Yes, Corporal?'

'Sir, I've got Owain on line one.' For a moment Lethbridge-Stewart was surprised at Bishop's casual use of the name, but then remembered that the corporal had met Owain in Bledoe. 'Says he needs your help, sir.' There was a hopeful tone in Bishop's voice.

'Very good, Corporal.' Lethbridge-Stewart pressed the button for line one, before Bishop got too excited at the prospect of some field work. It was good for the man to learn how tedious staff work could be at times.

'Hey, Uncle.'

Lethbridge-Stewart still didn't quite understand the link between him and Owain Vine, but they had agreed to leave it as an uncle-nephew kind of thing until it made more sense. If it ever would. As Lethbridge-Stewart understood it,

Owain had been, in a past life, the brother that Lethbridge-Stewart hadn't even known he had until a few months ago. There was a time when the notion of past lives, let alone aliens, would have made Lethbridge-Stewart laugh dismissively. More mumbo-jumbo for the new age crazies. But much had changed since February. 'Good to hear from you, Owain. How goes the travelling?'

'Still haven't left the UK, but me and Jennie are working on it. Actually, that's not really true. We've just returned from an island about eleven miles off the channel coast, so that's kind of like leaving the UK, right?'

'I suppose you could say that,' Lethbridge-Stewart said. This was a conversation for the Ordnance Survey rather than the British Army. 'What can I do for you?'

'I'm in Hove right now, but...' For a moment Owain went silent, and Lethbridge-Stewart could hear the background noise of people talking as they walked past the phone box Owain must have been standing in. Once the chatter had died down, he spoke again, his voice now low and secretive. 'Last night I saw a shooting star.'

Lethbridge-Stewart raised an eyebrow. He had a feeling he was about to be sent on another wild goose chase.

While Lethbridge-Stewart was busy pursuing the Grinning Man the night before, and Bishop returning from his first month at Sandhurst, Anne Travers was rubbing her eyes and wishing she worked in a better lit environment. The Vault, which is all anybody seemed to call it, was situated in a secret location in the Cheviot Hills, Northumberland. Run by a mysterious man called *the General*, it was permanently kept in a state of near darkness because, apparently, certain objects contained inside were sensitive to light. After a few months there, in which she had searched the storerooms several times, Anne still could not find the objects in question. She was beginning to think that the General just liked to keep his employers in the dark – literally. Most of those working in the Vault wore special night-vision glasses, but Anne had simply refused and argued her case until the General relented and allowed her some light in her private lab.

It wasn't much light, just a few low watt lamps, but it was enough for her to work with, as long as she didn't need to focus too hard, in which case the eye strain soon ended up in headaches. At least Sam Hawkins, the quartermaster of the storerooms, showed her sympathy and provided her with some pretty strong aspirin.

She had been busy the last few weeks, not only working on the crystal machine, but researching her family tree. An undertaking not made easy by the bad record keeping of the nineteenth century. She had contacted her brother, Alun, who had been able to help her a little and led her to various colleagues of his. From what she could work out there had been a lot of bad blood between the Goffs and Travers for a good hundred years or so before she was born. It was only the marriage of her parents that had healed the rift, and even then only so far. Nobody seemed to know the reason for the bad blood, although all indications were it began with a Vina Travers and Bethlem Hospital in the late 1820s. Alun promised he would keep digging for her. He was, after all, a history teacher at the Oxford College of Further Education, and he relished the idea of looking into his own family, something that had never really occurred to him before. That had made Anne smile – it was so typical of her brother. He was brilliant, but didn't have much by way of instinct or initiative.

She had more success with the crystal machine, although only marginally. She had managed to open it, with some effort, but what she found inside was even more alien than the crystalline protuberances outside. She did what tests she could; the Vault's powerful X-ray used synchrotron radiation, which sped up the tests somewhat, but unfortunately crystallography was not a major of hers, so she had to make a few cryptic calls to experts she had met over the years. As far as she could tell, the protuberances were a form of silica, and thus thermodynamically stable, however inside was what Anne could only describe as a circuit board of crystals – or, more accurately, polymorphic crystals, which seemed to be in a constant state of flux. At one point she had sat for a couple of hours watching the crystal circuit reform. She was told it was closer to allotropy than polymorphism. She had run every test she could think of, in an attempt to identify the structure of the crystals, and could only conclude that they were not from Earth. Or at least, not like any crystals yet discovered.

She had discussed her findings with Doctor Gautam Jhaveri, an old colleague from the think-tank in America. What he told her made her realise just how primitive Earth science sometimes was. 'It would seem to me, Annie, that whoever made this has a vast knowledge of what we would call crystal engineering. Also, a very advanced understanding of intermolecular interactions, in the context of crystal packing, and the utilisation of such understanding in the design of new solids, with desired physical and chemical properties.' What followed was a short discussion about the work she was currently involved in, at which point Anne had to end the call. She had probably said more than was safe already.

She was now strolling through the Vault, ostensibly to grab a strong cup of black coffee, but really to stretch her legs and think. She was considering the crystal machine. She knew it was engineered, which in itself suggested a purpose...

She stopped and looked around. She had been so caught up in her thoughts that she had accidentally taken a wrong turn and was now in the place known as 'the deep freeze'. It was really little more than a mortuary. She had once gone inside, morbidly curious to see what kind of people would be stored in a place like the Vault. She wished she hadn't.

Most of the names on the caskets she did not know, like *Sgt. Smith, M*, or *Krimpton, M*, or *D.I. Gascoigne, P*, but she soon came across names familiar to her. People she had, however briefly, known during the London Event. *Cpl. Lane, A* and *Cfm. Weams, S*... and, since March, *S/Sgt. Arnold, G*. She had sought to query this, incensed that the men were not laid to rest with honours as was meant to be the case. Somehow she doubted their families knew the bodies of their loved ones were stored here and not in the graveyards as they believed. But she was soon shamed into silence when it was made clear to her that her work with the Intelligence's web came at a price, and that price was the death of many soldiers in London who were covered in the substance and so stored at the Vault. To make it worse, the only way to remove the web from the bodies was to remove the skin to which it was attached. Ignorance was no excuse for her complicity in this.

She stepped back, once again feeling the weight of the Vault on her shoulders. Back in March she had been happy to join the Vault, to help with the research, with access to secrets hidden from most of the world, happy to uncover the secrets for her *real* employer. But since visiting *Morecombe & Slant* she found herself regretting her decision. The Vault was suffocating her.

Knowing about aliens was one thing; to be confronted, almost daily, with the detritus left behind by them was another. The deep freeze was the worst of it. There had to be some friendly aliens out there, surely. Aliens who wished to help, instead of invade and enslave.

She sipped her coffee in thought.

She looked up sharply, almost dropping her Styrofoam cup in shock at her own stupidity. The circuit board may have been unusual, but it did look somewhat familiar. The crystal sets she used to build as a little girl! That's what the crystal machine reminded her of! A crystal set – the most basic form of radio receiver invented. If she could build and adapt a crystal set to transmit and marry it to the crystal machine... Yes! Then perhaps she would get somewhere.

Renewed by the idea, Anne quickened her pace and went to search for Sam Hawkins. Hopefully there was something in the storerooms that would be of use to her.

For the first time since 1955, the craggy island off the coast of Hove was open for business. Against their better judgement, the custodians of Trinity House had been convinced of the good publicity of allowing the 'with it' students to throw a spring holiday party to celebrate the opening. What could possibly go wrong?

Stephen Worman expected disaster. He didn't feel safe on the rock, which was less than five thousand square feet across even at low water. More rock surrounded the largest part of the reef, but it was submerged, and it was because of this that the lighthouse loomed over the island, its only landmark, visible no matter where you were on the rock. The tower itself was rebuilt by 1961, the lamp automated to warn off any unwary mariners, but this was the first time it would be fully manned again. Automated or not, many accidents had occurred over the last eight years, and Trinity House had finally decided that occasional visits by repair crews to maintain the machinery and optics was simply not enough.

It was not without reason that Fang Rock became a 'lazaretto', a term Trinity House insisted he use in his introduction – a maritime word for a ship or island that was quarantined, although why they couldn't just say quarantine was beyond Steve!

He looked around at the student revellers, already drinking and smoking, as they stepped off the boats and made their way across the uneven rocks to the lighthouse. At midnight the stars of BBC TV's *Doctor Omega* were due to arrive, flown in by a helicopter which was to land on the helipad, the first of its kind to sit atop a lighthouse by all accounts. It was a silly publicity gimmick that would almost certainly be good for the BBC but, Steve was sure, would be less good for the reputation of Fang Rock itself.

The island had a reputation for being host to the most haunted lighthouse in the British Isles, a reputation earned after the strange events that occurred at the turn of the century, in which three light keepers and several civilians, including a lord and an MP, were found dead with little or no explanation. There were whispers of strange goings-on, of bright lights in the sky – even one mention of a shooting star. Such whispers, Steve believed, were the origin of all the ghost tales that haunted the isle, tales that didn't let up even after the lighthouse became automated in 1929. He didn't believe in ghosts, and Chris Finch, his producer, knew that, which was exactly why Finch had been so happy to give Steve this assignment.

Gimmicks stuck in his craw. What better way to re-open the most haunted lighthouse in the British Isles than have Doctor Omega himself arrive at midnight? It had been a couple of years since the height of what the BBC press had called 'Kleptonmania', when *Doctor Omega's* seminal monsters had become the most popular thing in the UK this side of The Beatles, and now the ratings of *Doctor Omega* were taking a dip. The BBC hoped this gimmick would raise the programme's profile and give it a much needed boost – although Steve was of the mind that perhaps it was time to change the star of the show and add some fresh blood. Not that Cyril Cusack would agree, of course. He'd played the part of Doctor Omega for three years now, and the kids loved him.

Steve sighed. He should have insisted Alastair Fergus be given the assignment – this was just the kind of nonsense he usually reported. He looked back at Jim Saunders, his cameraman.

'Come on then, Jim, let's set up.' He glanced up at the dark sky, littered with grey clouds. 'Seems to be a storm coming.'

Jim smiled and spoke around his cigarette, which he seemed to be chewing more than smoking. 'Perfect weather for ghosts.'

Steve shook his head. Ghosts! What a load of old tosh! The only problem he could forsee involved unruly students in the lamp room.

Sometime later, Steve was back outside. A few electric lights had been set up for the interview, with insulated cables running from inside the lighthouse. Steve stood as close to the tapering structure as possible, while Mark Powell, the attending official from Trinity House, stood with his back to the rocks, the English Channel churning behind him. All three men, including Jim, were well-protected against the increasing ferocity of the elements by yellow plastic rain macs worn over their usual heavy coats. For Jim the protection was more important, as he had on his shoulder one of those new Marconi VIII OB cameras, with a heavy backpack containing the electronics hidden beneath his mac. Usually a small crew would have accompanied Steve, but with Fang Rock having the reputation it had, Chris Finch thought it too much of a risk. He just hoped that between Jim, Steve and the new OB camera, they could get enough decent material to use for the programme. The sky was turning a dark shade of grey, and already the wind was biting.

'Fang Rock has a somewhat shady past, does it not, Mr Powell?' Steve asked. 'Going as far back as the 1820s, with reports of a beast that prowled the rocks. Indeed, is it not true that this Beast of Fang Rock killed two light keepers and left one mad in 1822? And in 1902 seven people died on this rock, six of them inside the lighthouse itself. According to all accounts, it is these lost souls who haunt the lighthouse. Given these facts, and taking into account the fire of 1955, which gutted the tower, one has to question the wisdom of opening the lighthouse once again.' Steve pressed the mic towards Powell.

The man from Trinity House looked at Steve with contempt in his eyes, but he nonetheless forced a smile as he answered.

'Well, for one thing, these *facts* are only supposition and hearsay. As you know, our clerical records were lost in 1940 when Trinity House in London was levelled during one of the worst air attacks of the war. Most of our archives were destroyed. We have, of course, worked hard to rebuild them, but we are reliant on a lot of *remembered* information, and memory is not always the most reliable source. As I'm sure you know, Mr Worman.' Mr Powell glanced up at the lamp room, but continued before Steve could think up a suitable riposte. 'As for the fire of '55, that was a real tragedy, and an accident. The light keepers barely escaped the fire, and had to spend the night alone on the rocks in the worst kind of weather. Things could have been a lot worse, as the heat inside the tower caused the fog signals to detonate, breaking the masonry of the tower itself. It could have been a *lot* worse,' he added again, his tone no doubt meant to make Steve feel guilty for his turn of phrase.

Steve ignored this and continued regardless. 'But the tales of ghosts are not the result of rumour. Every crew that has served Fang Rock since 1902 has told stories of the voices they have heard. Voices belonging to those seven people found dead in 1902, and not only them, but three other voices which still can't be identified. It is not without reason that Fang Rock is called "the most haunted lighthouse in the British Isles". Indeed, new facts have come to light regarding the events of 1902. Facts that strongly indicate that outgoing principal-assistant light keeper, Reuben Whormby, was responsible for all those deaths, before he killed himself in an act of remorse.'

'Really, Mr Worman? Is this the kind of journalism one can expect from *The Passing Parade*?' Mr Powell batted away the microphone. 'I was given to understand that this interview would discuss the history of the lighthouse, not the sensationalist reporting you are well-known for. Be assured, Mr Worman, Trinity House will be in contact with BBC 3, if you are the best they have to offer.'

Powell moved to leave but Steve blocked his way, keeping the mic between them. 'Many reports and accounts have been made, records of the voices heard in the last sixty-seven years, and they all indicate that Whormby, who was due for retirement, killed his fellow light keepers. Including Vince Hawkins, a young light keeper who was still in training, a man at the start of his career, because of greed. Diamonds brought to the isle by a Lord Palmerdale.'

'What rot! Please get out of my way. I have a call to make to the mainland to put an end to your nonsense.'

With a smile, Steve stepped aside and allowed Powell to make his way up the precarious path to the lighthouse. Satisfied, he turned back to Jim. His cameraman did not look best pleased.

'Do you believe any of that?' Jim asked, unplugging the mic from the camera.

'Of course not, lot of superstitious rubbish. But it seems

it's what the BBC want. The basis of this entire gimmick.' Steve turned away from the lighthouse and looked out at the English Channel. 'An old man driven by greed... More likely than some mythical beast that killed them all, wouldn't you say?'

Jim shrugged. 'I've travelled a lot, Steve, and I know what I know. People have done much worse for a lot less. But ghosts?' He shook his head. 'I ain't seen nothing that will convince me of ghosts.'

'Precisely. Superstitious nonsense. But it's what our employers want.' Steve patted his pocket to check he had his IE portable tape recorder on him. 'I'm going to head inside and talk to some of the kids in there, see if I can spook a few of them up. Get us some good copy.'

'Okay. I'll stay out here for a while longer, see if I can get some good pick-up shots of the tower.' Jim checked his wristwatch. 'Helicopter should be here in about an hour. Want to be ready for that.'

Meanwhile, back at the Vault, Anne smiled. With the help of Captain Hawkins, she had found just what she needed in one of the storerooms: a collection of damaged crystals contained in a box that someone had labelled *Krakatoa 1883*. She hadn't seen their like before, but a few quick tests showed they had similar properties to the circuitry of the crystal machine and, more importantly, shared some of the same elements as galena, the base component of cat's whisker detectors, which were used in the most basic of crystal sets.

She quickly fashioned a detector and connected it directly to the circuit board of the crystal machine.

She wasn't entirely sure what she expected to happen, but when it did she had to admit a little disappointment.

She scolded herself. She was forgetting her scientific detachment. It wasn't much, but it was something. And all great things started somewhere. So she smiled at the minor success. One step closer to whatever it was Archibald had been alluding to.

As she attached the detector to the crystal machine, her lab had filled with a steady hum and, beneath that, only just perceptible, a series of noises that sounded to her rather like a binary code. Short and long hisses. It could have easily been random, but she listened intently and was sure she could hear a pattern to the sounds.

She wondered what it could mean. Whatever it meant, it was a transmission. She smiled, feeling like she was finally making some progress.

On Fang Rock Jennie Rudge was also making progress. She was a great believer in ghosts – had been all her life. So when the opportunity came to spend a night at Fang Rock she'd jumped at it. Her mum thought her mad, but then she always did. The lamp room, although not out of bounds to them, was supervised, with the principal-assistant light keeper, Ivan Heggessey, stationed at the gate at the top of the steep steps.

Jennie smiled at him, and with a few muttered words of caution, the light keeper opened the small gate and allowed Jennie to enter the lamp room. She walked around the lamp, or the optic as the light keepers liked to call it, careful not to look directly into the light as it flashed every ten seconds. She always imagined the walk-space around the optic would be wider, but it would have been a squeeze to pass another while walking around. According to what she had read, the old lamp room, prior to the fire, had been a lot larger, and the lamp itself much smaller.

She looked out of the window at the gallery beyond. Entry onto the gallery was strictly prohibited, but she had to admit that's where she wanted to be. She knew the stories of Fang Rock well enough, knew that if you stood on the gallery long enough, facing east, you would hear the voice of Lord Palmerdale, his tortured screams as he was attacked and thrown over the gallery railings to meet his painful death on the rocks below.

She looked back. The light keeper was still standing there, but he was looking away, facing the ladder. Jennie turned to the small brass plaques screwed to the iron wall beneath the windows. There were four such plaques, each of them indicating which way you were facing on the compass. She walked around the lamp room until she was facing east. Beside her was the hatch that led to the gallery.

'I imagine it's lonely up here, eh?'

Jennie turned around at the voice, expecting to see the light keeper approaching her. But she was alone. Another voice responded, this one younger, his accent more befitting someone from Hampshire.

'You make do, sir.'

'I don't suppose the wage is very good, either.'

Jennie stood still, listening intently. The two voices continued, drawing closer to her.

'Oh, it could be worse,' said the younger voice. 'They keep you in steady work.'

'I daresay a bit of extra for the pot wouldn't go amiss,

though, eh? Fifty pounds, perhaps?'

Jennie smiled. She had read about this. It was Lord Palmerdale, trying to bribe the expectant light keeper, Vince Hawkins. A shiver passed through Jennie.

'It is important I get a message to London. You are familiar with the apparatus downstairs?'

Jennie mouthed the words along with Vince. 'It's the Trinity House telegraph, sir. Not for civilian use.'

'Fifty pounds is all I have about my person, but I can give you another fifty pounds when I return to London.'

Jennie closed her eyes, imagining Palmerdale showing Vince the money. She'd seen daguerreotypes of the two men, Palmerdale looking smug and all entitled with his stupid moustache, while Vince always looked to Jennie like a man who was just a little too trusting... but definitely cute with it.

'That's a... I don't want to be caught up in anything illegal.'

Jennie took a deep breath and opened her eyes. It was exactly as she had heard. With one last glance at the light keeper by the ladder, Jennie crouched down and opened the hatch.

'Illegal! Don't be so daft, Hawkins,' the voice of Lord Palmerdale said.

Outside it was cold. Jennie wrapped her arms around herself, wishing she had dressed a little more appropriately, and peered over the guardrail. Inside the lamp room it was hard to truly get a sense of height. Even though she knew the lighthouse was 132 feet high, looking out through the window with the English coast a vague shape in the distance, there was no tangible feeling of being high up. But now, standing on the narrow gallery with only the guardrail stopping her from toppling over, Jennie felt the height. Luckily any chance of her actually falling was curtailed by the scaffold-like cage that surrounded the gallery: the support struts for the helipad that now sat atop the lamp tower. She looked up. There was a ladder that led to the helipad, but she didn't want to risk climbing it in this wind. She was pushing her luck as it was.

'Gear!' she said, trying her best to hold back the smile on her cold lips, the light air almost taking the word from her.

She looked down, placing her hands firmly on the railing, and couldn't help but feel the urge to jump. Just at the thought of it, her heart was in her throat. She'd never do it, of course, but she knew she wanted to.

'...if the Beast has come back, well, we all know the legend. Two keepers dead, one driven mad by fear.'

Jennie looked around slowly and almost slipped in surprise. Through the window, inside the lamp room, she could see Vince Hawkins. The young man, looking not much older than Jennie, was dressed in a white polo-neck jumper and a thick woolly hat. He stood there with his arms folded, looking both perplexed and worried. He was talking to another man, a little taller than Vince, dressed in a grey frock coat, with a head of dark unruly curls.

'Reuben is out of his mind, Ben's dead. I'm the only one left.'

'That's superstitious rot,' the other man said, his voice deep.

'It's not! Look at Ben.'

'Eight of us, Vince, against one of it. When it attacks,

we'll be ready.'

Jennie frowned. She had read transcripts of many of the conversations overheard from the ghosts, and they were always the same. Replayed over and over again like an 8-track on repeat. But she had never read anything about nine people being in the lighthouse in 1902, or that an unknown something was attacking them. The transcripts made it clear what had happened, and it was a conclusion many people across England had drawn. Reuben had killed them.

So who was the man talking to Vince? Jennie had spent many hours, days, months even, researching the haunting of Fang Rock and she knew the faces of all seven people involved. But the man in the lamp room – he was new!

And just what was this 'it' the man referred to?

Movement dragged her eyes and mind back to the gallery. Beside her, looking much like his photograph, dressed as he was in his Edwardian dinner suit, stood Lord Henry Palmerdale, a somewhat unscrupulous financier from London at the turn of the century. Jennie had tried to look him up, but there was scant information on him. Had he lived, perhaps Palmerdale would have amounted to something, but he was cut off before his prime and, even then, he had a reputation for cheating his way into his money.

For a brief moment Jennie was eye to eye with Palmerdale and, despite his mode of dress, it was clear that before her was a man with something to hide. Palmerdale looked out across the English Channel, peering through the night, looking for… Jennie wasn't sure. Probably the fortune in London to which he had been trying to return before his yacht came afoul of Fang Rock. For many years it was believed to be Palmerdale who had killed the other six people; so much of the recorded ghostly conversations and arguments were concerned with his aggressive need to return to London, talk of bribes and blackmail. But more recent observations had revealed the truth about Reuben.

Jennie knew that ghosts were often considered malevolent, but she believed they were simply echoes of the past. Not lost souls tormented in their isolation. And so she stood there watching, keyed but not fearful.

Then it happened.

A strange green glow emanated from below the guardrail. Jennie looked over, careful to maintain her balance, and saw what looked to her like a large green jellyfish complete with tendrils that writhed around it. But it was no jellyfish, Jennie knew that. It was... alien somehow. Palmerdale was also glancing over the edge, his upper torso passing through the cage – it hadn't existed back in 1902, of course, there had been just a simple guardrail – but before he had time to consider what he was seeing, a tendril lashed out and wrapped itself around his neck.

Electricity arched all over Palmerdale's body and he let out a piercing scream. Jennie knew she'd never forget the sound. It was full of so much pain and horror. The sound of a man who knew his life was about to be painfully torn from him. Just like his body, which was violently torn from the gallery and flung over the railing.

Jennie couldn't watch any more. She knew she could do nothing, that Palmerdale had died almost seventy years ago, but nonetheless it seemed so real – like it was really happening now!

It was exactly *why* she had insisted to her friend that they take up the offer for a visit.

132 feet below, Jim repositioned his camera for a better shot of the lamp room, a task not made simple by the uneven craggy ground that made up Fang Rock.

He looked through the camera. "Ere, ain't that one of your lot up there?'

He was accompanied by one of the students, a teenager from Cornwall called Owain, who seemed more interested in walking about the rock than drinking with the rest of his lot inside the lighthouse. Even now they could just about hear the distant sounds of *The Dawntreader* coming from the lighthouse. Jim wasn't too sure if he liked Joni Mitchell's music or not, a fact he and Owain had been discussing before Jim spotted the figure outside the lamp room. Owain did; he especially liked *The Fiddle and the Drum* from her new LP, an anti-war song aimed at America and its war in Vietnam, and had recommended that Jim listen to it. Jim liked peace as much as the next person, but he was old enough to remember that sometimes you just had to say no, and that war was not always as avoidable as so many young people liked to believe.

Owain shielded his eyes from the wind and rain and looked up. 'Could be,' he said in his soft Cornish accent. Jim let him look through the camera. Owain laughed. 'Yeah, that's Jennie Rudge. Good chick, really great on the guitar. She's teaching me how to play. All the way here she's been going on about visiting the gallery, though. Looks like they let her in after all.' He wiped his long wet fringe out of his eyes.

Jim pointed at Owain's earring, the silver semaphore symbol used by the followers of the Campaign for Nuclear Disarmament. 'Ain't that cold out here?'

'Yeah, man, but you know that's how it goes when you're on a rocky isle in the English Channel, right? Which bit of you isn't cold? Stung a bit at first, but getting used to it.'

Jim laughed. He liked Owain; he seemed to have his head more screwed on than most of the students he'd been introduced to since arriving on Fang Rock. Mostly the event seemed to attract the hippies, with their bright glasses and clothes not even slightly suited to being on a rock like this one. Obviously Owain was as much one for peace and one-love as the rest of the beautiful people, but he at least had the good sense to dress in a manner suitable for a rock lighthouse. Owain handed Jim the blunt they had been sharing, but Jim shook his head. There was only so much of that he could stomach. Owain shrugged and returned it to his mouth.

'You believe in ghosts?' Jim asked.

Owain considered this, his eyes distant. 'Kind of, yeah. But not in the way some people do. I think ghosts are more echoes of people that once existed, than any kind of supernatural creatures. There's a scientific reason for them. You've heard of the stone tape theory?'

Jim had to admit he hadn't.

'It's the idea that emotional or traumatic events are stored in rock and can be played back in certain circumstances, which is why you get haunted houses... or *light*houses.' Owain smiled. 'Not my first haunted gig,' he said.

Jim pursed his lips. He wasn't convinced, but it was clear Owain was. Well, Jim had travelled enough to know that people usually had good reasons for what they believed, and it wasn't up to him to judge them on that.

He turned back to his camera.

He blinked.

'What the hell!' He pointed. 'Look!'

They both watched as a flash appeared in the dark sky. It was an odd reddish colour, and it stretched out, leaving behind it a red trail of light.

'A shooting star?' Jim wondered out loud.

'A red one?' Owain shook his head and looked through the camera lens. 'Can you zoom in?'

'I can, yeah.' Jim barely got a chance to before Owain stepped away from the camera with a huge grin on his face.

'That is no shooting star. Look,' he said, and Jim looked at it through his camera. He swallowed. There was a shape inside the light.

'It's a bleedin' UFO!' he exclaimed, and wondered at the strength of the blunt.

'Mint,' Owain said still smiling. 'Knew something like this would happen eventually. My uncle's going to dig it.'

'Your uncle?'

'Yeah.' Owain pointed at the light as it dropped closer to the English Channel. 'Keep filming,' he said, 'the colonel needs as much proof as he can get.'

Jim kept filming. Suddenly the assignment had got interesting.

— CHAPTER THREE —

No Coincidences

Normally the word of one civilian would never have been enough to rally Lethbridge-Stewart into action, but Owain was a special case. A meeting was immediately arranged with Hamilton, while Bishop was tasked with dredging up all information that could be gleaned about Fang Rock, which had, according to Owain, something of a strange history. Once again Lethbridge-Stewart got the feeling of grasping at straws, but he would rather trust Owain's word than another Mr Woodward.

Hamilton pulled in a few favours and Fang Rock was once again off-limits for all but essential personnel and Owain, who Lethbridge-Stewart had asked to remain at the lighthouse, along with the BBC 3 cameraman, one James Ratcliffe Saunders. Meanwhile a D-Notice 05, covering United Kingdom Security & Intelligence Special Services, was given to BBC 3. All those on the rock, including the keepers and the chap from Trinity House, had been held for a few hours while statements were taken; they were all released with a strong warning to keep their silence on what they'd seen. Hamilton had made calls to the Royal Navy, and HMS *Warspite* had been pulled from her usual duties and sent to comb the waters surrounding Fang Rock for any sign of the UFO.

After a long day in Fugglestone, Lethbridge-Stewart now sat back at his desk in Chelsea Barracks, itching to make his way to Fang Rock himself. While he awaited news on the air-lift he'd requested from the RAF, he occupied himself by looking over the witness statements he had brought back from Strategic Command.

The statements weren't especially helpful. It seemed to Lethbridge-Stewart that most of the students, a term used a little too freely in his view since it was clear that not all of them were actually in any form of education, had been inside at 23:23 hours when the light appeared in the sky. And those near the windows didn't take much notice of it, since they just thought it was a natural thing and they were more interested in the 'jam'. The only really useful statements came from the principal-assistant keeper, a Mr Ivan Heggessey, who had been up in the lamp room at the time, and Miss Jennifer Rudge, who had been outside on the gallery without permission.

The statements matched in all relevant ways, echoing what Owain and Saunders had said. Both Miss Rudge and Mr Heggessey had seen the light in the sky, Heggessey at first believing it to be a reflection of Fang Rock's own optic, and watched its descent into the waters barely a mile from the outer edge of East Crag. Both described the light as red, with a trail like a comet. Miss Rudge went on to explain that it had happened shortly after she witnessed the death of Lord Palmerdale. This had surprised Lethbridge-Stewart, as Owain had not told him about a murder, but then General Hamilton had explained that Palmerdale was one of the infamous seven who had died in 1902. This did nothing to assuage Lethbridge-Stewart's concern. He did not believe in ghosts – evidently Miss Rudge had been high on something else. He knew all about the current counterculture of young people and their interest in hallucinogenic drugs. Kids in his day knew better than to play around with such things, an attitude that made him sound like a 'fuddy-duddy' according to Sally, but he didn't care. He had no time for these flower children. And besides, after his own recent experiences with psychoactives, he knew of what he spoke.

Given the nonsense about ghosts, coupled with the fact that, as per Mr Heggessey's statement, Miss Rudge was not supposed to be out on the gallery, her statement wasn't the most reliable. Even if it did match up with Heggessey's, Saunders' and Owain's. Well, apart from the foolishness about seeing a dead man.

Lethbridge-Stewart sat back in his chair and put his hands over his eyes. Who was he to talk about the foolishness of seeing dead men? His mind cast itself back, unbidden, to Bledoe and the spectral form of his dead brother. True, that had turned out to be the Great Intelligence using the form of a dead child, but later, had Lethbridge-Stewart not seen James alive and well and in his thirties?

He shook his head and yawned. He was tired. Too tired to be thinking about the possibility of ghosts and dead men walking.

It was only twenty-hundred hours, a mere ten hours since Owain had called him, and already hundreds of man hours had been used up, costing thousands of pounds. He knew there had to be an easier way to do this, which is why, once again, he had stressed to Hamilton the need for a special unit dedicated to looking into such incidents. Eventually questions would be asked by those at Chelsea Barracks; Lethbridge-Stewart was not the only one there with connections at High Command. Both he and Hamilton could only field questions for so long before their unofficial activities would be brought to account.

His phone rang, interrupting his thoughts. It was an outside line. Very few had his direct number. 'Hello, Lethbridge-Stewart?'

'Alistair,' said a voice he recognised immediately. Sally, his fiancée. 'I'm just calling to check up to remind you about tomorrow.'

He placed his head in his free hand. Tomorrow... He had totally forgotten their plans for Bank Holiday Sunday. A picnic in Kensington Gardens, followed by a trip to the pictures to see *The Royal Hunt of the Sun*. He had, in fact, been looking forward to it – a chance to make up for what happened between him and Kyle, not that Sally knew of that, of course, but that was beside the point. He was, after all, an officer and, apparently, a gentleman. Honour was important, and he had to honour the relationship he had with his fiancée.

'Ah, well, about that...' He didn't like making excuses, but he owed her the truth. 'You see, something has come up, and I'm not entirely sure how free I'm going to be tomorrow. If at all.'

'Oh.' For a moment Sally was quiet. 'This is starting to become a regular thing, Alistair. It's not just you that has to set time apart, you know.'

'I am aware of that!' he snapped. 'But you need to understand, the work I am engaged in is vital to the safety of the United Kingdom. I'm afraid I can't be held responsible when personal plans have to change at the last…'

On the other end of the line Sally had started laughing. 'Don't flip your wig, Alistair, I was only teasing you. I know about your meeting with Hamilton today.'

Of course she did. Lethbridge-Stewart smiled ruefully and berated himself for allowing his guilt to put him on edge. Of course Sally would understand, it was part of the reason he dated somebody in the forces. Because they would understand the responsibility on his shoulders.

'There is always Monday,' Sally said, once Lethbridge-Stewart had apologised, blaming stress for his snippy response.

'I suppose there is. All depends on how things go at Fang Rock, of course, but whatever happens we will make it to the Serpentine at some point in the next week, I promise.'

'Good. I'm looking forward to it. As long as the weather holds up.'

They continued with a bit of small talk, before they agreed that Lethbridge-Stewart would call Sally as soon as he returned from Fang Rock – regardless of the outcome of his visit.

He replaced the receiver, feeling more relaxed now he had been able to hear his fiancée's voice. He had clearly been reading too much into things, putting off his time with her for no reason. The thing with Kyle was over, if it ever happened at all. He shook his head and made an effort to settle himself on the notion that he probably would never truly understand his recent experiences in Germany. Some things were simply beyond his ken, as his great grandfather used to say.

*

Anne was tired. The Vault had kept her busy all day, what with a new arrival, *another* dead body of interest. Anne was becoming sick of the way the General treated the dead.

The body in question had been a man called Ed Hill, once a member of the pop group Kathmandu, although looking at the size of him Anne found that hard to accept. He was killed the previous weekend at a concert in Wembley Stadium. She was told to examine his brain chemistry, although she felt sure the bullet wound in his forehead may have left quite a bit of damaged brain tissue, and was handed a small flower that looked a little like a white butterfly wing. 'What is this?' she had asked.

'The Miracle Flower,' she was told by Tim Gambrell, one of the research scientists. 'The most common name is Om-Tsor.'

Anne supposed she was meant to recognise the name, and Tim laughed at her ignorance.

'It is a powerful narcotic which can produce telekinetic abilities in the user and has been known to assist a very advanced level of astral projection. Unfortunately it does have some side effects,' Tim said, and pointed at the body of Ed Hill.

'He was shot,' Anne had pointed out.

'Twice, yes. Extreme prevention measures,' Tim had said, but wouldn't say any more on the subject.

For the rest of the day she and Tim worked together, running a multitude of tests on the flower. The results reminded her of a drug she had come into contact with the previous year in China, while working with noted pharmacologist Hong Ping Li. Tim once more refused to comment when she asked about that, except to say the flowers had first come from Tibet. For now the tests were simple enough, straightforward and harmless, but soon she knew they would need to test the effects of the Om-Tsor on living subjects. And she didn't like it. Not one bit. Developing new defensive weapons was one thing, and what she had signed on for, but weapons of the mind... No, she didn't like it at all.

At Chelsea Barracks Corporal William Bishop was giving his report to Lethbridge-Stewart. 'Finding something concrete has not been easy, sir,' he said. 'But I have uncovered some interesting facts about Fang Rock. Troubled isn't the word.'

Even as he spoke Bishop found himself wishing for something a bit more. Finally promoted to junior NCO and here he was chasing paper trails. When Major General Hamilton had approached him and told him he was being transferred, complete with promotion, Bishop couldn't have been more excited. But then Hamilton had explained the particulars of his transfer, and he had got even *more* excited than before. His experiences in Bledoe had opened up new possibilities for him. As much as he enjoyed his service with the Green Jackets, he'd been wanting something more. Another taste of the world in which aliens existed. Serving with Colonel Lethbridge-Stewart would provide that, or so Bishop had thought.

Paper trails, answering phones, more paper work. Not quite the alien-fighting he'd hoped for. Still, the colonel seemed sure the business at Fang Rock was a sign of alien activity. Bishop wasn't entirely sure he agreed, based on his research.

'The lighthouse at Fang Rock was originally designed by John Smeaton in 1789, initially based on his work with the Eddystone lighthouse, and it was first lit on March 18th, 1790. Some say that when Alan Stevenson designed his lighthouse at Skerryvore in 1837, he was heavily inspired by the work done by Smeaton at Fang Rock and...'

'Get to the interesting stuff, Corporal,' Lethbridge-Stewart said, obviously impatient to get on.

'Yes, sir,' Bishop said. He rifled through the papers in his hands. In his attempt to please, he realised he may have been a little bit too thorough. 'Tragedy and Fang Rock seems to go hand-in-hand, sir, with many minor incidents throughout its history, although most notable are the events of 1822 when it was said a beast of some kind prowled the crags of the rock...'

'A beast, really? Out in the middle of the English Channel. It's hardly Loch Ness, Corporal Bishop.'

'Quite so, sir,' Bishop said. 'However, whatever happened on the isle that night, it left two keepers dead and one driven quite mad. Unfortunately very little documented evidence exists; the records of the Fang Rock lighthouse were among the many that were lost in 1940. Even the names of the light keepers have been lost.'

'I see. And these names may be relevant to last night?'

'It's not impossible, sir. After all tragedy struck the rock again eighty years later in 1902. And at least one of the keepers is connected to us... in a manner of speaking.'

Lethbridge-Stewart raised an eyebrow and leaned forward, reaching for Bishop's notes. Bishop handed them over and indicated the relevant section. Lethbridge-Stewart nodded slowly.

'His grandfather?'

'No, sir. It took a lot of checking, birth records being what they were at the turn of the century, but it would appear that Ben Travers is the uncle of Professor Travers.'

Lethbridge-Stewart nodded and continued to read the notes. 'I don't suppose Travers was at Fang Rock last night?'

'Erm, no, sir. Why would he be?'

Lethbridge-Stewart brushed it aside. 'Doesn't matter. I'm sure he'll turn up eventually. But it would have tied things up neatly. So, other than the filial connection, what bearing do these tragic events have on last night?'

'Well, sir, it would seem that back in 1902 many people along the channel coast, in Hove and Brighton especially, witnessed a strange light in the direction of Fang Rock. Many called it a shooting star, sir, and at least a few accounts said the star appeared to be an off-red colour.'

Lethbridge-Stewart put the paper down on his desk. 'And your supposition is that Fang Rock has been visited by aliens more than once?'

Bishop shrugged. 'Wouldn't like to assume, sir. But the reports from 1902 and what happened last night... Coincidence?'

'Which you know I don't believe in. Pity there is nothing on record from... when did you say, 1832?'

'1822, sir.'

'Yes. Then.' For a moment Lethbridge-Stewart sat there. He raised an eyebrow and looked up. 'What do *you* think, Corporal?'

'I think, sir, given the obvious connection between last night and 1902, and the obvious need for at least one scientific mind… Perhaps Doctor Travers should join us on Fang Rock?'

'Us?'

There was something in Lethbridge-Stewart's tone that was daring Bishop, so the corporal nodded. Lethbridge-Stewart smiled and shook his head.

'Very well, Corporal. Good thinking. Miss Travers could do with a bit of field work, and her help has proven invaluable on more than one occasion.' He checked his wristwatch. 'We're due at RAF Odiham in a couple of hours. I'll put a call through to the Minister of Technology…'

'Sir?'

'As I understand it, only Mr Benn knows where this Vault is. He will give me Miss Travers' contact details, and if he refuses I will ask General Hamilton to apply some pressure. I'm sure the general holds a few secrets he can barter.'

Anne returned to her private lab, Tim having finally decided it was 'time to crash', as he put it. She was more than happy to leave him to it, since she too needed some sleep. She hadn't slept much the night before, the noise of the crystal machine keeping her awake into the early hours. It seemed to increase in power at about half eleven, before settling into a steady hum for the rest of the night. It was still humming as she entered the lab, but Anne was so tired that she found she didn't mind it too much now.

She turned to her bed, in the corner of her lab, and let out a sigh. Perhaps she should leave the lab for the night, go and sleep in her own flat a few miles away in Kilham. The rest and, albeit temporary, peace of mind would do her some good. She understood the importance of why she was at the Vault, and she was happy to do her duty, but sometimes she wished she could just walk away from it.

Just then the phone rang.

'Hello?'

She wasn't sure she was in the mood for any kind of phone call, but the voice on the other end had her smiling at the first hello. It was William Bishop, her favourite 'soldier hero'.

'How was your first day, Bill?' she asked. They had remained in contact since Bledoe, and she was aware of his promotion. She was also very aware of Colonel Lethbridge-Stewart's 'secret mission', although she could never tell Bill that. It wasn't just the military that had orders that bound them. She found Bill interesting, and was happy at the friendship they had developed since. She knew he didn't like 'Bill' as a diminutive, which only made her use it more.

'Slow, but it's proving interesting. In fact I'm calling you on behalf of the colonel.'

Anne sat on her bed. More work then. 'What is it? As long as I can sleep, Bill, then I...'

'I'm afraid it's bad news then, Anne,' he said, and she could tell he meant it. 'A car has been dispatched already, and will pick you up from the Vault in about thirty minutes. It will take you to RAF Boulmer, where a chopper will be waiting. We need you on Fang Rock within a couple of hours.'

'Listen, William, you can tell the colonel from me, that I have had a...' She stopped abruptly, Bill's words sinking in. 'Wait a minute. Did you say Fang Rock?'

'Not surprised you've heard of it. There was an incident

50

last night, and we're off to investigate. The colonel believes your expertise will be needed.' He paused. 'And so do I.'

Anne failed to spot the implication in Bill's words. Her attention was dragged back to the crystal machine, still sitting on the table, still humming away. 'I do so hate coincidences,' she muttered. 'Very well then. But tell the colonel I want to talk to him *before* we get to Fang Rock. Something very odd is going on here, and I think we all need to compare notes.'

Owain leaned against the wall of the lamp room and wiped his forehead. Jim laughed. 'Heavy bit of equipment, eh?'

'You could say that.' Owain had agreed to help Jim lug his camera and attendant equipment up to the lamp room after Jennie had told them about what she had seen the previous night. Owain didn't want to believe her, but he'd promised the colonel he'd get as much evidence as possible. Many people had transcribed Fang Rock's ghostly conversations over the years, but nobody had managed to record the voices. It was hoped that now that the ghosts had manifested once, they would do so again and Jim would be able to get it on camera. There was just one problem: the only place a manifestation had occurred was the lamp room. And so the lugging of equipment up almost 132 feet of stairs.

Ivan, the keeper, watched them set up. He was now acting-principal light keeper, and had been left behind to keep an eye on things. He took his responsibility very seriously.

He eyed Jim as the man set the camera up on its tripod, then turned to Owain. 'I've got work to do in the service room, so I'll leave you to it, but remember, no going out on the gallery without me.' His Hampshire accent added a rough edge to his tone. 'The weather could turn at any time, and you don't want to be out there on a stormy night. Damn girl was lucky last night,' he added.

Owain nodded, but couldn't help himself. 'Tell it like it is, Ivan,' he said, before the man descended the ladder.

Jim watched him go. 'Maybe you shouldn't wind him up. We're here on sufferance.'

'More like we're here because my uncle has the authority. We're ghost hunters,' Owain added with a grin. 'It's all copasetic.'

Jim frowned. 'It's all what?'

'Sorry, been caught up in all this hippie stuff in the past couple of months. Starting to talk like them, I think.' Owain laughed. 'You wouldn't believe I came from a small village, would you, way I talk these days.'

'How did you end up in London?'

Owain's answer was drowned by a deep whistle. They looked around the lamp room. Nothing had changed. The whistle came again, followed by the sound of footsteps. Owain spotted it first. The speaking tube, which hung near the stairs. A ghostly hand reached out for it.

'Ahoy there,' said an older man's voice, the Southern accent so thick that the words seemed to rumble out.

'Far out,' Owain said, and indicated for Jim to start filming. The man aimed his camera at the speaking tube.

'Tell her to use the bunk room below the oil room.'

The sound of footsteps on the floor echoed towards him. Owain stepped back. Despite his rational explanation for ghosts, he swallowed, feeling his pulse race. A man was beginning to manifest before him. Old, white hair, somewhat large in stature. From what Jennie had told him, Owain guessed it to be Reuben, the man responsible for all the deaths in '02.

'Problem with the toffs,' he said, 'always want more.'

'Are you getting this?' Owain asked in a whisper. Jim just raised his thumb, his eyes never leaving the image on his camera.

'Reuben,' said another, much younger, voice.

'What?'

'There's someone on the rocks.' The second voice took form. It was the man Jennie had seen last night, the expectant (or trainee) keeper. He unfolded his arms, and pointed out of the lamp room to a point on the rocks below. 'Lights, you see?'

'No doubt it's…' Reuben's voice cut out, although his lips continued to move. Vince responded, but again no words came out.

The two men didn't look especially close, but it was clear Vince respected Reuben, probably looked up to the old man and his years of experience with lighthouses. Owain shuddered. Respect that came to naught, if history was right.

'…can't say as I didn't tell 'em.' Reuben's words came through again.

'Told them?'

Reuben looked away from the window, his old face crumpled into a deep frown. 'About the Beast, boy.'

Vince almost laughed. 'Old keepers' tale!'

'It's not a tale, boy,' Reuben said, turning back to Vince. Owain felt a shiver go down his back. Reuben was deadly serious. 'The girl saw it. Heard her talking to her friend. Glowing green, she said, just like the legend says.'

Owain looked out of the window for any sign of the lights they were talking about. But there was nothing. Just the dark rocks below, with the water foaming over them.

'How can she see what's not real?' Vince said, clearly more to convince himself than anything else.

'Eighty year since the Beast was last seen, and then two men died.'

Vince shook his head. 'That be an old wife's tale. Ain't no one died on Fang Rock. Not from a beast, anyhow, and that's for…'

The two men dispersed, fading like a bad dream. For a moment Owain and Jim remained as they were, but then Jim straightened up and moved from the camera. He walked over to the spot previously occupied by Reuben and Vince. He looked around, his face a mixture of shock and excitement.

'Well, I've seen it all now. Ghosts. Blimey!'

Owain wasn't sure what to think. His experiences with the spectral form of Gordon had not prepared him for this. Gordon hadn't been a ghost, just a form taken by the Great Intelligence. A copy of someone it once killed. But these… They were actual ghosts! He could see through them, probably walk through them too, and their voices were not quite real, more like an echo he had heard from a distance.

'The colonel is going to…'

A scream echoed from the service room below, cutting Owain off. He went to move forward but was stopped by Jim's hand on his arm.

'That wasn't Ivan,' he said.

Jim was right. The scream had been female.

'Then who…?' Owain crossed the lamp room, Jim hot

on his heels. They were barely past the obtrusive camera when a woman appeared, climbing up the steep ladder, glancing behind her frantically.

For a moment Owain expected it to be Jennie, that she'd somehow hid away and stayed behind. But it wasn't Jennie. Her hair was too short for one thing, darker too. And her clothes… They were more expensive looking, a nice orange top over a short but respectable skirt.

The woman didn't stop when she reached the lamp room. She kept on, passing right through them. They turned as one.

'Charlie!' the woman called. 'It's coming!'

'Jim, the camera, we need to get this on film!'

But Jim wasn't fast enough. Before he had a chance to turn the camera around, the woman faded just like Reuben and Vince had. For a moment Owain and Jim stood there. Owain felt a shiver pass through him. So much for rationality.

'Who was she?' Jim asked.

'I don't know, but… did you notice the way she was dressed?'

'Yeah, all modern.'

Owain walked across the lamp room, and turned on the spot where the woman had, only a moment ago, stood. 'I'm sure I've seen her before.' He looked back at Jim. 'But I can't quite…'

'Somebody here last night?'

Owain shook his head. 'I don't think anybody died here last night, did they?'

Jim shrugged. 'If they did, someone would have noticed.'

'Yeah. But somehow she looked familiar.'

— CHAPTER FOUR —

Strange Visitors

Anne wasn't sure she'd ever get used to flying by helicopter. This was her second consecutive flight now, and she couldn't wait to get her feet back on solid ground. She had been flown to RAF Odiham, where Colonel Lethbridge-Stewart and Bill were waiting for her. She barely had a chance to say hello before Lethbridge-Stewart bundled her into a waiting helicopter. Now they were flying through the night sky over Headley, on course for the south coast.

Bill sat opposite them in the hold of the Whirlwind HAR10, while she and Lethbridge-Stewart sat next to each other so they could talk shop before they arrived on Fang Rock. Both men were dressed in fatigues, their tartan-banded dark blue glengarries tucked beneath the epaulettes of their green combat jackets, while all she had to protect her against the weather when they landed was a parka. But for now her main concern was the noise inside the helicopter. Flying from Boulmer to Odiham it hadn't been a problem, since the pilot had not engaged in much conversation, but now she and Lethbridge-Stewart had much to discuss, and both had to talk in raised voices to be heard about the noise – even with the aid of the radio headsets they all wore.

She explained about Archibald Goff and everything she had learned from Rupert Slant. When she came to the letter and the crystal machine, which sat behind them protected in a canvas holdall, she could see the colonel's puzzlement.

'How can your great-great-great grandfather know about you?'

'That's just one of the mysteries, I'm afraid.' She went on to tell him about her experiments with the crystal machine. 'Other than a humming sound, nothing has happened, and it's been active since late last night.'

'Last night, you say? When?'

'About eleven. Why, is it important?'

'It may well be. That was shortly before the UFO was spotted over Fang Rock.'

Anne let that sink in. 'A response to whatever the machine transmitted?'

'It would seem reasonable.'

Anne agreed. Only... 'What's so special about Fang Rock? It's a long way from Northumberland, so why would the you-fo appear here?'

'All good questions, Miss Travers.'

'We have a few too many for my liking. But what connects all these things together?'

'Your family, it would seem.'

'Well, yes, Archibald, me... But I still don't understand how.'

'And your great uncle.'

'My...? Which one? My mother had two uncles, both died a long time ago.'

'Your father's uncle, I believe. Ben Travers.'

It was another name she had never heard before. Like

Archibald. When this was all over, Anne determined she would join her brother in looking up their family tree. There seemed to be a lot of relatives, on both sides, whom she had never even heard of before. 'What does he have to do with this?' she asked, acting as if he was familiar to her.

'He was a principal light keeper when he died in 1902. On Fang Rock.'

For a moment Anne sat in silence, just the noise of the helicopter rattling around her. The colonel was right. It all seemed to go back to her family, to people she had never even heard of until a few weeks ago. Her family and Fang Rock.

'What do you know, Colonel?'

She listened as Lethbridge-Stewart explained all he had learned about the events of 1902, as told to him by Bill. The information was pretty scarce, but it was enough.

'Why has nobody ever told me about this before?' she asked rather lamely when Lethbridge-Stewart had finished. He shook his head. He had no answer for her. 'Ever had the feeling you're being manipulated?' Anne asked.

'In my job, Miss Travers, quite often. But this is new. For whatever reason, your family are very connected to Fang Rock and the tragedy that has happened there over the years.' Lethbridge-Stewart shouted over at Bill, 'Corporal, in your research did you come across a Travers on Fang Rock in '55?'

'Or a Goff,' Anne added for good measure.

Bill shook his head. 'No, sir.'

'Why '55?' Anne asked, once Lethbridge-Stewart turned back to her. He explained about the fire. 'Well, at least that's one tragedy not involving my family.'

'Quite, which leaves us with a mystery, Miss Travers. A mystery that connects your family to Fang Rock, and one that an ancestor of yours is sure you can solve. An ancestor who died over a hundred years before you were born and yet, somehow, knew exactly who you were and how to contact you. The same ancestor who left you a piece of alien technology just before a UFO was seen over Fang Rock.'

Anne smiled grimly. 'Believe me, I don't like how all this is connected, not that I know how it is.'

'I should think that crystal machine of yours is connected to the UFO. The odds of it not being so...' Lethbridge-Stewart let that hang in the air for a while.

Anne waited for the colonel to continue, but it was clear he was lost in thought. 'Another thing that puzzles me,' she said eventually, 'is that Rupert Slant never said anything about Archibald being a keeper, so what was he doing on Fang Rock in the first place?'

The answer lay in 1823. Archibald Goff had been warned off the east crag of Fang Rock – it had claimed the lives of many, not least several of the men who built the lighthouse. He guided his little boat due south, as far from the east crag as possible. The weather was taking a turn for the worse, and the water around them was rocking the boat more and more violently. Despite this, or perhaps because of it – Archibald knew very little about the nature of water currents, but he imagined the undertow by the reef would do more than darken one's daylights – the boat reached a relatively smooth edge of Fang Rock. He berthed the boat as best he could and helped his companion out. The reef beneath them was wet, and they had to move carefully in case they slipped and ended up in the English Channel.

He gathered his greatcoat about him, lowering his hat against the hard wind, and looked up towards the lighthouse. The light flashed at regular ten second intervals, casting a red glow due east to warn mariners of the extra danger presented by the rocks beneath the water. It stood like a bastion of hope, a safe haven in the storm. Archibald glanced back at his companion, who was looking around him in fear. He wasn't as barmy on the crumpet as when Archibald had first come across him, but there was still a hint of crazed thoughts behind his eyes.

'Make haste, Jacob, old fellow,' Archibald said, and set off across the rocks.

Jacob held his ground, shaking his head slightly.

This wouldn't do at all. The man was still at sixes and sevens, just as Archibald had expected. But Jacob had assured him he could hold it together. Well, never mind.

'Perhaps the chaps inside will be of a mind to have stocked some strong port, get you foxed,' Archibald said loudly for Jacob's benefit, then muttered to himself, 'Who needs a sound mind when one's mind is as broken as yours? Perhaps I ought to have left you at St George's Fields.' He shook his head. No, he needed Jacob here with him. Without Jacob there would be no...

'Ahoy there!' called out a new voice. Archibald turned to see a light apparently floating its way towards them. Soon two figures could be seen, one holding the lantern aloft, the second, a much younger man, with rope hanging over his shoulders.

'Ahoy there!' Archibald called back, waving a hand. He waited until the two light keepers were near enough, then asked, 'Where are we? Our vessel came aground some miles out.' He looked around, feigning surprise. 'Lucky to happen upon this rock.'

'Luckier than you know with slack water like this,' the older man said, indicating the water lashing against the rocks. 'Mean high water is at its worst this time of the night. Not much of Fang Rock to see.'

Archibald knew this, which is why he had chosen this time to visit the rock. Nobody else would be visiting and he could carry out his work without concern of being interrupted unnecessarily. As long as the light keepers believed his fabricated tale. He looked around. It was true, the tide was high and most of Fang Rock was covered in water. But enough to explore under the cover of darkness. First, though, he needed to get the light keepers on side.

'God steers the faithful,' he said, and fingered the crucifix around his neck, intentionally worn outside of his shirt for that very purpose. Light keepers, much like sailors, were ever a superstitious bunch in his experience. For his own part he liked to consider things a little more rationally.

'You are the only survivors?' asked the younger keeper.

'As far as we know.' Archibald nodded towards the lighthouse. 'Perhaps others will be guided here yet.'

'Perhaps,' the old keeper agreed, although much doubt clouded his tone. 'Follow me, but tread carefully.'

They followed the man, Jacob first, with Archibald and the young light keeper taking up the rear. 'I'm Charlie Crane,' the young man said, 'assistant light keeper. That buffer is Edgar Wishart, principal-assistant keeper. Don't mind him, he don't much care for visitors is all. But he'll do his duty.'

'We owe a debt to you both. I was of a mind that there was no light out here. I figured Casquets were our only hope. But it lifts the heart that you were closer.'

Crane smiled grimly. 'Yes, sir, that we are.'

They continued the rest of the way in silence. As they walked, Archibald took in his surroundings. He could see what remained of the iron track that had been laid prior to the building of the lighthouse – used to move the granite blocks from the boats during construction. He'd never seen a lighthouse being built, but looking up at the 132-foot structure before him, he imagined it must have been a very hazardous job. Just the men against the elements, with nothing but their wits to protect them. Was it any wonder such men were often so religious? When faced with the ferocity of a storm, what else could one put his faith in other than one's fellow man and God. He had heard many stories of the lives lost during construction – accidents could happen so easily when out at sea. Just looking at the waves crashing against the reef, he didn't doubt the ease of such accidents for a second. He would have to be mindful of himself during his search.

They were soon four storeys up, safely ensconced in what Archibald initially took to be the crew room, before he was told by young Mr Crane that it was, in fact, the library, where the keepers tended to spend most of their banyan time. They had passed through the water and coal room, before climbing the narrow curved staircase, in single file, past the provisions store and the kitchen before coming to the library. Due to the conical shape of the lighthouse, with each floor the space became tighter, the steps narrower.

Several times Archibald had almost bumped his head on the ceiling before rising onto the following floor. He didn't suppose he would ever get used to being in a lighthouse, and wondered how the fellows managed.

The library was a circle of a room. There was but one window, beneath which sat a handsome oak table. A marble bust of John Smeaton, the engineer who designed Fang Rock lighthouse, hung over the window. The room was fitted with an elegant Turkish carpet and oak chairs. There was also a bookcase, full of technical manuals and various reading materials, no doubt to keep the light keepers entertained on their long weeks of service with only two others to keep them company, and one cupboard. Archibald asked the nature of the cupboard, and Crane explained that the iron chimney from the kitchen ran through the library, safely inside the cupboard, which helped to warm the library up a little. A little was right. If it wasn't for the fact that his greatcoat was soaked through, Archibald would have kept it on. His tails and waistcoat simply didn't provide enough warmth, the coldness outside seeped through the granite walls.

Jacob took his place on one of the oak chairs and rested his head in his hands. Wishart and Crane looked at him, the older man frowning. Archibald stepped forward. It wouldn't do for Wishart to look too closely.

'I say, do either of you chaps have some port, or fizz? I fear Jacob's nerves have taken quite a knock, and he could do with a bit of bolstering.'

Wishart didn't seem convinced. 'We only have beer here, and not much of it at that. Charlie, go and fetch some for this man.'

Crane dashed out of the library and set off down the steep steps to the kitchen below, leaving behind him a room full of tension. Archibald was usually quicker than this, a sharp response never far from his tongue, but he felt himself withering under Wishart's gaze.

'Where were you heading anyhow?' the light keeper asked.

'Back to Hove,' Archibald quickly supplied. 'I'm a little plump in the pocket and chartered a ship to and from Deauville. Jacob here likes to…'

'Money is no help to you here,' Wishart cut in. A bell rang out, and whatever else Wishart wanted to say was dismissed quickly. 'You'll be safe here this night. We have a bunk room for visitors. Ask Charlie and he'll fix you up. Especially this one,' he added nodding at Jacob. 'It's my watch now.'

With that, Wishart left the library and ascended the steps outside. Once he was safely out of the way, Archibald closed the door of the library and turned to Jacob.

'Pull yourself together, man, now is not the time to be off your onion.'

Jacob looked up. His eyes were haunted by a pain Archibald knew he would never express. But damn him, he wasn't about to go soft now! Archibald needed him. They hadn't risked the English Channel just for Jacob to get a case of the devil's blues.

'Tonight we can get to the bottom of this, find out the truth. We have talked about this, Jacob. It's what you wanted as much as I,' Archibald reminded him. 'Remember your promise to Vina. She is waiting for you.'

Jacob still did not speak.

64

The door opened again and Crane re-entered, carrying two metal mugs of beer. Archibald gratefully accepted one, but Jacob refused. Crane didn't look like he knew what to do with the other, so he brought the mug to his lips. Judging by the look on his face, young Crane had never supped on beer before.

'Wishart said something about a bunk room,' Archibald said, hoping to get Jacob out of sight before the principal keeper returned from the first watch – the one-hour shift during which the lamp was lit for the night. Of course, the man could simply go to his own bunk for a banyan, but Archibald knew it was too early in the investigation to leave things to chance. 'If you could show my companion here to…'

'I will have some answers first,' said a new voice from the doorway.

Archibald turned, and the mug stopped at his lips. Standing in the doorway was a rather short, slightly rotund man with thinning hair and thick grey mutton chops. He was looking at Jacob with recognition in his eyes, eyes which turned a steely, accusatory stare on Archibald. 'What sort of josser would bring him back here?' he demanded.

Let it never be said that Archibald Goff was one to hide when he had been rumbled. He held out a hand towards the principal light keeper, a man of some repute even to Archibald. Alfred Scott, the youngest person to ever work on lighthouse construction, at the age of fourteen years. A long time ago, of course, as the man was now forty-seven years of age, and not one for a Banbury tale. The truth was, therefore, the only way to appease him.

Archibald introduced himself. 'I am here to solve your

mystery for you, to capture the Beast!'

Scott looked down at the proffered hand and ignored it. 'Is that so? The spirits of many a dead man walk these shores, Mr Goff, and they are not to be disturbed. If you need any further proof of that, then consider the fate of Davy Williams.'

He was talking about the light keeper who had died the year before, when it was said the Beast first prowled the rock. It killed him and left another man completely off his chump, while the third light keeper had been ashore at the signal house in Hove.

Scott, the fortunate third keeper, brushed past Archibald and approached the man who had survived the Beast's nocturnal call. Jacob looked up at Scott. It was a reunion Archibald had hoped to prevent, at least until he had begun his search. It was the one problem in his plan; he'd known it as soon as he learned that Alfred Scott had returned to Fang Rock for his six weeks at the lighthouse. But by then it had been too late. The ship had been chartered, and the most useful weather conditions forecasted. The kind of weather that would keep most on dry land.

'Travers, old chap, you should be safe at Bethlem; why the devil would you return here?' Scott asked.

Jacob Travers looked away, his eyes resting on the window. 'The Beast is out there, and it calls for me,' he said, the fear in his voice palpable. Archibald swallowed, dousing his own fear with the force of his will. He had spent months in Jacob's company, and still he got the willies whenever Jacob talked of the Beast. He looked over at young Mr Crane – the assistant keeper had turned a new shade of pale, realisation dawning. He crossed himself.

'Calls for you? Dash it, Travers,' Alfred Scott said, obviously trying his best to keep his tone one of incredulity, 'why would it call to you?'

'It wants me back.'

The Whirlwind HAR10 came to a gentle land on the helipad atop the lighthouse. Lethbridge-Stewart looked at Miss Travers, who was a little green around the edges. All things considered the flight had been smooth, bearing in mind the choppy weather they had hit once they began to cross the channel. It was still raining buckets outside, and even over the noise of the helicopter they could hear the wind howling.

'Soon be on firm ground,' he shouted. 'Don't worry, though, the HAR10 is used for search and rescue. It's built to withstand worse storms than this.'

'Thank you,' Anne shouted back tersely, her nerves getting the better of her. 'It's not the first Whirlwind I've been in, Colonel,' she added, with a forced smile.

Lethbridge-Stewart nodded sharply at Bishop. The corporal gave him the thumbs-up. He removed his headset, manoeuvred the khaki hold-all over his shoulders, and slid open the hold door. Bishop reached out a hand for Miss Travers. She pulled up her parka hood.

Lethbridge-Stewart waited as they made their descent down the narrow ladder to the lamp room gallery, where a tall man with ginger hair waited for them. Lethbridge-Stewart picked up the holdall containing the alien machine.

With the added weight of the bag, it took Lethbridge-Stewart a moment or two to steady himself on the helipad. He gave the thumbs-up to Flight Lieutenant Nolan and his co-pilot, who returned the signal. Lethbridge-Stewart followed in the direction he'd seen Bishop go and found the ladder. As he descended, he looked up and watched the chopper take off, the down draught only making his climb more treacherous. He glanced down, careful with his footing. 132 feet below him the rocks looked like pebbles.

The keeper closed the hatch behind him, and Lethbridge-Stewart straightened up, soaked through. 'Welcome to Fang Rock, Colonel. Ivan Heggessey, currently acting-principal light keeper.' Mr Heggessey offered a friendly hand, which Lethbridge-Stewart shook. Bishop and Miss Travers were shaking themselves dry, Miss Travers having already removed her parka.

Lethbridge-Stewart introduced himself. 'And these are my... staff, I suppose you could say,' he said, his voice hoarse from all the shouting on the chopper. 'Lance Corporal Bishop and Doctor Anne Travers.'

Heggessey looked Miss Travers up and down. She immediately realised why, and held her hand out. 'Ben Travers was my great uncle,' she explained, her voice equally rough. 'I'm the colonel's science advisor.'

Mr Heggessey smiled warmly. 'A pleasure to meet you, Doctor.' He looked back at Lethbridge-Stewart. 'Warm blankets on the way, Colonel. Oh, and I have this for you.' He handed Lethbridge-Stewart a telegram.

Lethbridge-Stewart read it twice. 'How can that be?'

'What is it?' Miss Travers asked.

'It's a message from HMS *Warspite*. They did a thorough search of the surrounding area and found nothing unusual. There's no UFO, crashed or otherwise, in the vicinity of Fang Rock.'

'But we saw it,' Heggessey said. 'Or at least, I saw it fall. But Saunders filmed it. We've connected the camera up to the TV in the crew room... We'll show you.'

'I'm not doubting you, Mr Heggessey. Nonetheless, the UFO is not in the English Channel now.'

'Then where did it go?'

Lethbridge-Stewart looked at Miss Travers. 'One more question to add to the list.'

'Or perhaps not,' she said, straightening the collar of her orange top, which had become dishevelled in the climb. 'The letter from Archibald mentioned a fallen star in 1822... And didn't you say that one was spotted in 1902? Perhaps it's the same star?'

'A time travelling star?' Lethbridge-Stewart asked with some amusement.

'Colonel, it's a you-fo. Is it not possible that it *could* be...?'

'Really, Miss Travers,' Lethbridge-Stewart said, cutting her off, his tone now one he tended to use on foolish privates. 'The next thing you know you'll be expecting a police box to turn up, too.' He could tell Miss Travers was disappointed with his response, but he still wasn't convinced by the idea of time travel, regardless of what Professor Travers had once told him. Nonetheless, three fallen stars since 1822. Another connection to bear in mind. 'Now then,' he said, and turned back to Heggessey, 'about these blankets.'

'Sounds like them now.'

And indeed footsteps could be heard as someone climbed into the lamp room. It was Owain, carrying with him a pile of thick grey blankets. He smiled when he saw Lethbridge-Stewart.

'Hi, Uncle,' Owain said, and stepped forward. His eyes came to light on Miss Travers, and he blinked. Surprise or shock, Lethbridge-Stewart couldn't tell. 'I've seen you before.'

Miss Travers smiled. 'Yes, we met in Bledoe. I came to *save* you,' she said.

Lethbridge-Stewart chuckled slightly. Miss Travers had arrived a little too late on that occasion. Between him and Owain, they had dealt with the Great Intelligence before Miss Travers had turned up with her invention.

'No,' Owain said, shaking his head. 'Right here, in this lamp room. But... You were dead. I saw your ghost!'

CHAPTER FIVE

Ghost Facing

'A ghost? As you can see, I'm quite alive,' Anne pointed out, once they had all climbed down from the lamp room to the crew room five floors below.

Owain had tried to explain what he had seen, but the colonel had suggested they continue in a warmer area than the lamp room, so Heggessey told them to go down to the crew room, where Mr Saunders was setting up his equipment. Owain led the way, with Bill and Anne following, Lethbridge-Stewart behind her. Mr Heggessey remained upstairs, as he had to attend the light. As soon as Anne entered, Mr Saunders had looked at her with shock, pointed, and said, 'Lads, look, it's that ghost again.'

Owain smiled an apology at Anne and turned to Mr Saunders. ''Fraid not, Jim. She's as real as you or me.'

'Yes, she is,' said Lethbridge-Stewart as he entered the crew room behind Anne, a grey blanket over his shoulders, his wet combat jacket in one hand. He looked around. It was a small room, circular, as one would expect in a lighthouse, with only one window. Below the window was a plaque of dedication to John Smeaton. Despite the smallness of the room, or maybe because of it, it was cosy, with a little sofa left of the window and a small table in the centre, atop a soft Persian rug. A small TV, black and white of course, sat on a stand opposite the sofa, to which Mr Saunders had attached his portable camera.

The BBC cameraman was still looking confused. Owain patted him on the shoulder. 'Welcome to the world of the weird,' he said, and nodded towards the colonel. 'That's my uncle, Alistair Lethbridge-Stewart. Weird is his speciality.'

Lethbridge-Stewart frowned. 'Well, I wouldn't say that, but it does seem to follow me around.' He rubbed the back of his neck. 'For some reason.'

'A pleasure, Colonel. Jim Saunders,' the cameraman said, holding his hand out. 'Brilliant work in London, if you don't mind me saying so.'

Lethbridge-Stewart shook his hand, and looked over at Owain. The young man held his hands up. 'Wasn't me. Didn't say a thing,' he said, and took care of Lethbridge-Stewart and Bill's wet jackets, placing them on the small cabinet to one side of the room. Anne noticed a painted pipe rising up from the top of the cabinet, and she realised it was probably the source of the heat in the room. She handed her own wet coat to Owain with a grateful smile.

'Press gossip,' Saunders explained. 'Harry and Larry have been snooping around, but no one seems able to uncover what exactly went on, not even Steve, but we've learned enough to know that Londoners owe you their lives.'

'Yes, well, you know, just training exercises,' Lethbridge-Stewart said, not very convincingly in Anne's opinion. 'Now, what's all this guff about seeing Miss Travers here?'

'It's true, we did,' Saunders said, looking at Owain for support.

'We were in the lamp room, trying to catch some ghosts on camera,' Owain said. 'It was my idea. As you know, last night my friend saw some ghosts...'

They explained. Anne and Lethbridge-Stewart listened, both as credulously as the other. The story of the voices that haunted the lighthouse was new to Anne, but evidently not to Lethbridge-Stewart and Bill. Ghosts had never been of any interest to Anne – despite all the stories and old wives' tales, there was simply no scientific evidence to support the existence of ghosts, and so Anne did what every good scientist did: she dismissed any and every mention of them.

Of course, there were the events of Bledoe and the young boy who haunted the colonel's mother and Owain himself. A *ghost* in effect. Although it turned out to be nothing more than a manifestation of a super-evolved intelligence which manipulated matter. Could these ghosts of Fang Rock have a similarly rational explanation?

The colonel looked at her once Owain had finished, clearly expecting her to debunk the whole story. Could she though? Owain seemed certain of what he had seen. 'Perhaps you should show us what you caught on camera, Mr Saunders?' she asked, turning to the cameraman, who was now sitting on the sofa puffing on a cigarette.

'Jim, please,' he replied, and rose to his feet. He placed his cigarette in the ashtray and walked over to his camera.

Lethbridge-Stewart remained in the doorway, his arms folded. Bill, much more relaxed, perched himself on the arm of the sofa. Owain offered him a fag, which Bill accepted gratefully. Anne smiled, glancing at the colonel. He didn't seem especially bothered by the actions of his adjutant.

'Now, this is the most interesting bit,' Jim said, as he fiddled with the camera. 'About an hour before you arrived we caught a... *conversation* in the lamp room. From what

Steve Worman found out, seems the assistant-principle keeper was responsible for all the deaths in 1902, but recently new voices have been reported. Three of which can't be accounted for.'

'Yeah,' Owain said, sitting himself on the sofa next to Bill, using Bill's cigarette to light his own. 'There was no record of them in Jennie's book, so nobody can figure out how these three fit into things. Although, I have a feeling one of the three is you,' he added, looking directly at Anne.

'I don't see how. I'm obviously not a ghost.'

'You were earlier,' Jim said. He shrugged. 'Don't ask me to explain it, but it was definitely you. Calling out to someone called Charlie.'

Lethbridge-Stewart raised an eyebrow, clearly still not buying the story. Anne wasn't sure herself, but Owain and Bill seemed very certain of their facts.

'Okay, let's assume that somehow a ghost of me haunts the lighthouse… The question is, from where does this ghost come? I'm very much alive here, right now, and have never visited Fang Rock before.'

'Puzzling, isn't it?' Owain said with a grin.

'Right,' Jim said, switching on the television set. 'Ready. What you're about to see throws a little more mystery into the mix. Did Reuben really kill all those people, or was someone else involved?'

'Or something else,' Owain added with a wink.

'Aliens?' Bill asked.

Lethbridge-Stewart raised an eyebrow. 'More likely than ghosts, I should think. Wouldn't you agree, Miss Travers?'

'That's what we're here to find out,' she replied, sitting on the sofa next to Owain and nodding towards the TV screen, which had finally warmed up. The picture was fuzzy, lots of white snow obscuring the details. Jim tutted and fiddled with the tuning dial on the TV. Eventually he found the right frequency, and the image settled on a black and white image of the steep steps that led up to the lamp room.

'Is it working?' Owain's voice asked through the crackly TV speaker. A pause and then, 'Good.'

The image moved as Jim carried the camera up the steps. The image shook, as he tried to navigate them without looking. The camera drew closer to the lamp room and a voice drifted across the airwaves. Deep, almost rumbling, the words initially hard to understand.

'How can he be dead?'

'Generator electrocuted him,' said another, much younger voice.

'Ben knew that blasted machine better than anyone, boy. Doesn't make a lick of sense.'

A figure came into view, a rotund old-ish man in full keeper uniform, complete with coat and a dark woolly hat out of which poked white whiskers. He crossed himself and looked at the younger clean shaven man next to him, who was dressed in a light jersey and wore a similar hat on his dark hair.

'Reuben and Vince,' Owain explained to those watching.

'The doctor said that, too,' Vince said.

The picture seemed to jump. Anne looked over at Jim, and the man shrugged. 'It's not the camera,' he said, 'this is what actually happened. Look.' He pointed at the edge around the two men on the television. Anne wasn't too sure what she was looking for, but then she saw it. The lamp room wasn't jumping at all, it was just the two ghosts.

'Yeah,' Owain said. 'It's as if the ghosts were jumping forward, like you see in films sometimes. Sped forward.'

'Jumping a time track?' Anne suggested.

'I guess. Something like that.'

Lethbridge-Stewart looked over at Anne. 'Time track?'

'As if, as Owain said, they're being sped forward in their own timeline. Look,' she added, nodding towards the TV. 'They've changed position, too, like a bad film edit.'

Lethbridge-Stewart let out an hmm, and the ghosts on the television screen settled.

'I reckon it's spies,' Reuben said.

'Spies! On Fang Rock?' Vince asked.

'Krauts, Ruskies, the damn Frogs. Not to be trusted.'

'They're not spies,' Vince said, suppressing a laugh.

Reuben wasn't to be dismissed so easily and continued on, his tone grave. 'It all started when they came ashore. Remember that, boy.'

'You think they did for Ben?'

'Odd things are happening on Fang Rock this night, is all I'm saying, and...'

Once again the two men fritzed, their images becoming indistinct. They settled once more, and this time Vince was talking. It was clear a whole chunk of the conversation had passed without any record of it.

'Only until the Master of the Tender returns.'

'Ben won't rest, boy, not easily,' Reuben said, his voice full of doom. Vince looked at the old man, confused. 'His soul will be angry, killed by that damned machine.'

Jim turned the television off. For a short while the crew room was silent, except for the sound of the wind and rain lashing against the small window.

'Sounds to me like Reuben is trying to cast the blame away from himself,' Anne said eventually, and looked over at Lethbridge-Stewart pointedly.

Lethbridge-Stewart turned to Owain. 'You mentioned a book?'

'Yeah, *Horrors of Fang Rock*. My friend left it here since I figured it might be useful. Transcripts of all the conversations, theories on the haunting, all that jazz.' He stood up. 'I can go and get it if you like?'

With a nod from Lethbridge-Stewart, Owain left the crew room.

The small room fell into silence again. The only sound was the wind outside, accompanied by the distant waves lashing against the rocks. Lethbridge-Stewart stared at the television screen. He shook his head. 'Ghosts indeed!' He looked down at Anne. 'What do you think, Doctor Travers?'

He was looking for some rational explanation, and Anne couldn't blame him. The colonel was not a man prone to flights of fancy. 'I'm not entirely sure,' she said. 'Clearly what we saw supports the idea of ghosts, or at least what we would consider to be ghosts. Those two men manifested in the lamp room. Two men who died a very long time ago. We can't deny that.' Not the response Lethbridge-Stewart had hoped for, clearly. So Anne tried to explain it another way. 'What about Bledoe? The ghost of your brother.'

'That wasn't a ghost,' Lethbridge-Stewart pointed out.

'Then what was it?'

The colonel narrowed his eyes. 'I'm not the scientist, *Doctor* Travers. All I know is that, somehow, the Great Intelligence was able to appear as the image of a boy who died over thirty years ago.'

'Not to mention someone who probably died a lot earlier than that,' Anne reminded him, thinking of the man in the Victorian-looking clothes, the form the Intelligence had an 'affinity' for.

'Are you saying that's what we're dealing with here?'

Anne stood up and stretched her back. 'Not necessarily,' she said. 'But I agree it's unlikely to be ghosts in the conventional sense. We're clearly dealing with something alien, three possible you-fo sight…'

'You-*Eff-Oh*, Doctor Travers,' Lethbridge-Stewart said pointedly.

Anne rolled her eyes at him. 'Toe-mate-o, toe-mart-o,' she said.

'Not quite. UFO stands for Unidentified Flying Object. Surely you understand the difference between a word and an acronym?'

'Both are words, Colonel, surely how they're pronounced isn't relevant?'

'They are if—'

'Fine!' Anne snapped, no longer able to hide her exasperation. No doubt it was some strange military thing. She continued, after a glance at the awkward expressions worn by the other men in the room. 'Three You-*Eff-Oh* sightings over Fang Rock from three different eras. Perhaps these "ghosts" are projections?'

'From the past?' Bill asked.

'Why not? We know time travel is possible.'

'We know your father *believes* it possible,' Lethbridge-Stewart said. 'I'm still not convinced.'

'Evidence of time travel was found last month,' Anne

said. 'Not to mention London and the…?'

Lethbridge-Stewart raised a warning eyebrow and glanced over at Jim. Anne bit her tongue. She believed her father; she had heard the story of his adventure in Tibet in '35 too often while growing up to deny the truth. Especially when faced with evidence that proved his story nearly thirty-five years later, a man the army had codenamed 'Cosmic Hobo'. A man who had, she later learned, been involved in at least five incidents dating back to the 1940s, from London to Northumberland, even in South Wales. If she was right, then the Hobo had been on Fang Rock in 1902 as well. After all there was no record of a medical doctor being in the lighthouse at the time, so who else could Vince have been talking about…? Well, that would be proof enough. Unfortunately, the truth of the London Event was protected by the Official Secrets Act – which she had been encouraged into signing. Discussing it in the open was a no-no. For now.

She decided to move on. She'd get back to that discussion another time.

'Okay, then, so why the ghosts? Why did a UFO come to land in the water and then seemingly vanish?'

'And why is there a ghost of you?' Bill added, a frown above his eyes as he looked down at Anne from his position on the arm of the sofa. For a few moments he continued to look her in the eyes, before finally lowering his head and flicking cigarette ash into the ashtray.

Anne smiled sadly, and looked around the room. She wasn't sure how much she could reveal in front of Jim. She knew she'd have to couch her words carefully; after all it seemed the colonel liked to pull the Official Secrets card whenever it suited him. Still, she doubted any of the men had considered what she was about to say next. 'I have a thought about that. All these ghosts seem to come from 1902, and at least one person in 1823 knows who I am... If there is a ghost of me,' she said, her eyes coming to rest on the plaque of dedication. 'Well, I think under the circumstances it's reasonable to assume that at some point I travel into the past and die there.'

Meanwhile in 1823 Archibald stood on the exact same spot as Anne examining the bust of John Smeaton, while behind him Alfred Scott burned holes in his back. Archibald waited for the eventual barrage of insults once Crane and Jacob were out of earshot.

'What is this game you play, man? This is no place for Travers!'

Archibald turned to face the old light keeper. 'And an asylum is? This is precisely the place for Jacob,' he said, his voice firm and calm. 'He needs answers, and I am here to help him discover them.'

Scott shook his head and reached down for the empty mugs. He looked at them and screwed his face in disgust. 'We was present when he was returned to the mainland, almost a year gone now. We... I have had my portion of experiences, Goff, I have witnessed men haunted by fear. Many on this very rock. But I have never seen anything that compared to the look in Travers' eyes that night. He was delivered to Bethlem for his own safety. Do you know the assertions he made?'

Archibald could see he would have to deal with Alfred Scott carefully. The man had a lot of influence, especially at the lighthouse. If he wished it, neither Archibald nor Jacob would step outside the lighthouse until the next boat came. And that would not help anybody. Not Jacob, and certainly not him.

'I encountered him at Bethlem, Mr Scott, and he does not belong there.'

'The treatments are—'

'Excessive!' Archibald raised his hand in apologies. 'Forgive me using such a strong word, but when I happened upon him, he was in the wing for the criminally insane. To even suggest he is of the same calibre as people like James Hadfield is... Well, it is a claim not far from insanity itself.'

Scott lowered his head. 'This is knowledge we did not possess.'

'I have conversed with him innumerable times, I know much of his experiences. Or at least as much as he will tell. I have made a name for myself for getting to the bottom of spectral occurrences, and I have seen the peace such understanding can bring. Doctor Hoenneger released him to my care, Mr Scott. I *can* help him find peace.'

Scott's eyes were cold. 'People should leave the dead alone. Sometimes they walk, and sometimes they do worse... Dead men walk these shores, Mr Goff, more than you can count. Including my brother. Do not disturb them, or you may be sorry.'

Archibald stepped forward, coming to a stop mere inches from Scott. 'Is that a threat, sir?'

'If you wish, but I mean only to warn. The veil ought not to be violated.' Scott turned away and picked up a lantern. He began to leave the library. He looked back before descending the steps outside. 'Travers *is* mad, he is accursed with delusions, and ought not be back here.'

'Delusions, yes. They call it clinical lyca—'

'You disturb things here,' Scott said, his tone cutting Archibald off. 'Continue on your course and there will be nobody left to be picked up when the next boat arrives.'

The light of the room dimmed with the departure of Scott and his lantern. Shadows danced across the walls, distorted by the single candle and the curvature of the wall. Archibald felt a shiver down his spine. And he wasn't sure it was from the cold air.

Someone said his name. He turned around, but there was no one else in the room. 'Archibald,' the voice said again, this time clearer. A female voice, strong and cultured. He stepped back, feeling his heartbeat increase. A woman stood before him. She was talking, but no words could be heard. Archibald stepped closer. She was dressed unlike any woman he had ever seen, her dark hair shorter than befitting a woman, an orange jersey of some kind and the skirt of a length that would bring shame to any man who held the arm of such a woman.

Finally words seeped through the veil. '…is instrumental in getting me to the past,' the woman said, looking down at something Archibald could not see. 'Archibald said it would help, that it was important I get…'

She faded away as quickly as she appeared.

Archibald felt a smile spread across his face. The ghosts of dead men walked these rocks, Scott had said. But why would a ghost of a woman be here? He swallowed. A ghost of a woman who knew him.

'Blimey,' he said to himself, wondering if perhaps Jacob's madness was catching.

Jim whistled in appreciation as Anne unveiled the crystal machine. She smiled. 'I'm afraid I can't take any credit. I just made it work again.'

Jim crouched down by the table upon which the machine now sat. 'What is it?'

'I'm not really sure,' Anne replied. 'It's alien, though, and from here.'

Jim looked up. 'Here?'

Anne looked over at the colonel, who was sat on the sofa, *Horrors of Fang Rock* open before him. Owain and Bill had gone down to the kitchen to make a brew, while the colonel read the chapter Owain had pointed him to. He looked up from the book, as if sensing Anne's gaze.

'What is it?'

'I'm just wondering how much I can tell Jim.'

'Ah.' Lethbridge-Stewart considered this for a moment. 'Well, at the moment he hasn't been read in, but General Hamilton approved his involvement with Fang Rock, so I suppose you can tell him whatever might help. But,' he added, looking sternly at Jim, 'be assured, Mr Saunders, when this is all over you will be required to sign the relevant papers.'

Jim shrugged. 'I figured as much. Well, if nothing else, at least *I* will know some truth of what's going on, even if my peers don't.'

'That's the spirit.' Satisfied, the colonel returned to the book, but not before saying to Anne, 'just remember, Miss Travers, even after signing the papers, Mr Saunders will not be privy to information pertaining to those who *assisted* the army in London.'

Anne took his meaning. She explained everything that had happened in the last few weeks, all about the visit to *Morecombe & Slant* and the work she had since done on the machine, and how it all pertained to her family.

'Everything that has happened, will happen?' Jim mused once Anne had finished. 'What do you think Archibald meant by that?'

'Time travel,' Anne said. She caught Lethbridge-Stewart's eye as he glanced up at her. 'I'm sorry, Colonel, but it's the only thing that makes any sense of this. How else does an ancestor of mine know me so precisely? Where else did the UFO go? And it's all connected to this machine. Archibald said there was a missing piece, and that the piece would find its way to me.'

Lethbridge-Stewart looked around. 'I don't see how. We're pretty much off the beaten track here. Unless Mr Heggessey has it?'

Now it was Anne's turn to raise an eyebrow. 'What about all this bothers you so, Colonel? The idea of ghosts, or time travel?'

'Both are absurd.'

'Really? After everything we have seen? I seem to recall how readily you accepted the idea in the London Underground when the… *Hobo* presented you with a way out,' Anne said. Now that Lethbridge-Stewart had promised to read in Jim later, she figured using the codename would be permissible.

'Born of necessity, Miss Travers. The Hobo had a craft that could help save my men, and with everything else that was going on I saw no reason to disbelieve him. But I have had time to think since, and I have seen nothing that convinces me that travel in time is real, let alone the idea of that such a thing can be achieved with a police box.'

Anne shook her head, hardly able to believe what she was hearing. But she supposed she could not really blame the colonel. He was a practical man, after all, a combat officer who was trained to accept the unacceptable only when presented with no other option. She, too, had spent a long time disbelieving the idea of time travel; it wasn't until London, and then the discoveries made in Wiltshire last month, that she'd finally started to accept it. And she at least had had her father's stories to prepare her; the colonel had no such thing.

Lethbridge-Stewart stood up and held the book out. 'Perhaps you should look through this, Miss Travers. See if it helps. Aliens I can deal with. Something tangible. But ghosts? It's absurd.' Anne took the book off him and he walked over to the little cupboard to check his jacket.

'But you saw the footage,' Jim pointed out.

'Yes, and I can't explain it. But I trust Miss Travers can. With a rational explanation instead of science fiction.' Lethbridge-Stewart pulled his jacket on and shook out his glengarry. 'Even if I accept the idea of time travel, which I don't, be assured that you are here under my protection, and as such you will *not* be dying on my watch.' He placed the glengarry on his head and nodded sharply, once again the commander in charge. 'Now, what's keeping those lads with the tea?' Colonel Lethbridge-Stewart left the room and descended the steps outside.

'Stubborn old goat,' Anne said behind his back, and turned back to Jim with a smile. 'Sorry about that, but I just don't understand why he's so against the idea, especially

85

after...' She stopped herself, reminding herself that some secrets had to be kept.

Jim took the book off her and sat down on the sofa. He began flicking through it. 'Okay, I can see how ghosts can bother him. After all I'm not so copasetic about all this either. But I don't understand why you're so sure about time travel.'

Anne regarded him for a moment, wondering if he was making fun of her or honestly interested. She decided on the latter.

'Experience, Jim. You see, before I was born, my father was an anthropologist. He was particularly fond of the myth about the abominable snowmen, and in 1935 he funded a trip to Tibet to find proof of their existence. Which he did, eventually, but not before encountering robotic yeti in the Himalayas.'

'Robots? In Tibet?'

'I know it sounds unlikely, but they were created as guards to protect a disembodied life form called the Great Intelligence. It possessed the llama Padmasambhava, and took over the monastery at Det-Sen.'

'Why?'

Anne smiled warmly. 'The less you know, the better. But the point is, in Tibet my father met a mysterious traveller, a rather brilliant scientist who helped him defeat this Great Intelligence. This man claimed to be a time traveller.'

Jim interrupted her with a nod towards the door. 'This Hobo person who *assisted* the army in London?'

'Yes. Anyway, all my life my father would tell me stories of this... Hobo and his two friends. Of course, as a child I believed my father. What daughter doesn't? But as I grew and became a scientist, partly because of the stories my father told me about this man, I'm afraid I became a bit more... rational about such things. The idea of time travel was ludicrous to me, and I never came across any evidence to prove its existence.'

'So what changed?'

'Meeting the Hobo and his friends in the London Underground. They were exactly how my father described them, *exactly*. For them only a couple of months had passed, but for my father... nearly thirty-five years.'

It was at this point of the tale that Owain returned, carrying a small tray upon which sat three cups of steaming hot tea. Anne gratefully accepted a cup. Owain considered the crystal machine.

'This is the thing that brought the you-fo to us?' he asked, with a cheeky smile.

Anne sipped her tea ruefully. 'That's the assumption, but I'm not too sure right now. It's clearly connected, certainly.'

Owain pursed his lips and nodded. 'Alistair and Will have popped outside, taken advantage of the break in the storm.'

'Good.'

Owain looked from Anne to Jim. 'Trouble in paradise?' he asked.

Anne rolled her eyes. 'Just your uncle. Stubborn old fool.'

Owain laughed. 'He can be. Military men always are, from what I can gather. Except Will,' he added, daring Anne to say something.

Anne refused to take the bait. Instead she returned to the earlier subject, leaning closer to examine the crystal machine. 'I'm sure this is instrumental in getting me to the past. Archibald said it would help, that it was important I get it working again. Something tells me he didn't send me a message from over a hundred years in the past just so I could attract the attention of an alien spaceship.'

The room was silent for a few moments, save for the steady humming of the machine and the distant howl of the wind outside.

'You know, I don't know much about time travel,' Owain said. 'Not really been into science fiction, but I've met some interesting people since I left home, done a few not so legal things, and... Well, have you thought of a trip?'

'A trip?' Anne asked.

'Yeah, like a flashback. That's kind of like time travel, right?'

It was not something Anne had considered before. So far her mind had been focused on the science of time travel, the kind of technology one would need, short of a police box. But there were all kinds of sciences, and not all of them involved technology. She hadn't considered the other disciplines, the science of the New Age, James Lovelock's theories. Once, while designing new software for NASA, she and a colleague had discussed some very interesting conjectures. If only she had access to...

She smiled and leaned forward to peck Owain on the cheek. 'Brilliant. Thank you.' Laughing at the looks of surprise on both Owain and Jim, Anne left the crew room and climbed the stairs to the lamp room. She needed to talk to Mr Heggessey.

Lethbridge-Stewart, warmed by the hot tea, had decided to take a quick recce of the rock, and took Bishop with him. If nothing else he needed to get a good lay of the land in his mind. The wind continued, but the rain had finally abated. Nonetheless the rocks beneath their boots remained wet and slippery. They walked carefully.

As much as he hated to admit it, he did think Miss Travers had a point, and he was reminded of their conversation on the Whirlwind about being manipulated. He refused to be subject to a whim of something unknown, and right now whatever was going on at Fang Rock remained unknown.

Despite what Mr Saunders had filmed, Lethbridge-Stewart refused to accept he was dealing with a haunted lighthouse. He had seen a lot of strange things in his time, but nothing he had seen would convince him that ghosts were real. There had to be a rational explanation.

Time travel.

Lethbridge-Stewart shook his head. Absurd.

'What do you think, Corporal?'

'About what, sir?'

Lethbridge-Stewart smiled. Good man, playing the innocent card. Best not to speak out of turn. 'About this whole time travel idea of Miss Travers?'

'Well, sir, I've been thinking about that, and it reminds me of a story I once read when I was about sixteen, I think. By Robert A Heinlein, although I can't remember the name of it.'

'A story?'

'Yes, sir, science fiction.'

'Hmm,' Lethbridge-Stewart said with a frown. He suspected that he wouldn't especially like where this was going. 'So, what about this story?'

'It's about a man whose future actions affect his past. From what Anne was saying about her grandfather, I've been wondering if that's what's happening here. In the book, a man called Bob is brought to the future by his future self, but this only happens because the future Bob remembers being brought into the future, so future Bob goes into the past to bring past Bob to the future. And around it goes. Archibald's present, our past, is being shaped by our present – *his* future.'

'I see,' Lethbridge-Stewart said, finding it somehow familiar. Something about Nikola Tesla and Professor Travers. He racked his brain, wishing he could remember exactly what had happened to him in Germany. It seemed the more time passed, the less he was able to recall. No doubt a result of the psychoactives that had been administered to him while he had been held captive.

Bishop tried to explain further. 'Would Anne have come here if not for the letter written over a hundred years ago? And if not, then the letter would not have been written.' He shook his head and offered Lethbridge-Stewart a weak grin. 'Kind of trumps the idea of free will.'

'We're all subject to rules and regulations, Corporal. But I don't see how what hasn't happened yet can determine what we once did. Yesterday only...' Lethbridge-Stewart stopped, as once again an image of Tesla came to his mind. *'Perhaps it would be more accurate to say we haven't launched any capsules yet.'* He shook his head, knowing the memory was somehow important but not able to make sense of it.

'You okay, sir?'

Lethbridge-Stewart nodded. 'Fine, Corporal, just a slight headache. Now, what was I saying? Oh yes, yesterday only happens once. It won't happen again.'

'Agreed, sir. I love science fiction as much as the next man, and I know that we're dealing with the unusual, the unexplained... But... What's happened has happened, and what we do today can't change that. I mean, if time travel was possible, then the past would be changed all the time. Wouldn't it?'

'Exactly my thoughts.' Lethbridge-Stewart wasn't entirely sure it made any sense to him, but evidently Bishop had given it much consideration.

'Besides, if time travel were possible, wouldn't we know? We'd have been visited by now,' Bishop concluded, although it sounded like he had confused even himself with his explanation.

They continued on in silence, walking further from the lighthouse, careful with their footing on the wet rocks. Above them the light continued to flash out into the English Channel.

'Sir, unless I have this wrong, haven't you met a man who travels through time?' Bishop asked, clearly having now warmed to the topic.

Lethbridge-Stewart stopped and looked at his adjutant. 'How the Dickens do you know that, Corporal?' he snapped. He knew he hadn't said anything. Yes, he had told Bishop about some of the particulars of the London Event, but he had intentionally left out certain details. Details that were filed under Top Secret on orders from General Hamilton. Only one person could have told the corporal. 'You do seem to be rather friendly with Miss Travers.'

'Um, yes, sir. Miss Travers and I have remained in contact since Bledoe.'

'I see, and you do know that the London Event falls under the…'

Movement ahead put an end to the approaching reprimand. Lethbridge-Stewart put a finger to his lips, and carefully pulled out his pistol. He preferred to use his grandfather's .38 calibre Enfield No.2 Mk I revolver, but it was currently being serviced and so he was stuck with the more advanced, but in his opinion less reliable, standard .40 calibre Hi-Power automatic handgun. Smaller it may have been, but it lacked the elegance of the Enfield.

Bishop followed suit. Lethbridge-Stewart indicated they both approach the source of the movement from different directions, and so Bishop branched left and disappeared around a large rock, while Lethbridge-Stewart took the more direct approach, his gun held at waist height.

What he saw gave him pause.

Robotic Yeti was one thing, the ghost of his dead brother another, but this…

A pool of water had been left over from the high tide. Beside it was what appeared to be a very large green jellyfish, its body glowing softly, its tentacles whipping about, blood and gore splashing everywhere. Beneath it lay the dead body of a man. It was nobody Lethbridge-Stewart knew, and for that he was thankful, but he still had to force himself to take in every detail regardless. Despite the damage to the body – charred skin, at least one arm missing, and his guts ripped open – the man wore clothes of an era long gone. They looked similar to those worn by Mr Heggessey, only, if Lethbridge-Stewart had to guess, he would say they were at the very least sixty years old.

Despite the rictus of horror, the face of the man looked

familiar. Lethbridge-Stewart had seen him before somewhere.

'Get off the body!' he ordered, once he saw Bishop had taken up position, his own gun raised and ready. The creature didn't respond. 'This is your final warning. Remove yourself from the body or we will open fire.'

The green shape turned to face him. Not that it had a face, but Lethbridge-Stewart had a sense that it was looking at him. The creature rose up, its tendrils acting like legs. A sound emanated from the creature. At first Lethbridge-Stewart wasn't sure what it was, but then he realised it was words. A kind of broken English.

'We not complete. You did this. The Rutan not complete. Where are we?'

The creature (the Rutan?) advanced. Lethbridge-Stewart and Bishop opened fire at the same time. Their bullets ricocheted off the rocks, passing through the alien mass.

I'll be damned.

'Cease fire,' he ordered. They could see the Rutan, hear it, but it wasn't really there at all. Much like the footage he had seen, the Rutan and the dead man were from the past. And though he didn't like it, Lethbridge-Stewart just knew that past was 1902. 'So much for science fiction ideas,' he muttered, holstering his pistol. The Rutan and the dead light keeper faded away into the soft fog that was slowly forming on the rocks.

'Well, that's that then,' he said, once Bishop had joined him.

'Sir?' Bishop asked, looking at the small dents in the rocks made by the bullets.

'Unless I'm much mistaken we're dealing with ghosts

and aliens after all,' Lethbridge-Stewart said. 'And it seems they can see us, too.' He looked over at the lighthouse, adding ruefully, 'Miss Travers will be happy.'

— CHAPTER SIX —

Portents

A rchibald climbed the steps, his mind furious with ideas. He had never imagined that the lighthouse was haunted. He had spent so many hours with Jacob, talking to him, hearing his tales of the year just gone. Archibald Goff made his fortune as a preternatural investigator, debunking spurious claims of the demonic and arcane. But he was not averse to the occasional haunted house, or contacting the dead... Mostly it was all flam, of course, but the grieving people who had lost loved ones were ripe for the plucking. So willing to part with their money for a fopsy, the assurance that their dear departed were happy. Of course, he had seen his share of ghosts, too.

When such things dried up though, as they were wont to do, he visited the many asylums of England, to see if he could exploit the insane. Those who ran such asylums cared little for those held within their walls, and were happy to take the extra coin Archibald offered. It was on one such a visit, to the most infamous asylum of them all – Bethlem Hospital in London – that he came across Jacob Travers. Chained up in the wing for the criminally insane. Driven mad by fear he may have been, but Jacob was not insane. Archibald had seen insanity enough to recognise it. And with Jacob, and the mysterious death of Williams, he knew he could really make a name for himself.

Jacob was a victim of the strange disease known as lycanthropia, the belief that he could transform into a wolf. The man was convinced that it was in such wolf form that he had killed Davy Williams. But long talks had proven the truth – that and the lack of transformation during a full moon. It was a delusion, but one, Archibald was sure, based on what he'd seen at Fang Rock. And so there was only one course of action: Jacob needed to be returned to Fang Rock, where they could reveal the truth of the Beast and find out just why Jacob was spared.

But now... The Fang Rock lighthouse was haunted. By a ghost that knew him! It was extraordinary. He needed to talk to Jacob, maybe get young Mr Crane on his side. Scott would stand against them, respectful of the memory of those who died building the lighthouse.

He listened at the curved door, but there was no sound of movement beyond. Archibald gently opened the door and entered the bunk room, the candle he held casting a spectral light ahead of him. He found Jacob crouched at the end of the bunk nearest the window, his head angled up, his eyes fixed on the moon poking out from behind grey clouds outside.

'Jacob,' Archibald whispered. 'It is time. We must go find the Beast.'

'Scott was right,' Jacob said, his voice even lower than Archibald's. 'It was an ill-considered thing, to return to this place. I should have ventured home to Vina... My dearest Vina.' He lowered his head and was silent for a moment, his thoughts returning to his wife.

'You speak of impossible things. You cannot share

blessed reunion with Vina until the truth is known. If we leave with the truth still unknown,' Archibald said, careful to stress his final words, 'it is not to Vina that you will return.' The implication was, he hoped, clear.

'Even now I can hear the Beast beckoning to me,' Jacob whispered. He turned his head sharply, the candle light reflecting in his eyes, and for a moment it seemed to Archibald as if they were yellow. 'Can you hear it?' he hissed.

Archibald listened, but heard nothing except the howling of the wind. He crept closer to Jacob. 'We must go now.'

Jacob shook his head. 'No. The Beast will come to me. It knows I am here.'

Still Archibald knew not what the Beast was. He had read the pathologist's post mortem in Hove, the details of the eviscerated remains of Williams. He would have said it was a mad wolf, only he could not work out how a wolf had ended up at such a remote location. He had considered other myths, like the *Bodu* of Guernsey, or the *Moddey Dhoo* on the Isle of Man. Such tales of black dogs were spread across the Channel Islands, and he believed that Fang Rock had its own. One that appeared in stormy weather. One that killed and drove men mad. Whatever it was, it was no wild wolf; neither was it a wolf who had once been a man. Of that Archibald was sure.

'There is more to this isle than the Beast,' he said. 'I think Scott is right. Dead men walk this rock. I have seen a ghost, Jacob, a ghost!'

Something clattered on the floor behind him. Archibald spun around to find Crane standing in the doorway, a metal plate and food on the floor. The young man's eyes were wide with horror, the lamp in his hand trembling.

'I seen them 'efore,' he said, his voice shaking as much as the lamp. 'The ghosts. And one of them looked like you!'

At first Archibald thought Crane was pointing at him, then realised the finger was directed at Jacob.

'A ghost of Jacob?'

Crane nodded and allowed himself to be pulled gently into the bunk room. Archibald closed the door. It wouldn't do to be disturbed again, especially not by Alfred Scott.

'Only he looked different. Hair longer, no whiskers...'

'Then you are mistaken. It was not Jacob,' Archibald said reasonably.

'It was. Looked younger, but was him. I swear!' Crane crossed himself.

Archibald turned away and smiled to himself. Such fear could be used. He pulled out his crucifix and made a point of fingering it conspicuously. 'The Lord has delivered me here, Mr Crane, to oust the evil from Fang Rock.' He looked back at Crane. 'How strong is your faith?'

Crane swallowed. 'The Lord is my shepherd,' he said.

'Good, then He has a task for you.'

Anne had a task for Ivan Heggessey, or at least a favour. He led Anne back down to the service room, making sure the hatch remained open, and pointed to the radio equipment. 'There it is,' he said.

'Thank you,' Anne said, looking it over. It seemed simple enough.

She waited as Ivan put her through to the mainland. He offered her the seat, and she sat down, relaying her message to the keeper on shore duty at the signal house in Hove. While she did so, behind her Ivan rummaged inside a small cabinet and pulled out a dusty folder.

While she waited for the signal house to relay her message to the Vault, Anne turned to Ivan, who handed her the folder. 'What's this?' she asked, flicking through the pages within.

'Keeper logs. Well, the remains of them. Most were destroyed in the fire of '55, but some were salvaged and placed in this folder for historical value.' Ivan flicked some pages over for Anne and pointed. 'It's not much, but these are all that remains from when your great uncle was principle keeper.'

Anne read the first few lines and felt a strange twinge in her heart. She had never really known her father's family well, since he was more enamoured with his in-laws than his own blood. She was still trying to get used to the idea that she was walking around the work place of an uncle she had never heard of before today. And now she had something written by that very same uncle, the brother of Lyndon Travers – her grandfather.

'Thank you,' she said, placing a hand on Ivan's.

The keeper smiled. 'Well, I figured you would never have met him, seeing as he must have died years before you were born.'

'It's very thoughtful of you,' Anne said. 'I didn't even know he existed until today. So this means a lot.'

The radio beeped behind her. She turned in the chair and flicked the send/receive switch.

'Hello? Anne?' Even among the crackle and distortion, Tim Gambrell's voice was distinctive. 'Are you there?'

'Tim,' Anne said. 'Listen carefully, I need you to do something for me.'

Crane had convinced Wishart that he was just showing Archibald around, and now the two men stood out on the gallery, while the assistant principle keeper continued to go about his business inside the lamp room. Jacob refused to leave the bunk, certain that the Beast would come to him. Archibald had no reason to argue with the man, and so he'd persuaded Crane they needed to talk in private. And the best place for that was outside the lamp room, as far from Scott as possible.

'I don't know, sir,' Crane said. He looked out to the channel. The waves were crashing against the rock, the tide moving ever-closer to the lighthouse. 'If this weather doesn't calm, we'll be lucky to have any rocks to walk on.'

Archibald couldn't let that bother him. One hand held tightly to the guardrail, while the other gripped the collar of his greatcoat in an effort to keep the wind out. 'Then entreat the Lord to give you the strength,' he said, searching for something to inspire the young man.

Crane lowered his head and closed his eyes. He began muttering to himself. '*The Lord is my shepherd; I shall not want. He maketh me to lie down in green pastures: he leadeth me beside the still waters…*'

Archibald rolled his eyes but remained quiet as Crane recited the 23rd Psalm. He looked out across the channel, the howling wind a strange accompaniment to Crane's fervent prayer.

'*Yea, though I walk through the valley of the shadow of death, I will fear no evil: for thou art with me; thy rod and thy staff they comfort me.*'

As Crane reached the end, Archibald lowered his head

and joined in for the final verse. '...*and I will dwell in the house of the Lord for ever.* Amen,' they both said, and Archibald turned Crane to face him, looking solemnly into the young man's eyes. 'If Shadrach, Meshach and Abednego could embrace the fiery furnace to prove their faith...'

Crane took a deep breath. 'I can do no less,' he agreed. 'But I am fearful.'

Archibald nodded and patted the younger man on the shoulder. 'It is wise to be fearful, but remember, *thy rod and thy staff they comfort me.* We are doing His work, and we are called to...' He stopped, his eyes finding something below. He pointed. 'Look, what do you see?'

Crane strained his eyes. He pulled back sharply, crossing himself. Down below, on the rocks, seemingly unaffected by the weather, was the woman Archibald had seen earlier. From the vantage point of 132 feet she was so small, an orange blot against the grey rocks. And there was someone with her. Archibald blinked the rain away. Surely it could not be!

'Quick, get me the telescope!'

Crane scrambled around the gallery and into the lamp room. He returned presently with the telescope in his hands.

'Who do you see?' Archibald asked, fearful of what he'd see if he were to look.

Crane put the telescope to his eye and focused it on the people below. 'It's...' He stepped back, lowering the telescope, his body rigid. 'I fear you are cursed, Mr Goff.'

'Who was it? Speak true!'

'You,' Crane said. 'An apparition of you, Mr Goff. A portent of your own death.'

*

The death of her ancestors was very much on Anne's mind when she returned from the service room, the log folder under one arm. She found Lethbridge-Stewart in the crew room on his own. His combat jacket was open, his glengarry on the table beside the machine, while he once again flicked through the pages of *Horrors of Fang Rock*. He looked up as she entered.

'I think I owe you an apology, Miss Travers,' he said.

For being stubborn? she wondered. She supposed she would have to get used to it, since she was rather stuck with him at the moment. She walked across the crew room and placed the folder on the cabinet. She would have a proper read of it later.

'This rock is indeed haunted. I just saw a ghost outside.' He stood up, flicked through the book and showed her a page. He pointed to a daguerreotype. 'Do you recognise this man?'

The man looked to be in his late thirties, with floppy thick hair and a handlebar moustache. There was something kind in his eyes, kind but firm. 'Should I?'

'*Benjamin Travers, principal light keeper*,' he read. '*The most gruesome of deaths occurred to Travers, the victim of a butcher.*' He ran his finger down the page, and read another line. '*Despite all the recorded hauntings, still no one can explain why Whormby attacked him so viciously. Reportedly first electrocuted by the generator, Travers was later eviscerated by Whormby.*'

Anne swallowed and took the book off Lethbridge-Stewart. She looked closely at the picture. On one level she felt an emotional distance, but on another she considered his immediate family, and the poor people who had to identify the body. After a few weeks studying the machine he had left, she had started getting used to the idea of Archibald Goff, but she still wasn't quite able to process the idea that her great uncle had died on Fang Rock. That, somehow, the two men had to be connected. The odds of both sides of her family being involved with the strange events of Fang Rock and *not* each other had to be astronomical.

'He wasn't killed by a man,' Lethbridge-Stewart said, breaking into her thoughts.

Anne looked up from the picture. 'Excuse me?'

'Bishop and I just saw what killed your uncle; indeed, we saw the thing *kill* him. Out there on the rocks.'

'Thing?'

'An alien, Miss Travers. And it spoke to us. I believe it's called a Rutan.'

Anne sat down. She glanced at her watch, feeling very tired all of a sudden. And little wonder; it was almost 2am. 'So, it *was* an alien spaceship that crashed in 1902. At least that confirms one thing. Still doesn't explain where our UFO went, though. Unless…' She flicked idly through the book. 'Is there nothing in this book about aliens?'

'Not that I can…' Lethbridge-Stewart stopped abruptly, looking around the room. Anne could hear it too. Distant voices. A man and a woman. She went to speak, but the colonel held up a finger of silence.

'…don't believe in mythical sea creatures either,' a deep male voice said.

'But you said we're in danger,' said the woman, her voice near hysterical.

'Out there is an alien life form from another planet that wants to kill us.'

A third voice spoke. Another man this time, softer, gentler, incredulous. 'An alien life form from a...?'

Silence.

Lethbridge-Stewart raised his eyebrows and looked down at Anne. 'Well, there we go then.'

She nodded, looking down at the picture of Ben Travers again. She could see a lot of her grandfather in his eyes. He had the strong jaw that was a common feature on all Travers' men. 'I don't think they're ghosts,' she said simply looking up.

At the look of surprise on Lethbridge-Stewart's face, she almost laughed. Ever since she had first heard Owain's story she had tried to convince the colonel they were dealing with ghosts, even though she had no real explanation for them, and now she was saying the complete opposite.

'Then what could they be?' the colonel asked, his tone impatient.

Anne shrugged. She had an idea, and it wasn't one Lethbridge-Stewart would like. 'How many hauntings are reported on a yearly basis?'

'According to that book, maybe half a dozen.'

'And there's been, how many? Four, five since last night?'

Lethbridge-Stewart nodded slowly, his eyes turning to the crystal machine. 'You think this has something to do with the increase?'

'Well, the first manifestation happened shortly after I activated the machine.' Anne stood back up to stretch. She would need sleep soon. Or a lot of coffee. For what she had planned, a sharp mind would be needed. 'That's it then. I'm certain of it. This is not a haunting.'

'Then how do you explain the manifestations? I saw Ben

Travers out there, killed before my very eyes. Bishop and I both shot the Rutan, and the bullets went right through it.'

'These hauntings... They haven't interacted with anybody, just acted events that transpired here in the past. Replaying events like a stuck record.'

'Except that Rutan spoke to me. It moved towards me.'

Anne took this on board; it still fit her new theory. 'Then it works both ways. It's time travel. I know it.'

The colonel sighed. 'Okay, Miss Travers, let us assume it is. Then how?'

'I don't know how, yet. But these Rutans must have the ability to travel in time.' She patted the crystal machine. 'Something is linking this machine with the past. And I believe I have an idea how we can find out what.'

Archibald left Crane in the lamp room to assist Wishart. He needed time alone, just to gather his thoughts. He had seen ghosts before, of course, exorcised a few of them, but never had he seen the ghost of a living man.

He was not a man who scared easily. But this had put the willies up him and no mistake. He clambered down the stone steps, turning past the keepers' room. He paused a few steps from the bunk room in which Jacob sat. Careful to make sure nobody was mounting the stairs either way, Archibald rested against the cold stone wall.

For the first time ever he questioned what he was doing. Not because of Jacob, not because he was disrupting the work of the light keepers, but because he didn't wish to die. His own mortality rarely occurred to him when he was working, though he had often found himself in the most dangerous of situations. But now... His future had shown itself to him.

He closed his eyes and his mind turned briefly to his family. His wife and his sons. Archibald opened his eyes. He had to put an end to this. If Jacob truly believed the Beast was coming for him, then who was Archibald to stand in its way? He had his family to think of.

He walked down the final few steps and pushed open the door to the bunk room. 'Jacob, old chap, I'm afraid I have decided to—'

The room was empty. Jacob was gone.

Lethbridge-Stewart couldn't believe what he'd just heard. 'You did what?' he asked again.

For her own part Miss Travers showed very little concern about her actions. And she repeated, calmly, 'I sent a message to the Vault to request the materials I need to confirm my theory. They'll be with us in about two hours.'

The Vault may have been a part of the Ministry of Technology, but Lethbridge-Stewart didn't trust those who ran it. Mostly because of the secrecy surrounding it. Ministers with secrets rarely boded well, in his experience. After learning where the Yeti and other technology used by the Great Intelligence had been sent following the London Event, he had tried to find out what he could, but he'd been stonewalled at almost every turn. Even General Hamilton refused to comment, merely explaining that the Vault was in service to the betterment of the UK. Not that he'd sounded very convincing.

Very well, then. Lethbridge-Stewart wasn't happy about involving the Vault in what was going on here, but the deed had been done. 'What exactly did you request?'

Now it was Miss Travers' turn to look like she didn't trust him. 'A sample of the Intelligence's web, and a rather unique flower.'

'A flower? What use would a flower be?'

'It has certain mind altering affects when ingested,' Miss Travers said, and raised a hand before he could complain about the use of drugs. 'It's also not from Earth originally.'

'Then how did...? I mean, just what is going on at this Vault?'

'I can't tell you that, Colonel.' Miss Travers sighed. 'You'll just have to trust me on this.'

Lethbridge-Stewart wasn't sure he could. Miss Travers hadn't given him any reason to distrust her before, but she had sent a message to the Vault without his authority, and this was his command. It was cause enough to doubt her loyalties at least. Of course, she maintained it was done to help them. But still...

'Trust is a two-way street, Miss Travers,' he said. 'You can't go behind my back and then expect me to simply trust you.'

'Behind your back? Have you any idea how pompous you sound? It will take hours to get the materials to us. I didn't think we could afford the extra time it would take for me to convince you to *allow* me to contact the Vault.'

'Which suggests that there is something suspicious about the Vault, if you need to convince me.' Lethbridge-Stewart let the silence sit between them for a moment. 'So, if you wish me to trust you, I need some kind of explanation.'

'We all have our orders, Colonel.'

'And who gives you yours?'

Again Miss Travers looked at him with distrust... No, it

was something more. She wasn't happy, like something was weighing on her. She let out a sigh and sat down. 'You need to ask your General Hamilton,' she said. 'How else do you think I got into the Vault?'

'Hamilton put you there.' It was a statement, not a question. This changed things somewhat. It was against Lethbridge-Stewart's nature to question the orders of his superiors, and he knew that Hamilton would have a very good reason for putting Miss Travers in the Vault. The general must have his own suspicions too. Lethbridge-Stewart made a note to ask him about this later.

'I'm sorry, Colonel,' Miss Travers said, her tone sincere. 'All I can tell you, and I'm probably saying more than I should, is that the Great Intelligence is far from the only alien to have visited Earth before.'

Lethbridge-Stewart accepted this without question. Hamilton had hinted as much several times. 'Like our Rutan friend in 1902?' he said instead.

'Yes. You do realise the—'

'*Hobo.*'

Miss Travers glared at him. 'Really, Colonel? Do we have to persist with this pantomime? Why can't we simply call him the D—'

Lethbridge-Stewart raised his eyebrow in warning.

'Oh, for heaven's sake!'

Lethbridge-Stewart sighed, reminded of why he didn't like bringing civilians into military operations. 'Because walls have ears, Doctor Travers, and we protect our secrets for a reason.'

'This is ridiculous, there's only us here and we know—'

'Miss Travers, I suggest you train your mind to *think* of

him as Cosmic Hobo. That way your mouth won't betray him.'

Miss Travers glared at him, but then something dawned on her. 'Of course, he's saved the UK more than once. No surprise the British government wants to keep him secret.'

'More than once?'

'Well, yes. Surely you have heard of his involvement in 1943? The incident at Llandrudnod Wells in 1959?'

'I have no idea what you're talking about.'

'Then maybe all that business with Chameleon Tours at Gatwick Airport a few years back?'

'Maybe I need to remind you that I serve with the Scots Guards, and we don't tend to handle civilian matters.'

Miss Travers studied his face, clearly trying to determine if he was lying. Once it was obvious he was not, she lowered her head. 'Then I'm obviously more informed than you.' She looked back up. 'Another question for you to ask Hamilton.'

'What question?'

'Why he would tell me all this and not you.'

A good question indeed. Lethbridge-Stewart knew he'd be overstepping his bounds, but he would need to have words with General Hamilton. Why was he looking for evidence if Hamilton already had some? Without saying as much, Miss Travers was confirming his suspicions. Despite the mandate of the Ministry of Technology, the Vault was not working for the benefit of the UK like they claimed. And if there was one such organisation… Lethbridge-Stewart would lay money on the fact that there were others. He stored that for another time. 'And just where did they find this flower?'

'Tibet, from what I can tell. I know, what are the odds? I'm not exactly sure how, but it's tied in with a man called Ed Hill, the so-called Revolution Man. Well, it was. But he's dead.'

Wembley Stadium, Lethbridge-Stewart thought. 'The former lead singer of Kathmandu, killed at Wembley last weekend.' Not a question. At least he had an answer to who had got there before him. The Vault.

He really didn't like the implications. How was he supposed to get the evidence Hamilton needed if he was always one step behind the well-oiled machine of the Vault? Hamilton must have known this. No doubt it was why he had put Miss Travers there.

'We can't allow the Vault to become a part of this investigation,' Lethbridge-Stewart declared, his tone making it clear there was no discussion otherwise.

'They won't be. I promised to share the results of my experiment with Tim Gambrell, and I will do so only as long as it pertains to tests Tim and I were conducting.'

'Hmm.' It seemed to Lethbridge-Stewart that he had no choice. 'What exactly do you expect to achieve with this alien flower and the Intelligence's web?'

'As you know, I'm convinced I somehow go back in time. All evidence leads to that. This machine is supposed to help, but it's missing an important piece...'

'Which is supposed to make its way to you,' Lethbridge-Stewart added, still sceptical.

'Yes. And maybe it has. I was only introduced to the Om-Tsor this morning. Before your summons, I'd been doing tests on it all day. Perhaps that's the missing element?'

Lethbridge-Stewart shook his head. 'I don't see how a

flower will help this machine.'

'Not in its native form, no, but when boiled into a solution and ingested it has been known to facilitate out of body experiences.'

It sounded like nonsense to Lethbridge-Stewart. 'I'm not a scientist, so if you could put it more succinctly?'

'An out of body experience, also called astral projection, is the way your *astral body* is able to exit your physical body. If you like, your mind, your soul, consciousness, whatever you wish to call it, can be free of your body and travel on its own.'

'Sounds like Eastern mumbo jumbo to me.'

'It's popular among Taoists and the Hindu religions, yes. But it's just another science, really, a science of the mind. And, as I understand it, essentially how the Great Intelligence came to be.'

'Hmm, not the best example.'

'Perhaps, but one to which you can relate.'

'Okay, and just how does this out of body experience thing help you?'

'Well, Owain gave me the idea. Astral projection through time.'

— CHAPTER SEVEN —

The Calm Between the Storms

Lethbridge-Stewart, resting against the crew room cabinet and enjoying the warmth of the iron pipe behind him, looked up from the log book he had been leafing through as Owain and Bishop returned from their quick recce of the lighthouse perimeter.

'Nothing to report, sir,' Bishop said, glancing at Miss Travers, who had fallen asleep on the small sofa, a grey blanket over her. 'All is quiet outside, no more sign of the Rutan or any other ghosts. Although it looks like the storm is about to start again.'

'Very well,' Lethbridge-Stewart said. He glanced at his watch. 'Unless the hauntings change in nature again, we have a little downtime until Miss Travers' materials arrive. I suggest you both grab some sleep while you can. Heggessey said you can use the bunks in the room above. Mr Saunders is using the keepers' bunk room.'

'Yes, sir.' Bishop saluted, and glanced at Miss Travers again.

'Wake us when her stuff arrives,' Owain said. 'Can't wait to see how this astral projection works.' He nudged Bishop with a grin. 'Come on then, Bill, let's see how comfortable the bunk is.'

The two young men left the crew room. Lethbridge-

Stewart stood there for a moment, smiling to himself, feeling oddly proud of Owain and the way he was handling the whole situation. He knew that technically Owain and he were not related, but nonetheless the sense of pride he felt was filial. Like Owain really was his nephew – or maybe even his brother. One day Lethbridge-Stewart hoped he would understand it. Perhaps he should get Owain to explain it once more. Reincarnation was just not a concept Lethbridge-Stewart could readily accept, much like the idea of ghosts and time travel.

'Open mind,' he said to himself. He had always been a pragmatic chap, accepting what was before him – just one thing that had made him a good officer, the ability to simply accept any order without question – but his pragmatism had been sorely tested in the past few months, and it seemed such testing was far from over.

He looked at Miss Travers. If only he wasn't on duty. Sleep sounded like a good idea. He flicked off the single electric light and left the room, taking with him the folder that Miss Travers had been holding when he'd returned from his recce of the lighthouse with Mr Saunders.

Scott's anger was palpable, so much so that Archibald had to draw from his own reserves just to not wither beneath the weight of it.

'What expectations did you bring with you, Goff?' Scott asked. His voice was low, but when it carried such force, shouting was not necessary.

Archibald felt like a school boy again, standing before his teacher. His hand twitched, as if he expected a cane to come crashing down on it at any moment. He steeled himself. 'Mr Scott, I came here to unravel your little mystery and…'

'Expand your reputation unto the heavens?' Scott shook his head. 'I am acquainted with your sort. Vain glory hunters. Only seeking fortune for themselves. It never occurred to you what effect returning would have on Travers.'

'That is not so.'

Scott snorted. 'It is so! Travers' mind is broken, any man with an ounce of intelligence can see that. Broken by whatever it was that happened to him on this rock. And you have delivered him back to it.'

'Would you prefer him to remain enchained at Bethlem?'

Scott's tirade halted for a moment, as something stirred behind his eyes. 'Of course not,' he allowed. 'But he is a danger to himself. The man believes he can transform into a *wolf*!'

'And you believe him?'

'I… Of course I do not. But he is unhinged, and he is out there. And out there he will meet his end.'

'Then help us,' Archibald said, looking at Crane. But the young man was sitting at the small wooden table, his head lowered into his hands. 'We need to venture out there and bring Jacob back.'

Scott shook his head again. 'No. I warned you. Dead men walk Fang Rock, and they're vengeful of those who disturb them. Travers must have done so, and now they want to avenge themselves.'

At this Crane looked up. 'He's right, Mr Goff. You and I have seen them. They appear in all forms. Even yours.'

Scott raised his eyebrows, turning to Crane. 'What is

this?' he asked.

Archibald tried to wave it away, but Crane continued and explained what they had seen earlier.

'A good omen indeed,' Scott said after a moment's thought. 'Perhaps I was wrong.' He opened the library door and waved Archibald out. 'Go, face your demon, Mr Goff. And allow Crane to accompany you. But I warn you, stay away from West Crag. There you will only find death.'

Archibald went to move forward, but stopped as the words sank in. 'What mean you, a good omen?'

'No man sees his own ghost. But if those dead appeared as you, it means they will spare you. So go, find Travers; bring him back.'

'But what of the woman? Who was she?'

Scott looked at Crane. 'May we never know, boy. No woman has ever stepped foot on Fang Rock. Now go,' he said, and ushered Crane out with Archibald. 'Find Travers, bring him back. But be mindful of the Beast. If it is out there, it wants Travers back. Goff is safe, but you are not.'

Archibald stopped at the door. 'What of you? What will you do?'

'It is almost midnight, the changing of the watch. I will take up the watch and send Wishart out to help you.'

'But it is my watch,' Crane said, obviously looking for an excuse to remain in the safety of the lighthouse.

'It is, boy. But you are younger, and the rocks are dangerous.' Scott offered Crane a smile. 'Mind your step out there. And remember, stay away from West Crag.'

Archibald didn't argue. He clapped a hand on Crane's shoulder. 'Come on, Charlie boy, let us do God's work,' he said with more gusto than he felt. Despite Scott's words of encouragement of the 'good omen', there was something in his expression that Archibald did not trust.

He had never been a fan of twilight, that period between dawn and sunrise when it wasn't quite night or day, and during his many missions overseas he'd seen more than he could count. Lethbridge-Stewart rested his hands on the guardrail and looked towards the Atlantic. With the arrival of Morning Nautical Twilight he could see the rock below more clearly, the sky a strange mix of blue and red. What was that old saying? *Red sky at morning, sailors' warning.*

He checked his watch. 04:38, which meant it must almost be time for…

'There!' Heggessey was the first one to notice the helicopter approaching. The man didn't miss a thing – which, Lethbridge-Stewart decided, made sense considering his job. In the hours before dawn the two men had talked a lot about the life of a keeper, drinking way more tea than Lethbridge-Stewart was used to, and having heard about Heggessey's duties, he had decided he'd probably enjoy the role himself. It was a regimented position, one with a lot of responsibility, although many of the duties had been replaced by automation, which on one level made Heggessey's job a little perfunctory. And some of the practicalities worried Lethbridge-Stewart – the bathroom was on the lowest level of the lighthouse; what would happen should one feel the call of nature while on watch? Heggessey had explained that usually the night watch was split into three short shifts, which eased that problem, although in case of emergencies they had a bucket. As it happened though, with so many in the lighthouse at the moment, Heggessey had been spared the use of the bucket. Something Lethbridge-Stewart was very grateful for – the stench in the lamp room would have been horrendous!

Knowing he'd be the only keeper on watch through the night, Heggessey had slept during the day and was still quite lively, having only been awake for eight hours. Lethbridge-Stewart wished he felt the same, but he'd been awake now for close to twenty-four hours; he'd need something stronger than tea once he awoke his staff.

Lethbridge-Stewart walked around the gallery and joined Heggessey facing north. The keeper handed him the binoculars and went to prepare the helipad. The approaching craft was a Whirlwind, although Lethbridge-Stewart didn't recognise the markings. Privately owned? If so, evidently the Vault's influence went further than tracking down alien technology. Fortunately the storm had died down, despite Bishop's warning, and so the chopper made an easy landing.

Lethbridge-Stewart returned to the lamp room, placed the binoculars on the side, and descended the ladder to the service room below. It was time to rouse his staff.

Over half an hour later and Miss Travers, still bleary from the little sleep she'd had, was staring daggers at Lethbridge-Stewart. He didn't blame her, but his decision had been made.

He had let Miss Travers sleep a little longer than the men, so she would have the freedom of the bathroom without half-asleep men getting in the way. Lethbridge-Stewart had spent enough time in various barracks and camps over the years to know how a group of men could act first thing in the morning, and he didn't think it was something Miss Travers needed to see. By the time she woke, the sun was shining through the small window, and the men had all but finished. Only Saunders was lagging. Heggessey was now in the kitchen preparing some breakfast for them all, with the help of Bishop, while Owain and Jim retrieved Miss Travers' supplies from the service room, where Heggessey had left them.

Miss Travers had returned to the crew room, looking surprisingly fresh all things considered, and eager to begin her experiment. That was when Lethbridge-Stewart had told her his decision.

'I don't think you understand, Colonel. I have to go back,' she said defiantly.

Lethbridge-Stewart had expected no less. 'I don't agree. You're here under my command, my protection. From what we talked about earlier I now understand you're very important to General Hamilton, and I suspect he wouldn't be best pleased if I got you killed.'

She narrowed her eyes. 'I thought we had already established that this lighthouse isn't haunted. That it's simply time replaying itself somehow.'

'We don't know that for sure.'

Miss Travers folded her arms. 'Then I refuse to conduct my experiment with astral projection.'

Lethbridge-Stewart raised an eyebrow. 'That is your prerogative, of course, but if you don't, then you'll never know what happened in 1823.'

'Neither will you.'

Stalemate.

The two of them continued to stare at each other, neither

118

wanting to be first to look away, both feeling they'd won. Of course, Miss Travers was right; if the experiment wasn't conducted, then Lethbridge-Stewart would have no proof of aliens to take back to Hamilton and his mission here would be considered a failure. Little more than another wild goose chase. Just like Wembley Stadium, just like Llandudno... And he would remain one step behind the Vault.

But then he was right, too. Miss Travers had a more personal stake in this investigation, one Lethbridge-Stewart had not considered when he'd first told Bishop to contact her. She needed to know why her family was so connected to the strange happenings of Fang Rock, why her great uncle was killed by an alien, and why Archibald Goff had been on Fang Rock in the first place. Lethbridge-Stewart knew that kind of pull – the desire to discover the truth about one's history. He'd been subject to it before. It was a potent pull. Even more so, he'd wager, than his current mission.

Miss Travers let out a sigh. 'Fine. What do you suggest instead?'

Lethbridge-Stewart resisted the urge to smile. He had won his point, but there was no honour in boasting. 'Owain has already volunteered to go in your place. Jim, too, but I want him here to film whatever happens as a result of this experiment. I need as much evidence as I can get for General Hamilton, and what can be better than something recorded on film?'

'So, you're unwilling to risk me, but you're willing to risk your nephew?'

'Not quite. I'm sending Bishop with him. Of everybody here, he's the only person other than myself who has any kind of training.'

'I don't think anybody has training that covers time travel.'

'A fair point.'

Miss Travers looked down at her machine. 'It should be me,' she said.

'I'm sorry, Miss Travers, but one way or another, I refuse to let you go back to the past. And that's final.'

Archibald wished he hadn't gone back outside. He reached out to grab hold of Crane's arm. He barely managed to lock his fingers around the younger man's wrist before the waves crashed up the side of the rock and knocked them both to the ground.

They both lay there, soaked through, Archibald's other hand holding fiercely to an iron ring cast into the rock, a small reminder of the old beacon that had housed the construction workers when the lighthouse was built. The beacon itself was gone now; all that was left were a few iron rods and rings struck into the rock, and one weathered wooden beam that had been one of the original support struts for the beacon.

Once the water had calmed a little, Archibald pulled himself to his feet, not letting go of Crane's wrist until both men were standing again, braced against a larger rock.

Archibald smiled. 'Scott was right to extol the dangers.'

Crane clearly didn't see the humour. His lantern had been swept away, but fortunately, once he had spotted the approaching wave, Archibald had placed his own a short distance up the rocks. The two men carefully made their way to a safer position, and Archibald picked up the lantern.

With no further words needed, they continued on in their search.

They had called out Jacob's name several times, but the roar of the wind must have been drowning out their voices. Once or twice Crane had thought he'd heard a howl, but Archibald persuaded him it was only the waves. But he wasn't convinced himself.

Crane stopped. 'Over there!' he shouted.

Archibald followed the direction Crane was pointing in. It was indistinct, but there was a shape, as if someone was lying on the rocks. 'Careful,' he said and pulled out a pistol he had hidden about his person.

Crane looked at it in horror. 'A barking iron! You can't shoot Travers.'

'If it *is* Jacob,' Archibald said. 'And if it isn't, then the Beast will feel the weight of my iron.' They approached the shape, Crane holding the lantern out before them, while Archibald prepared his pistol.

He didn't need to use it. The shape was a person, but it wasn't Jacob Travers. He had seen the person before, of course. Twice now. The orange clashed horribly with the black rock beneath her. Seemingly unconscious, the shape before them was the ghostly woman he had seen in the library.

Anne looked up from her pottering as Owain returned to the crew room. 'Is this what you wanted?' he asked. He looked around at the expressions of those watching Anne. His uncle was looking both bemused and pensive, while Jim, standing behind his camera, wore a look of concentration. Bill, checking his gun, kept throwing concerned glances at Anne. Owain wasn't sure why Bill was so concerned about her; she wasn't the one about to be astral projected through time.

The only person missing was Ivan, who, now that he wasn't needed, had decided it was his turn to sleep.

Anne took the folder off Owain. 'This is the one, thanks,' she said, rifling through it.

Owain sidled up to Bill and nudged him. 'What's wrong?' he asked in a whisper.

'It's nothing,' Bill said, and placed his gun in its holster.

Owain glanced down at Bill's weapon. 'You do realise our bodies aren't going anywhere, right? Your gun won't be any use to us.'

'Oh.' Bill smiled at himself. 'I should have worked that out.'

'Yeah, obviously distracted,' Owain said, suddenly realising the real cause of Bill's concern.

'Don't know what you mean, mate.'

'Of course not,' Owain said, offering the most innocent smile he could. He walked over to the machine and muttered to himself, 'Always somebody else.'

A lattice of copper, covered in the pulsating sticky web, had been constructed above the machine. Multi-coloured wires were clipped to the web. At the end of the wires were small suction pads, four of them, which reminded Owain somewhat of the device the Great Intelligence had set up in the small pyramid at Remington Manor. He shuddered at the memory. The web had killed his brother, and now it was an integral part of Anne's experiment in astral projection. An experiment Owain had volunteered for. He shuddered again.

'Would you care to explain what you are doing?' the colonel asked Anne, nodding towards the camera. 'For posterity's sake, of course.'

Owain smiled slightly. Any explanation would be beyond his uncle, but after experiencing the effects of trips himself, not to mention seeing what the web could do, Owain had a general idea of how the experiment would work.

'I don't suppose you have heard of the stone tape theory?' Anne began, and Alistair shook his head, but from behind the camera Jim said he had. He glanced at Owain and winked.

'We were talking about it the other night,' Owain explained.

'Good,' Anne said. 'Well, this is a variation of that idea. Many cultures believe that objects can retain the memories, a trace, of the deceased, and you can contact the dead with such an object... A hair brush, an old medal, anything of personal value to the deceased.'

'Sounds like magic to me,' Alistair said.

'I suppose it could be, or is it just some level of technology that is so advanced it looks like magic?' Anne countered.

'Psychic energy isn't magic,' Owain said, having spent some time reading Paramahansa Yogananda. 'Just a different kind of science.'

His uncle didn't look convinced.

'How did you feel when you saw the very first television programme?' Owain asked.

'Ah,' his uncle said, and nodded. 'I never did understand how television works, if I'm honest. Even now.'

'Just like magic,' Anne said with a grin, 'unless you understand how the technology works, then it's just science. Apply that principle to what I'm doing here.' She turned back to her experiment. 'I'm now covering the pages of the log written by Ben with web, and as we know the web was an extension of the Great Intelligence's mind. Synaptic and neural pathways, and the like, facilitating the transmission of its will into the Yeti and others to extend its reach. What I'm hoping to do is use the web to access the memories of Ben as retained by his logs, and those held by this machine, and use them to guide Owain and Bill back in time. To the time when these memories actually happened.'

'Which is where this miracle flower comes in?' Alistair asked.

'Yes. It's been known to produce astral projection, so combined with the web and this machine, I can hopefully direct Owain and Bill to a specific time. To 1823, when this machine was first on Fang Rock.'

'I see.'

Anne tried to suppress a smile. 'Do you?'

'Not really,' Alistair replied, 'but I trust you know what you're talking about.'

'So do I,' Anne said, and turned to Owain. 'If you and Bill could take a seat?'

Owain glanced at Bill, and the two of them shrugged, equally unsure, but game if the other one was. They sat on the sofa as instructed. Anne placed the pads on Bill's temples and he frowned. He was now connected to the web.

Anne went to do the same to Owain, but pulled back. 'What is it?' she asked. 'You've gone very pale.'

Owain wasn't surprised. He felt very light headed too.

'Did someone turn up the temperature?' he asked.

Bill looked at him. 'You'll be fine, mate. It's just a trip.'

But it wasn't that. The trip itself wasn't the problem; he was sure he'd indulged in worse in the past few months with Mike, Daisy and the gang. It was the web wrapped around the wires that Anne held before him. The same web that was woven around the crystals of the machine, the same web that had wrapped itself around Lewis and killed him.

Owain closed his eyes and held up a hand. 'Give me a moment,' he said. He focused in on himself. He had spent a lot of time listening to George Harrison lately, and learned much from Yogananda's autobiography, which even now sat in his backpack in the bunk room. *Offer inhaling breath into the outgoing breath, and offer the outgoing breath into the inhaling breath, and you neutralise both these breaths; you thus release the life force from the heart and bring it under your control.* He cleared his mind as much as he could, focusing on his breath, imagining his diaphragm. In, and out. Out, and in.

He opened his eyes again, feeling centred. 'Okay, I can do this.'

Anne looked at him with fascination, then grinned. She gently placed the pads on his temples and turned to the cup of steaming water that sat on the table beside the machine. There wasn't much water in the cup, Owain knew, but then there didn't need to be. It was the boiled petals of the Om-Tsor which mattered the most. She handed the cup to Bill, who took a sip. Owain did likewise.

For a moment nothing happened. But then he felt it. A strange pull. Like he was being dragged out of himself. Anne and Alistair watched him, one looking intently, the other looking concerned. Anne nodded and turned on the crystal machine.

The last thing Owain remembered was four words. He wasn't sure who said them; it sounded like a million voices overlapping. Some male, some female: 'And now we wait.'

Despite what he had said, Scott did not climb the stairs to relieve Wishart of the watch. Instead he walked down to the provisions store. Once there, he carefully enclosed his candle in a metal lantern casing. At the far end of the store, hidden in darkness, were a few wooden crates, nailed down by him almost a year ago.

He pulled the nails out and opened the largest of the crates. Inside, surrounded by various bits of technology of a type never even thought of on Earth, was a metal box, out of which protruded several crystals of various shapes and sizes. He crouched down and placed his palm onto it. A brief hum of power emitted from the box, and Alfred Scott was covered in a soft green glow. He closed his eyes.

Yes, it was as he thought. For the first time in almost a year, the osmic projector was picking something up. It didn't last long, but he recognised it for what it was. Somewhere, out there, an identical machine was transmitting a signal through time.

Bishop wasn't sure where in time he was exactly. He looked around, a strange feeling when you didn't have actual eyes through which to see. He felt like he had eyes, hands, legs – a whole body in fact. He could see it when he looked down, but he knew it wasn't really there. He clapped his hands together, and even though he could see his hands connect, he felt – and heard – nothing.

So, this is what astral projection feels like.

Beside him stood Owain, also looking normal. They were both standing outside on the rocks, the lighthouse close by. It looked different, although it took Bishop a moment to work out how. The dome at the top was bereft of its helipad. It was strange how much of a difference this made. In his own time the dome was more or less hidden by the helipad and the scaffold-like structure that supported it. But now, in front of them, the dome on display as it ought to be, the lighthouse of Fang Rock was a thing of beauty. The way a lighthouse was meant to be.

'Well, we definitely moved,' Owain said. 'It's night time again.'

'Looks like,' Bishop agreed, and pointed to the lighthouse. 'Although it could only be a matter of months. The helipad is a recent addition.'

Owain nodded. 'The paint job looks different, though, so at least before '55.' He paused, staring up at the lighthouse with a troubled expression, before turning to Bishop and forcing a smile. 'Well, shall we find out *when* we are?'

— CHAPTER EIGHT —

Before the Horror

T he first obstacle they faced was the door to the lighthouse. It was locked. Bill looked around, wondering about another possible way in, but Owain shook his head. 'There is no other way, other than scaling these walls. Which,' he held his hands up and showed his well-bitten nails, 'I just don't have the claws for.'

'Then what do you suggest? I can't see how we'll discover *when* we are unless we get inside.'

Owain agreed. Beyond the lighthouse the rocks all looked much the same to him. The tide wasn't in as much as in their time, so that at least suggested a different time of the year. But what year? 'I suppose we can look around the rocks, see if there's any sign of the launch that Trinity House constructed a couple of years ago?'

'We could,' Bill said slowly, extending a hand out for the door. 'But I've got a more interesting idea.'

Owain smiled when he realised that Bill wasn't reaching for the door, so much as putting his hand out before him, testing the door's solidity. His hand passed through the iron. 'Of course! We're not physically here, we just think we are.'

Bill nodded with a grin. 'Yeah, I was thinking that your hair should be blowing about by now, but it's as lifeless as if we were still standing inside the lighthouse.'

'My hair is not—' Owain stopped himself, realising that Bill wasn't insulting him. It was just as well; Owain prided himself on his hair, refusing to let it become as greasy as most boys his age. He smiled, thinking of the way Daisy would spend hours with him, sitting and talking, while she ran her hand through his soft hair.

He watched Bill pass through the door, and took a deep breath, feeling oddly exhilarated by the idea. He followed Bill. It was a bit disappointing. He had expected to feel *something*, a bit of give perhaps. Like the sensation of air lightly brushing past your face – that feeling you got in the street when you were sure you'd walked into a rogue cobweb. But there was nothing. One moment the door was before him, the next it was behind him and he was inside the generator room.

It was darker than he'd ever seen it, only a small lamp to one side giving it any light at all. It looked old, dirty, as if soot sat on the walls. To his right, and taking up most of the room, was the bulky generator. He was no expert on advances in electrical generators, but even to him it was antiquated. And yet it looked brand new.

Bill looked around. He moved to touch the generator, but his hand passed through. He snatched it back quickly in surprise. 'Oh yeah,' he said.

'Definitely in the past,' Owain said.

'Yeah, but I don't think 1823. Pretty sure they didn't have electricity back then.'

'Certainly not in common usage, no. Let's look around then, see what we can find. Must be keepers upstairs.'

'Do you reckon they can see us?'

Owain shrugged. 'Don't know, never astral projected

before. Probably not, though.'

'Only one way to find out,' Bill decided, and walked towards the stone steps.

Owain went to place his hand on Bill's shoulder, to get his attention. Not being able to touch would take some getting used to. 'But what if they can see us? How're we going to explain...?'

They both stopped. Bill a couple of steps up, Owain still at the bottom of the stair. They had both heard it. Footsteps. Somebody was coming down the staircase.

Bill stepped back, careful with his footing so that he didn't slip down the steep steps. Owain frowned at that. Not because the idea of someone without a body slipping was crazy, but that Bill had even managed to mount the stair. Why hadn't he simply passed through them and stepped through the wall?

Such a question would have to wait. A light keeper came into view.

The man, dressed in a black uniform, jacket open and showing his waistcoat, looked familiar to Owain. He had seen the man in *Horrors of Fang Rock*. The dark floppy hair, the handlebar moustache, the cheeky glint in his eyes.

It was Anne's great uncle, Benjamin Albert Travers.

He showed no sign of seeing either Owain or Bill, and passed by them, holding something in his hands. Owain leaned close to Bill. He whispered, telling Bill who Ben was, and added, 'Which means we're in 1902, at the latest.'

'Makes sense, I suppose,' Bill whispered back. 'After all, it was his memories that the web was locked in to.'

'But what about the crystal machine? Weren't the memories held by that supposed to...'

130

'What's he holding?' Bill asked, and walked over to Ben. The keeper stood next to a small table, shot a furtive glance towards the stair, and gently placed the object on the table. Bill glanced over at Owain. 'Look.' Owain joined him. 'Look familiar?' Bill asked.

Owain moved around Ben to get a better look. The object was a long cylindrical thing, made of shiny, almost see-through metal with what looked to be a crystal running through the centre of it. Owain hadn't seen anything like it before, except...

'It's a piece of Anne's machine!' he said, louder than he'd meant to. He clasped his hand to his mouth and snapped a look at Ben. The other man hadn't heard a thing. Instead he reached into his blazer and pulled out a small piece of paper.

'Probably why we were brought here. Both Ben and the machine are here. Well, a piece of it,' Bill said.

Ben dipped a quill in a small ink pot on the table and started writing. After a quick glance between them, Owain and Bill read as Ben wrote.

Anne, I still don't understand how or even why I have to do this, but I made a promise to my father, and he made a promise to his closest friend. I spent many years wondering about this, and finally on my last visit to the mainland I decided I would do as asked. After all, what harm could it do? I hope you know what to do with this.

Ben stopped writing and looked up. He laughed. 'I must be crazy,' he said in a thick Hampshire accent. 'Spending too much time on this here rock.' He laughed again.

You won't be born for over thirty years, so I've been told. I really do not know how any of this makes any sense, but perhaps you will. If you ever find this, or indeed if you ever exist. Perhaps it's all a joke? If it isn't, and you really are the future daughter of my three-year-old nephew (the idea of Teddy having a child is really beyond the pale – he's three years old!), then all I can do is wish you good luck and success in what you have to do.

Nice to know the family's future is in safe hands.

Ben signed the letter and then carefully folded it.

Beyond the generator was the door that led to, in their time, the bathroom. Owain hadn't spotted it before; his attention had been held by the generator, which took up such space. He hadn't even considered that the generator room was laid out exactly the same as in 1969. Ben opened the door and entered the smaller room beyond. Owain and Bill looked at each other.

'Why in there?' Bill wondered.

They soon found out. Inside the room was the coal store. It was black and filthy, and probably the perfect hiding place. They watched in silence as Ben moved a sack of coal aside and worried at a loose rock in the base of the wall. It revealed a small space, just big enough for Ben to stash the metal rod and his letter. Once they were snug, he put the rock back in place and rearranged the coal sacks. He looked around the small room and nodded.

'Should do the trick. Or so I'm told.'

He left the room, passing through Bill as he did so. Bill emerged from Ben, a spectre of green and khaki coming out of a shadow of black, looking faintly disgusted.

'What's wrong?' Owain asked.

'Nothing. That was just... Odd,' Bill finished lamely. 'Can't say I much like being a ghost.'

They passed through the door, back into the generator

room. Ben was climbing the stairs.

'We should probably follow him,' Owain said. 'Can't do anything about that message for Anne until we're back in '69, so may as well discover what we can. Maybe find out what actually happened here.'

'What killed them?'

Owain nodded.

'I've already seen it,' Bill reminded him.

'Yeah, but that was only Ben. What about the others, Bill? Not only the keepers, but that Lord Palmerdale and his crew. Maybe we'll even find out who those strangers were – the male and female voice than nobody can identify.'

Bill didn't look like he was sure, and Owain could only imagine how damaging it was to see a man die before your eyes. He'd been spared that in Bledoe, but death was no stranger to him, and he knew how it could haunt a person. He nodded towards the stairs. 'Come on, Bill, let's follow Ben.'

Bill let out a sigh and set off towards the stairs. 'Flobbalob' he said as he passed. Owain blinked, then laughed. He shook his head.

'Never thought of that.'

'Come on, Weed,' Bill said, glancing back at Owain. 'And don't complain; your fault for calling me Bill. Only Anne gets away with that.'

'Yeah,' Owain muttered, as he followed Bill, 'she would.'

As they continued up the round staircase, Bishop reflected that, considering the lighthouse was over sixty years newer, he would have expected it to look a lot cleaner. But it looked like the inside of a chimney. He supposed if Owain was right, then they'd only recently turned over to electricity, which meant that since it was first lit in 1790 the lighthouse had been using an oil lamp. After over a hundred years of burning oil, he guessed it wasn't really surprising that so much soot was ground into the walls. Fortunately it would all be cleaned by his own time.

They passed the usual rooms; most of the doors were closed so neither Bishop nor Owain got to see the difference, although they did get a glimpse of the crew room. It looked so much smaller in the past, full and cluttered. It seemed to be used as a dining room and washroom, as evidenced by the small table in the middle of the room, around which sat four chairs, and the porcelain sink at the far end. The room was cluttered with equipment and supplies. Far from the tidy crew room they had got used to in '69.

A flash of light caught Bishop's eye as they passed one of the small windows. He stopped and looked out. Ben hadn't seen it; he had already passed the window by the time the light appeared. A straight, reddish streak of light in the dark sky.

'Just like the one I saw the other night,' Owain said beside him.

It did look like the one Jim had shown them on the television, although seeing it in glorious *technicolor* made it seem more alive somehow. Bishop strained his eyes. He couldn't make out any shape within it, but if it *was* the same as the falling star in '69, then it carried within the craft that was no doubt operated by the Rutan he and the colonel had seen kill Ben.

Bishop nodded. 'That's definitely three of them, then.'

'But why? What's so special about Fang Rock? And why

does it centre around Anne's family?'

'Beats me.' Bishop resumed his climb. 'Maybe we'll find some answers in the lamp room. Looks like that's where Ben is heading.'

They continued up in silence, past the bunk rooms, but as they neared the service room Bishop spoke. 'I wonder how that rod-thing came to be in the possession of Anne's paternal family.' He scratched his head. 'You know, I've read lots of books about time travel, everything from *The Time Machine* to *A Sound of Thunder*, and I always thought I had a pretty good handle on it, but actually coming face to face with the realities of time travel... Not so simple to get your head around.'

They reached what was to them the service room, but Owain explained that in 1902 it was still the oil room. The room was a lot different from how Bishop remembered it. There was no sign of any radio equipment, just a few tools used to maintain the new electric lamp in the room above. Ben was still ahead of them, and he walked the curved room until he came to the ladder that led up to the lamp room. A voice drifted down from above.

'...shot across the sky. Went under the sea, it did.' The voice sounded familiar to Bishop, one of those ghosts he'd seen on Jim's footage. Vince Hawkins. 'And the sea was all glowing. Over there.'

'Now there's nothing there,' an older voice said. Reuben Whormby, Bishop recalled. The one wrongly blamed for the murders.

They climbed the ladder behind Ben and entered the lamp room. It was more cramped than in '69, and the early electric lamp much bigger than the optics used in the future.

Out on the gallery stood two men Bishop had only previously seen as ghosts. He looked back at Owain, who shook his head and offered a smile.

'Weird. Guess we're the ghosts now,' he said, and they followed Ben out onto the gallery.

'What did they call 'em, meteors? Could be one of them,' Reuben was saying.

Vince peered through a wooden and brass telescope. 'Hmm. Weren't far off.'

'What's this? Spot of sightseeing?' Ben asked as he came upon Vince and Reuben. Bishop smiled at the humour in Ben's voice. 'Hoping to spot some of them bathing belles on the beach, eh?'

Reuben glanced at Ben, then nodded out towards the dark sky. 'Vince here has been seeing stars.'

'I saw a light,' Vince said, trying his best to convince. 'It came across the sky, it did, went into the sea.'

'Shooting star, eh?'

'Weren't no shooting star,' Vince said, clearly used to Ben's mocking tone. Bishop knew how he felt. Vince was the younger of the two, his experience barely touching that of Ben and Reuben, and was almost certainly the object of much joshing by the more-experienced keepers. Bishop had been the butt of such ribald comments himself since enlisting with the British Army.

Reuben said, 'Bit of luck coming for you, boy.'

'On this rock? Not till my three month is up.'

Reuben grunted and squeezed past Ben. Bishop and Owain steeled themselves as the old man walked through them and clambered into the lamp room. Moments later the lamp came on.

'Well, whatever it was, it's gone now. So long as it isn't a hazard to navigation we don't have to bother with it,' Ben said.

'It were all red and glowing.'

Ben clearly wasn't convinced. He laughed and patted Vince on the shoulder. 'Aye, well, I've heard enough about it now, lad. I'm off downstairs for my supper. You just forget it.'

Owain looked out across the rocks, in the direction Vince had been aiming the telescope. Ben passed through Bishop.

'What do you reckon?' Bishop asked.

'I think we should go and see what it was,' Owain said.

'Lot of rock out there.'

Reuben walked past them. 'I'm getting food, too. Will you be okay on your own, boy?'

'Course I will,' Vince said. He lifted the telescope to his eye again. 'But I saw something. Down by East Crag.'

'Weren't nothing. Now keep an eye on those rocks.'

With that dismissive instruction, Reuben left the gallery and crossed the lamp room. Owain watched him.

'East Crag. I know where that is.'

'Let's go then.' Bishop looked back at Vince, who was still squinting through the telescope. 'See if we can spot ourselves a Rutan.'

'Yeah. Should be safe enough, as it'll not be able to see us.'

Owain went to leave, but Bishop shook his head. 'How are we even up here? We have no form, so how did we walk up the stairs?'

'I did think about that. Force of will? We walked up them because that's what we expected to do.'

Bishop thought about this. It was always something he'd never quite understood when watching films with ghosts in them. How the ghosts never fell through the floor when they could so easily walk through doors and walls. 'I've got an idea. We're basically ghosts, right?'

'Yes,' Owain said slowly, suspiciously.

'Kind of like how Vince is a ghost in our time.'

'Same reason?'

Bishop nodded. Seemed reasonable. Well, as reasonable as any of it. 'So, if we're ghosts, we don't need stairs.' And with that, Bishop walked through the guardrail and off the lighthouse.

He was well aware of the irrational desire to jump that people often got when standing on a great height – a tall building, a cliff's edge – and knew it was believed to be an ancestral impulse from a time when humans used to live in trees so many millions of years earlier. He'd had the impulse himself before now, and given into it when parachute training. But this was different, this was the first – and only – chance he'd have to simply walk off the edge and see what happened.

He was disappointed with the result. He expected to float down, like the cliché sheet-like ghost of kid's cartoons, but instead one moment he was walking through the guardrail and then next he was on the rocks below, standing next to the lighthouse. No falling, nothing. Just one step, and then he was at ground level. He looked up.

Far above he could just about make out Owain. Bishop waved. He couldn't be sure, but it looked to him like Owain made a rude gesture in response.

*

'You're bloody insane!' Owain said, not for the first time.

Bill looked at him. There was a glint in his eyes that Owain had not seen before, like he'd got a real buzz out of jumping from the lighthouse. Not that it was a jump, as it happened, but the intention had been there. For his own part Owain had simply run down the steps and met Bill back outside.

'What harm was there?' Bill asked. 'After all, we're not here in any way that counts, as you pointed out in the first place, remember? We're still in the lighthouse in '69. Nothing we do here will affect that.'

'How do we know?'

Bill shrugged. 'This isn't like stepping on sea gull wings. We can't affect anything in the past. Nothing we do will change the future.'

'Stepping on sea gull wings?'

'Yeah. The Deterministic Non-periodic Flow?' Owain was clearly none the wiser. Bill explained further. 'The idea that one flap of a sea gull's wings could be enough to alter the course of the weather forever. Apply that to time travel, like in Bradbury's *A Sound of Thunder*, what if we broke the wing of a sea gull in the past...'

'And the flight of the sea gull was important for some weather conditions in the future?' Owain said, and nodded. 'Like a hurricane or something.'

'Right, a hurricane that may kill someone who was supposed to die. A fireman who was supposed to save hundreds of people, for instance. But if we change that...'

Bill waited for Owain to catch up. The younger man was nodding slowly. 'Where do you get all this stuff from?'

'Books, you know. You don't read much, do you?'

139

'Nope. Give me a football magazine or the sport's section of a newspaper and I'll read for hours.'

Bill shook his head. 'Mate, you need to read more. Maybe some scientific papers. Edward Lorenz could be very helpful if these are the kind of situations we're going to get into with the colonel.'

Owain shrugged. 'Nothing I can learn in a book that I can't learn by travelling. Although, travelling to the past wasn't on my…' He stopped at a sound ahead of them. A strange slithering. Like something was sliding across the rocks.

'Come on,' Bill said, reaching for his gun instinctively.

Owain followed him, not bothering to point out that the gun didn't actually exist. It was only here because it was part of Bishop's astral image, a reflection of how he looked back in the future.

They stopped and watched the creature slink forward. Owain hadn't seen anything quite like it before. A strange, giant jellyfish pulsating with a green luminescence. It was the Rutan he had heard about. The alien responsible for all the deaths on Fang Rock in 1902. He moved forward.

'Owain!' Bill hissed, his gun aimed at the Rutan.

'It can't see us,' Owain reminded him, stepping closer to the alien as it continued towards the lighthouse. 'We may as well get a good look at…' His head snapped around. A strange noise echoed across the rocks. It wasn't a natural sound, a strange wheezing, rising and falling asthmatically, as if the very air itself was being torn apart by something.

Bill was looking around. 'It came from over there,' he said. He set off at a run.

Owain glanced down at the Rutan, shook his head and

set off after Bill. They turned a small group of rocks and skidded to a halt. Before them stood the most incongruous sight – even stranger than the Rutan. A police box.

Standing on a rock island in the middle of the English Channel... in 1902 was a police box!

Before they could take another step, Bill faded from sight. Literally, like dust on the wind, he simply disappeared.

'Bill!' Owain called.

— CHAPTER NINE —

Executive Decision

Bill returned first. He opened his eyes, blinking like he'd just been asleep, and looked around the crew room. Anne walked over to him and gently removed the pads from his temples and handed him a glass of cold water. He drank it gratefully.

'How are you feeling, Corporal?' Lethbridge-Stewart asked from behind Anne.

'Colonel, if you could give him a moment to get his bearings,' Anne said, her tone protective, not offering another option.

Lethbridge-Stewart wasn't happy, but stepped back with a nod.

Bill sat forward and placed his head in his hands. 'Headache,' he said, and looked up. 'That was... Very strange. I think—'

'Bill!' Owain's eyes snapped open and he shot forward, crashing off the sofa onto the floor. Lethbridge-Stewart was at his side in an instant. The young man was unconscious. Lethbridge-Stewart looked up at Anne enquiringly.

'I imagine no two people experience astral projection the same. Like taking LSD, or any other kind of drug really, the effects are slightly different for everybody. All depending on how the drugs interact with the brain chemistry, the body, all kinds of variables.'

Lethbridge-Stewart looked over at Jim. 'Mr Saunders, help me get Owain up to the bunk room. He can recover there.'

Anne waited until the two men had carried Owain out of the crew room, then knelt before Bill. She placed a hand on his, and he lifted his face to look at her. 'So, Owain calls you Bill now? Knew it'd catch on,' she said with a smile.

Bill shrugged. 'It's okay, Sam calls me it, too.'

'Sam?'

'My sister. Well, she calls me Billy, which is much worse.'

Anne had forgotten he had a sister. Brothers, too, as she recalled. 'How was it?' she asked, returning to the matter at hand.

'Strange. We were there, but not there.'

'Did you talk to Archibald?'

Bill shook his head. 'We couldn't interact, just watch. We were the ghosts this time.'

'He saw you?'

Again Bill shook his head. 'No.' He took another sip of the water. 'But we didn't see Archibald, we saw Ben. Your uncle.'

Anne frowned. 'But he died in...'

'1902, yeah.' Bill explained what he remembered of the trip. Seeing the falling star, what Vince had said, seeing the Rutan approach the lighthouse. 'Seemed like a nice guy, your uncle. You'd have liked him. Great sense of humour from what I saw.'

Anne felt a little disappointed. She had hoped to learn more about Archibald. The events of 1902 had been well-documented; what Bill and Lethbridge-Stewart had discovered about the Rutan solved the mystery of how they had all died, and if she was right about the Hobo's involvement, then they could safely assume he had dealt with the Rutan. But 1823 still remained the mystery. Why had Archibald come to Fang Rock? What did all this have to do with the Beast?

'Did you see anything helpful? Anything we didn't know, something that will at least help us solve the mystery of the Beast.'

'I don't know, I think...' Bill screwed his face up, concentrating. His eyes lit up. 'Of course! Ben, he left something for you.'

That was not what Anne had expected. 'What? For me? How can he know about me?'

'The piece missing from this machine,' Bill said, nodding at the apparatus. 'Well, I think that's what it was.'

'Ben was the *he* Archibald mentioned in his letter? But how? That was a long time before Ben was even thought of.'

At this Bill laughed. 'What, and someone knowing about you in 1823 is normal?'

'Good point. Well, where did Ben leave this missing piece?'

Bill stood up. 'In the generator room.' He took Anne's hand and led her out of the crew room. 'Come on!'

On the stairs outside they bumped into the returning Lethbridge-Stewart and Jim.

'What the devil?' Lethbridge-Stewart said. 'Where are you two going?'

'Ben Travers left something here for Anne,' Bill said. Lethbridge-Stewart noticed the hand-holding, and Bill quickly let Anne go. He looked down, chastised by Lethbridge-Stewart's glare.

'What something?'

'The missing piece,' Anne said, setting off down the stairs. She didn't care for the look Lethbridge-Stewart had given Bill, but forced herself to keep her tone civil. 'Come on, Corporal,' she called behind her. The sound of multiple footsteps let her know that the men were following. Anne smiled. She didn't like the idea that this whole situation had been manipulated in some way by Archibald, that she was simply a pawn in a paradox she was only beginning to understand, but she was looking forward to finally getting the crystal machine working properly.

Once in the generator room she realised she was not sure where she was supposed to be looking. She couldn't imagine the room as it stood now much resembled the generator room of 1902, especially when one took into account the great fire of '55, which had all but gutted out the lighthouse.

'In here,' Bill said, passing Anne and heading to the bathroom door.

Lethbridge-Stewart glanced at Anne. 'Are you sure this *trip* hasn't played with his mind?'

Anne didn't think so. But then she considered Owain. Despite the recent events in Wiltshire, she was far from an expert in time travel. She wondered what Kashchei Stravinsky, the Russian scientist who had assisted her and her father at the Joint Warfare Establishment, would think of all this. He certainly knew quite a bit about the applications of time travel, and its consequences.

Astral projection on the other hand… Much was written about it, and she couldn't recall ever hearing of any bad effects. But, of course, there was also the inclusion of Om-Tsor, and that was known to have detrimental effects on some people.

Instead of answering, Anne simply crossed the generator room and walked into the small bathroom. Lethbridge-Stewart and Jim joined her; she could feel them both looking over her shoulder from the doorway. The bathroom was not big enough for more than two people at a time, especially now that Bill was on his knees by the side of the bath tub, his left arm reaching beneath the tub. She glanced back at Lethbridge-Stewart and offered a smile. He didn't look too impressed by the actions of his adjutant. Because of the uniqueness of Bill's appointment, Anne knew his responsibilities were much less than if an officer was in the position, but, Anne reasoned, they were out in the field (in a manner of speaking) and as such Bill had more duties than just answering Lethbridge-Stewart's calls. She'd have thought Lethbridge-Stewart would be impressed with Bill's initiative, with his willingness to take control of the situation.

Bill finally withdrew his arm and turned around, a beaming smile on his handsome face. In his hands he held a metallic rod – no more than four inches in length, covered in dust – and a faded piece of paper. 'One piece of alien equipment,' he said, 'and one letter for you.' He handed her the letter and clambered to his booted feet.

'Where did they come from?' Lethbridge-Stewart asked.

'Buried there by Ben Travers in 1902, sir,' Bill said.

'You saw him bury them?'

Bill nodded.

'I see. Then how did they survive the fire of '55?'

Jim answered. 'It never quite reached the generator

room, luckily. If it had, I doubt there would have been much of a lighthouse to reopen.'

'Then it's a lucky hiding place.'

'Not really, sir,' Bill said. 'Not if Ben Travers knew it'd be safe.'

'How could he possibly have known that?'

'Maybe the information came from someone who knew,' Anne said. 'Someone from the future? Like me.'

The men looked at her. It was clear that the colonel was having trouble getting his head around it, but Jim and Bill both looked back with understanding.

She unfolded the paper gently. It was surprisingly well preserved. She read the words. A surge of emotion erupted in her and she brushed past the two men in the doorway, walking across the generator room to sit on the bottom stone step.

This was different from the letter she had received from Archibald. It was the use of the word 'Teddy' in reference to her father. Of course she knew that Ben was her father's uncle, but that one word brought home the fact that her father and Ben had actually known each other. For the first time since all this had begun, she was hit by the reality of it. No longer was she dealing with the abstract, with sketchy figures from history, but her own flesh and blood. It all went some way to explain why her father had never mentioned Ben; he was only three when Ben had died. *Three.* So young. If the Rutan had never visited Earth, then her father... *she* would have got to know Ben Travers. Their uncle.

She read the letter over again and took a deep breath.

For the first time she truly understood why Hamilton had set Lethbridge-Stewart on his mission, why he had put her inside the Vault. She understood it... on a very visceral and personal level.

She looked up. The men had gathered in the room but were keeping a respectful distance. Lethbridge-Stewart and Jim both looked uncomfortable with her display of emotion, but not Bill. There was concern in his blue eyes. If his superior officer were not standing by him, Bill would probably have been by Anne's side. She felt another rush of emotion, but shook it off before it could take hold. It wouldn't do to be like this. She was a scientist, and she was here to solve a mystery, not indulge in personal fantasies. One day there would be time enough to worry about her personal future. Right now it was her past she needed to work out.

She stood up, face determined, and stepped forward with her hand out. 'Archibald didn't lie, Colonel. He said the missing piece of the machine would find its way to me, and here it is.'

Bill moved to give her the rod, but instead Lethbridge-Stewart took it. 'So it would seem. Nonetheless, my previous decision stands. You are not going back into the past, Miss Travers.'

Anne narrowed her eyes. 'But I must. Both Archibald and Ben,' she said, raising the letter in her hand to punctuate her point, 'have now sent messages from the past, beyond the grave itself, to tell me that I *have* to go back.'

Lethbridge-Stewart shook his head. 'I'm sorry, Miss Travers, but I will not allow it. There is no indication whatsoever that you can come back, and this may seem selfish to you, but you are needed here.'

Anne could not believe it. 'You really are the most

obstinate man I have ever met,' she snapped.

Lethbridge-Stewart raised an eyebrow. 'You are my responsibility, and as such you will do as I say.'

Anne glared at him and folded her arms. 'Is that right?'

A short time later, once Lethbridge-Stewart and Jim had left the generator room, Anne and Bishop discussed the issue of time travel and Anne's role in the events of 1823. Bishop knew he was probably talking out of turn, maybe even going against the orders of the colonel, but he didn't believe the colonel was right.

'You not going back could change the past,' he said.

Anne agreed. 'I have been thinking that, too. Remembering something my father said recently. The past isn't set in stone, as one would think. It doesn't just happen once.'

'Not for those who can travel there, no. All evidence would suggest that you were involved in whatever happened in 1823, perhaps played a pivotal role. If you don't go back, then what happens? Archibald would never know to leave the letter with your solicitor, or that machine. Ben would never know to hide the rod. And who knows what actually happened in 1823? Why you're needed there?'

Anne reached out and patted him on the knee. 'I know what you're saying, Bill. If I don't go back, all this,' she waved her hands around, 'could change. A completely different future would unfold. Would we even know that it had?'

Bishop shrugged. 'I don't know. I've read books, but they're just fiction. This is reality now. How can we know what will happen?'

'My father has read about such theories, and Stravinsky seemed to agree with the notion behind them.' Abruptly, Anne stood up and walked to the door that led outside.

Bill joined her as she stepped through to the outside. For the first time since they'd arrived, Fang Rock looked beautiful. The sun was rising in the sky, heralding a lovely day ahead for those on the mainland. The air was clear, and looking out they could see the distant shores of Hove and Brighton. In silence they walked along the damp rocks, until Anne found a small pool of water left over from last night's storm.

'What if time is like a stream?' she said, kneeling down by the pool. She picked up a small rock. 'Imagine that the centre of this pool is the past, say 1823, and the edge of the pool is now. Today.' She dropped the rock in the middle of the pool and they watched it splash. She pointed at the ripples in the water. 'You see? The changes ripple out until they finally reach the edge. If I don't go back, and the past is changed, then perhaps those changes haven't reached us yet.'

Bishop nodded, pretty sure he'd read something similar. 'Ripples in time.' He helped Anne to her feet. 'Then what do we do? I can't go against the colonel.'

'No.' Anne looked back at the lighthouse. 'I have to do this myself.'

For a little while Owain had spent some time living out of a VW van with some friends, and they had introduced him to certain mind-expanding substances, but none that had adversely affected him like the Om-Tsor. After one attempt at standing from his bunk he remembered why he'd so soon tired of drugs, and collapsed back into bed. He'd always found himself more drawn to the Eastern philosophies anyway; he supposed it was inevitable considering what he had learned about his reincarnated soul. Clearly, though, Om-Tsor was a lot stronger than any Earth-going drug.

His uncle now sat on a small stool beside the bed, explaining what had happened since Bill and he had returned to the present.

'You believe in time travel now?' Owain asked, trying not to laugh at Alistair's obvious resistance to the idea.

'Well, I'm more inclined to believe you and Bishop than an old man close to senility and a man I've only met once, however brilliant they may both be. But,' the colonel added, his tone one of seriousness, 'I'm still not entirely convinced.'

'Despite what Bill and I have told you?'

'As I said, that's convinced me somewhat. Besides, the two of you weren't really there.'

'No, but Anne would be. We have letters that prove that. She'll be there, she *has* to be there.'

'But how? That rod thing?'

'Makes sense to me,' Owain said. 'She needed the Om-Tsor to project us back, but now the machine is complete...'

'She can really travel into the past?'

Owain didn't push any further, he could tell his uncle still wasn't quite believing yet. Instead he asked what the next course of action was. It seemed that Alistair was still debating that, but what he had decided was that Anne was definitely *not* going into the past.

'I bet she took that well. What *are* you going to do then?' Owain asked.

'Well, that's it, isn't it? *What*. I do, after all, have a mission to complete.'

Owain nodded, and sipped the coffee Alistair had brought him. 'Well, surely what's past is past? I mean, you can't change what's already happened, can you? Whatever happened in 1823 has always happened.'

'That is my thinking, yes.'

Owain thought about it more. 'Anne might be the sea gull,' he said, and got a blank look from his uncle. 'What if Anne was always part of events in the past. If so, then doesn't that mean stopping her alters the past?'

Alistair was obviously not following. Which Owain could appreciate; he wasn't sure he was following it either. Anne was the scientist, and Bill the one who read fiction about time travel and science journals; he was just a guy from a small Cornish village, same as Alistair for that matter. Although, of course, his uncle had a great deal more experience than he. He must have seen a lot of strange things during his military service, and if he couldn't follow this...

'All I know is that I need evidence of alien threats to Britain,' Alistair said. 'And, it would seem this rock has been visited by aliens at least twice. And I have a method by which to bring back evidence.'

'You mean go yourself?'

Alistair stood up. 'Why not? I'm better trained to handle any hostilities in the past. I'm sure I can help Archibald Goff with this Beast as easily as Miss Travers can. Probably better.' He pulled out his gun. 'A few shots of this will take care of an alien jellyfish.'

On the floor below, Anne stopped outside the crew room.

152

Jim was in there, playing around with his camera. And so was the alien rod. It rested on the cabinet beneath the window, not far from where Jim was sitting.

'Hey, Jim,' she said as she walked in. 'The colonel wants you and your camera. Owain's remembered something, and Lethbridge-Stewart wants to get it on film.'

'Oh, right.' Jim stood and grabbed his equipment.

Anne smiled. 'I'm going to make some tea,' she said, putting on her best 'little lady' voice. 'Fancy a brew?'

'Wouldn't say no.'

'Okay, I'll bring it up to the bunk room,' she said and turned to leave. She walked down a few steps, around the curved wall so she was out of sight. She stopped and listened until she was sure Jim had left the crew room.

She crept back up. Sure enough the crew room was now empty. She crossed the room and picked up the rod. She had no time to waste. Anne turned back to the machine and searched for the slot into which the rod fitted. Upstairs she heard the sound of a raised voice: Lethbridge-Stewart, no doubt realising what she was up to.

She found the slot and pushed in the rod. Ideally she would have liked more time to explore the machine, test it, but the colonel had left her with little other option. She was needed in the past, so she had to go. It was that simple. The machine hummed in a crescendo of power, then stopped abruptly. The crystals lit with energy, different colours dancing around within them. Anne looked up as Lethbridge-Stewart entered the room.

'Miss Travers, just what do you think you're—?'

Anne barely got a chance to smile before the entire room disappeared around her.

CHAPTER TEN

Family Ties

Anne awoke and looked around the dark room. Nothing was familiar to her. She wasn't on the small cot she'd set up for herself at the Vault, neither was she in her more familiar bedroom at Kilham. She sat up and removed the rough blanket from over her. As she threw her legs onto the cold concrete floor she felt it very keenly through the thin material of her tights. To her right was a small window, through which moonlight cast into the room. It wasn't much, but as her eyes adjusted to the dark, the moonlight helped bring a few small details into focus. The room was functional, bereft of any of the small touches one would expect in a well-used bedroom, with a small wooden writing desk to one side, on which sat, unless she was mistaken, an ink-pot and quill. A small metal pot was on the floor only a short distance from the wooden bunk she was sitting on. She had an uncomfortable feeling that she knew exactly what the pot was used for, and it wasn't rubbish.

She shivered suddenly. Not from the coldness around her – there was no heating in the room – but from the realisation of where she was. Her geographical location hadn't changed, but her temporal one...

Had she really travelled in time?

She looked around for her shoes, wondering why it was

she had woken without them. There they were, underneath the bed. Slipping them back on, she crossed the room and picked up the ink-pot. It looked like an antique, but not in the least bit old. Used, certainly, but still relatively new.

'It's true,' she said to herself. 'Time travel.'

She silently apologised to her father for all the years of doubt. Despite coming face to face with the time traveller he had always spoken about, she now realised a part of her had still doubted her father's stories of Tibet, of the man who had travelled from 1630 to 1935 to return the Holy Ghanta to Det-Sen. A man who had then travelled forward another thirty-four years to help them in the London Underground... Travelled in *time*. Just as she had.

'Here's to the... *Hobo*,' she muttered, adding the proper noun with some reluctance. She didn't expect the walls around her now to have ears, despite the colonel's claims, but she had to reluctantly admit he was probably right in his advice. Knowledge of a friendly time travelling alien was probably not something that should be advertised, especially when travelling in time yourself.

She turned the ink-pot around in her hand. Even after last month, examining the capsule which had come from a past that had never existed, even with the soldiers from the past appearing in the present... Even after all that, she found herself in awe of the truth. Time travel *was* possible and she had travelled through time. Her. Anne Travers. She shook her head, imagining the next report she'd have to write for General Hamilton.

She replaced the ink-pot and looked around the dark room. Nothing to light her way; no candle, and definitely no electric light. Confirmation, if any were needed.

She stepped out of the bunk room and considered which way to go. Presumably at least one keeper was on watch above, while below... She turned left and began her descent. She needed to find Archibald Goff, and it seemed more likely he'd be in the library or, if not, outside.

As she descended, Anne was once again reminded of the coldness of the tower. It wasn't especially warm in her own time, but it was warm enough to not need an overcoat. But here, in the past, it was a different matter. She didn't know much about the 1820s, but she did know that Faraday had only recently discovered a way to convert electrical energy into mechanical energy, and it seemed unlikely that the practical application of such a motor had found its way to rock lighthouses already. And she doubted gas was used at Fang Rock either; she couldn't imagine them using the highly explosive acetylene gas in such a remote location. It was all oil here, which accounted for the smell, Anne decided as she continued down the curved steps. She removed a hanky from her skirt pocket and placed it over her nose, grateful for the scent of Yves Saint Laurent which hid at least a bit of the cloying stench of oil.

She stopped a few steps from the library at the sound of two men speaking. She listened, unable to steady the uneven beat of her heart. Anxiety? Yes, Anne realised, she was a bit anxious. Not only was she actually in the past, but she was about to meet one of her ancestors.

'You ought not to have brought her here,' said an old gruff voice, his accent betraying his southern origins.

'What would you have me do, Scott? Leave her out there on the rocks?' The second voice was younger, more well-travelled, the accent harder to place.

'Yes, dammit!'

Silence followed for a moment, save for the steady breathing of a man trying to contain his frustration. Scott continued, calmer now. 'You gave thought to her being a ghost, but that is clearly not so. Who the devil is she? How did she come to be on this rock?'

'I cannot say. But contend with this we must. She is real, yet I beheld her as a ghost in this very room!'

'Dash it, Goff, you have delivered unto Fang Rock much trouble. Consider Crane. The boy looks to be in a fit of the vapours.'

Anne's heart steeled at the mention of the name Goff. Gingerly, like she was once again a little girl sneaking into her father's laboratory, she descended the last few steps. This was it, the moment she had been, on some level, expecting ever since Rupert Slant had told her about Archibald Goff. Meeting the man who had guided most of her thoughts for the last few weeks, the man who held the answer to the bad blood between her paternal and maternal families.

She paused at the door. She was better than this, not the easily impressed child she had once been. She was thirty years old, a respected scientist in her own right; she had stepped out of the shadow of her father long ago, and she would not now wither in the shadow of another of her ancestors, no matter how small she felt at the idea of meeting a man who had died almost a hundred years before she was born.

She stepped boldly into the library and regarded the three men. 'Gentlemen,' she said, and found herself enjoying the looks that passed over their faces as they turned as one at the sudden interruption.

All three men, although vastly different in stature and bearing, had some startling similarities. All had some kind of facial hair, be it the mutton chops of the elder two or the ridiculous moustache of the youngest; all were dressed in many layers to combat the coldness of the lighthouse, and all were dirty, their faces and hands covered by sweat, soot and dirt, with missing or yellowed teeth. A far cry from the men of her time. The oldest, Scott, was white haired and slightly plump in the stomach; he looked at her with something like apprehension, mixed with an odd distance, as if he knew more than he wanted to admit. The youngest, Crane no doubt, a man who could be no more than his very early twenties, looked at her with fear, his hands clenching and unclenching as he sat on the stool at the far end of the room. The third man, who had to be Archibald Goff, gave a curious look, rubbing his dirty beard as if unsure quite what to make of her. There was no fear in his eyes, however, despite his talk of ghosts.

Anne stepped forward and held out a hand politely. 'Anne Travers,' she said. '*Doctor* Anne Travers, actually,' she added, unable to resist winking at her three-time-great grandfather's look of incredulity.

'What the deuce!' Archibald said, his brow furrowed. 'You're a woman!'

Anne looked down at herself. 'Am I? Good grief!'

'But...' Archibald shook his head and looked to Scott for help, but the older light keeper had none to give. He barely even acknowledged Archibald, his eyes set firmly on Anne, the thoughts behind them no doubt manifold. 'How can you be...? This is absurd. I beheld you a ghost.'

'Yes, this is not the first time I've heard such a thing.' She held out her hand again. 'And you are Archibald Goff?'

'I am. Well, yes, but how did you know…?'

'What manner of dress is this?' Scott said, finally finding his voice.

Anne lowered her hand again with a sigh and looked down at her orange top and green skirt. They did rather stand out against the drab, muted colours worn by the men. And, no doubt, the women these men were used to barely showed their ankles in public, let alone the amount of leg her skirt revealed.

'It's how all women dress where I'm from,' Anne said, hardly able to help herself from teasing the men further.

'And just where is that?' Archibald asked.

'Well, and this is the bit you may find hard to believe,' Anne said, brushing the hair behind her ear coyly. 'If I am a ghost, then I am a ghost from your future.'

'What rot!' Scott exclaimed.

'I really am. In fact, I'm you're great-great-great granddaughter,' Anne said, looking directly at Archibald. 'And I came here because you told me to.'

Lethbridge-Stewart stormed into the bunk room. 'She's gone, and she's taken that blasted machine!'

'Where has she gone?' Owain asked, looking up from his guitar.

'If she's right, then I suppose she has gone into the past.'

Owain nodded slowly, placing the guitar to one side. 'That's us stumped then. We definitely can't follow her there.'

'No.' The colonel took to pacing the room, muttering to

himself. 'Stubborn woman. She just wouldn't listen, would she? And now look. Who knows what she'll find in the past? We'll probably never see her again...'

'Only as a ghost.'

Lethbridge-Stewart stopped pacing. 'What?'

'Well, not a ghost, an echo or whatever it is Anne called them. I've already seen hers once before, remember? Before you got here.'

'Of course. So, does that mean from our point of view she's dead? That we give up?'

Owain shrugged. 'I don't know. But if she *is* in 1823, then what can we do? It's already happened. Whatever it was, it's done with. A long time ago.' He could see his uncle wasn't keen on the idea, but what else could they do? The web and the Om-Tsor would be no use without the machine to direct them. 'Perhaps you need to contact your boss, let him know what's happened. I mean, I wouldn't mind getting off this rock.'

'Hmm. Perhaps, but we still haven't completed our mission.'

Owain couldn't help but laugh at that, wondering when it had become *their* mission. 'We have some answers, maybe not all of them, but some. We know that it was aliens who came to Fang Rock, that they were somehow stopped in 1902, and that Anne ended up in 1823 as she was supposed to.'

The colonel shook his head and sat down on the stool by the small table. He tapped his swagger stick on the surface. 'This is all absurd. Miss Travers dying over a hundred years before she was born; how is that possible?'

Owain looked down at his hands. 'Time can be changed,'

he muttered. 'Like it did with your brother, remember?'

The tapping stopped. Lethbridge-Stewart stood up and closed the door. He looked back at Owain and the façade of the soldier dropped. Now it was just Alistair and Owain, uncle and nephew. 'You know I don't remember, Owain. All I know is what I've been told. Without the stories of Ray and the photographs, I wouldn't even believe James existed.'

'Existed, and was supposed to die in 1949, but the Intelligence killed him ten years earlier. And now Anne has died in a past she doesn't belong in.' Owain shook his head and laughed with humour he did not feel. 'Not saying I understand how it works, but apparently it does.'

'Yes. I met him again, you know. James. *Major* James Lethbridge-Stewart of the Coldstream Guards, no less. Well, I *think* I met him. At least, that is to say, I thought it was all some hallucination, but now with all this...' He stopped, noticing the blank look Owain was giving him. 'Recently, well, some weeks ago now, I think I may have somehow found myself in the past. In 1959...'

Owain listened as Alistair explained his recent experiences. It was a confused tale, and Owain wasn't entirely sure he followed it. Soldiers from the past appearing in the now, only a now that was actually 1959, which at the time seemed perfectly normal to Alistair, until his brother turned up. Alive and well and in his mid-thirties.

'Since I returned to the UK I have gone over it many times, trying to make sense of it all. After everything in the last few months, the hallucinations made a kind of sense. Time travel, James, even a younger Professor Travers, but... But I was sure it was some plot by the Eastern Bloc to extract secrets from me. Only...' Alistair shook his head and sat on the bed beside Owain. 'Time travel is possible,' he said, his voice disbelieving still. 'Did I travel into the past?'

'A past in which James didn't die. He died early in your past, after all.' Owain was silent a moment, concerned by the look passing over his uncle's face. Doubt – doubt and grief. 'The Intelligence came from the future, travelled back to kill James. What if it hadn't? James would have lived and I... Would I have even been born if James lived? After all, he was my previous life.'

'How readily we learn to accept such things.'

'Just like Alice,' Owain said with a smile. 'I have book knowledge after all.' He paused as a thought struck him. 'Have you spoken to Anne?'

'Why would I do that?'

Owain was probably betraying a confidence, but he couldn't back out now. 'She told Bill about something that happened to her a few weeks ago, something about General Hamilton bringing her in to investigate soldiers from the Great War that had appeared in the present. She and her father found a capsule in Arctic, a capsule from the past. A past which never happened, I think Bill said. Like the one you found in Deepdene.'

Alistair frowned, clearly hearing this for the first time. 'Then what I experienced was real,' he said, relief in his voice. 'Only... This is incredible. No, it's impossible.'

'Implausible, maybe, but obviously not impossible. I think you need to have a word with your general, as well as Anne.'

Alistair nodded. 'Yes, I think you may be right. Hamilton's been holding out on me.' He looked down at the guitar between them. 'How is your family?' he asked

Owain suddenly.

For a moment Owain wasn't sure what to say. It wasn't often that he and Alistair got to chat in such personal ways; indeed, he couldn't remember a time since that match between Arsenal and Southampton back in March. The odd phone call and letter didn't allow for much real conversation. Owain shrugged again. 'They're okay, I suppose. I think my mum misses Lewis a lot. She doesn't say it, but when I talk to her on the phone I can hear it in her voice. I think part of her believes she's lost both of us, and I have to remind her that she hasn't. I'm still here, just travelling. Living my life. Doing the things Lewis never got to do.'

'And what of the things you want to do?'

Owain smiled. 'I'm doing them.' He lifted his guitar. 'Learning new things. Not all of them good.'

'No, but sometimes we need to experience the bad to realise who we are.'

For a moment the two of them held each other's eyes, and with a shock Owain realised how much pain his uncle carried within. He was a man who had seen much misery in his years, experienced more loss than Owain could imagine. Yet the most personal loss was one that Alistair couldn't even remember. Owain wasn't sure how the colonel carried on. If it was him, Owain wasn't sure he could manage. He had lost family, of course, grandparents, all people who had lived long lives. The only loss that had ever hit him was his brother. His twin, the one absolute constant throughout his entire life. Gone forever.

And now Anne. He couldn't say he knew Anne that well, but she seemed nice, and now she was gone too. Dead. Only

163

it didn't feel like she was dead. How could one quantify a death that occurred one hundred and forty-six years before? It was as abstract as reading about the death of a stranger in the papers, or hearing about it on the radio.

A knock on the door pulled Owain out of his thoughts. Lethbridge-Stewart, once again the soldier, stood sharply and called out 'come'. The door opened and Bill entered. He looked at Owain briefly before saluting the colonel.

'What is it, Corporal?'

'I was just coming to see how Owain is, sir,' Bill said.

'I see.' Lethbridge-Stewart looked back at Owain and gave him a smile. 'I'll leave you lads to it then, while I contact General Hamilton, appraise him of our current predicament.'

Owain offered a mock salute. The colonel went to leave the room, but first stopped by Bill. 'Do try to not give away any more secrets, Bishop,' he said sharply.

Bill closed the door behind him. 'What was that about?'

'No idea,' Owain said, feigning ignorance. He'd put his foot in his mouth enough for one day, and the day hadn't even begun for most of the UK. 'You okay?'

Bill crossed the room and moved the guitar out of the way before sitting next to Owain. 'I don't know. This is... It's unreal. We're supposed to think Anne is dead, but she was here less than half an hour ago.'

'I know, it's kind of like some strange trip.' Owain sighed, and looked Bill in his blue eyes. 'I'm sorry, I don't know what to say.'

'Nor me.'

So the two young men just sat in silence.

*

164

Archibald had heard it all now. In his life he had experienced things that would drive most men insane, things that would leave women a helpless mess on the floor. Seen things that couldn't be explained by a rational mind, but he had never heard such as this before. A woman from the future!

'Never mind Charlie having a case of the vapours,' he said, trying his best not to laugh at the absurdity of the woman's claim. 'I think I must be blotto. From the future? My, what did you say, great-great-great granddaughter? A *doctor* no less.' He could no longer contain it. A deep belly laugh erupted from him. 'Footle!'

'Then, how do you explain my clothes? My hair? Heck, how do you explain my hygiene?'

Archibald waved it all away. 'I don't.' He took to a stool himself and continued laughing.

Behind him Charlie finally stirred. He got to his feet and stumbled towards the woman. 'You can't take me,' he whimpered, crossing himself.

The woman frowned, and then nodded to herself. 'Charlie. Of course! It was you I was with when Owain and Jim saw me as a ghost.'

'You see!' Archibald snapped his fingers and pointed. 'She confesses; a ghost.'

Scott reached out and touched the woman's arm. 'A bit too solid for a ghost, I'd wager,' he said, then snatched his arm back when the woman turned to face him. 'Forgive me,' he rumbled.

'I'm not a ghost. I'm as real as any of you.'

Charlie reached out his own hand, but he couldn't bring himself to touch her. The woman shook her head, now clearly frustrated, and reached out to grab hold of Charlie's hand. He shrieked in terror, but she wouldn't let go.

'You see? I'm real.'

Archibald watched as slowly the terror drifted from Charlie's face. He offered a weak smile and the woman returned it. Archibald stood up and pulled Charlie away from her.

'Enough of this. You claim to be my descendent?'

'I am. My mother is—'

'Didn't you say your name is Travers?'

'Yes. Anne Travers.'

Archibald laughed, and looked to Scott and Charlie. 'Then you are quite mistaken, young woman,' he said looking back at Miss Travers. 'The person you seek, if we really are to entertain the notion that you are from the future, is out there on the rocks. If anybody has claim on your ancestry it is him.'

'But you are Archibald Goff. Aren't you?'

Archibald bowed. 'At your service. But I am not the man you seek.'

'Then who is?'

'Why, Jacob Travers, of course.'

'What?'

'Ha!' Archibald waved her away and turned to Scott. 'You see how easy it is to reveal her lies.' He pointed at the woman. 'If you were who you claim to be, then you would have knowledge of Jacob Travers.'

'But...' The woman stopped to think. 'So, it's not just Ben, my family's connection with Fang Rock *does* go back to...' She shook her head and looked directly at Archibald. He stepped back, shocked at the fierce intelligence in her

166

eyes. 'It begins here, it must do. You and... Jacob? This is where the Travers and Goffs first meet. You and him. What is going on here?'

'Tell her,' Scott said.

Archibald was surprised. He had expected more resistance from the old buffer, but now the man was before this woman who claimed to be a Travers, he seemed content to stand back. To let Archibald handle things. 'Very well. What do you know of the Beast?'

'That it...' She blinked. 'Are you telling me the Beast is here, now?'

'That is why I stand before you, dear lady,' Archibald said, puffing himself up with pride. 'I am here to locate the Beast, to discover what manner of being it is and why it wants Jacob.'

As he spoke Archibald observed Miss Travers' face. He had seen such expressions before, on the faces of learned men as they put together new theories with the facts they already held. Like Doctor Hoenneger at Bethlem Hospital after Archibald had explained all he had learned about the events of Fang Rock a year ago. But to see such intelligence sweep across the delicate features of a woman... She was, without any doubt in Archibald's mind, the most intelligent person on Fang Rock at present. He found himself wondering if perhaps she had spoken true; after all her bearing, her clothes, they were nothing like any woman he'd ever met. He thought briefly of Rebecca, his wife, who he had always considered of above intelligence for a woman; next to Miss Travers she would look like a simpleton. Could the woman before him really be from the future? And if she was, what became of men when women ranked the most intelligent? He shook himself from his reverie. Miss Travers was ruminating aloud, but more to herself than to any of the men.

'Of course, that makes sense. Here and 1902. But why did the Rutan come back to Fang Rock in seventy-nine years' time?' Miss Travers turned to the door, her mind evidently made up on something. She made to leave, then glanced back, genuinely surprised to see that the men were not following her. As if leading men was a natural thing to her! 'We have to go and find him before the Rutan does. The future of our family might depend on his survival.'

Jim was balanced halfway up the ladder, his head poking through the open hatch of the helipad, enjoying the bracing air on his face. Ivan was carefully cleaning the helipad of any dirt and water left over from the previous night's storm. He wore a brace, which was secured by rope to a stanchion next to the ladder. 'What do you make of all this?' Jim asked.

Ivan glanced over at him and shrugged. 'Well, I've heard plenty of strange tales of lighthouses in the past. You wouldn't believe some of them. Never thought I'd become part of one though. And mark my words, tales of the vanishing woman will be told for many a day yet.'

Jim didn't doubt it. He was still trying to sort it all out in his own head. Lethbridge-Stewart had been less than impressed, and Jim doubted he had helped much with his endless questions and it wasn't like Lethbridge-Stewart had any answers. The only person who could have provided answers was in the past.

Jim chuckled, surprised how easily such thoughts came to mind. How easily he accepted it as fact. He'd have loved to talk to Harry Chorley about all this, catch up over a pint with Steve Worman, too, compare notes, but he would soon be read into the Official Secrets Act and that would be it. Never to talk of such things again. Not if he wanted to avoid ending up like Harry, anyway. Harry had no doubt spoken out of turn, pushed his luck – getting Larry Greene in trouble while he was at it – which is why he was now *persona non grata* at most papers; even BBC 3 didn't want him. Jim wasn't so stupid. He liked his job, had been to a lot of interesting places thanks to the Beeb, and he didn't intend to risk that once this was all over. He knew things that only a few others knew.

'Ivan, when you're next on the mainland we should grab a pint. I'll invite Owain and Bill.'

Ivan smiled at him. 'Sounds like a plan,' he said. Then his smile faded. 'Oh s—' His words were obscured by a loud boom.

Jim looked up and didn't blink for several minutes. All he could do was stare. He had seen it before, of course, through the lens of his camera, but this was different. It was closer, realer... A UFO descended from the sky and soared a couple of hundred feet above the lighthouse, heading east towards the channel off Fang Rock.

'*Another* one?' he said, when he finally was able to find his voice, by which time the UFO had sunk beneath the waters.

'Colonel!' Ivan shouted, leaning over the side of the helipad.

He wasn't going to leave Fang Rock, not again. Last time he was lucky to escape, although he knew that he never truly escaped. Not all of him. It had taken a long time to realise this, many days and months of talking to Archie. Poor Archie, he really believed he was going to help Jacob, but Jacob knew better. He had lied to Archie, told Archie what he wanted to hear. Lying became easy when Jacob understood the truth.

Hoenneger was wrong, believing Jacob had inherited a disease from his father, Lawrence Travers, which he had contracted in India. Jacob hadn't even known that such a disease existed until Hoenneger had told him about his father's trip. But he was wrong. This was not a case of lycanthropia, although it was an easy mistake to make considering the state Jacob had been in when he'd been found by the Master of the Tender and Alfred Scott a year ago.

The Beast was real, and it kept a part of him on Fang Rock. But now it wanted all of Jacob.

He stopped and looked up. He wasn't far from West Crag. He sniffed the air, ignoring the water spraying on his face. He could feel it; the Beast was out there. Distant yet near. He could hear it growling, pressing ever closer. He moved on, but before he could take more than a few steps he stopped and doubled over in pain.

It was excruciating, like his muscles were on fire. It was a singular pain, one he could never forget. He had felt it before. A year ago, when the Beast had first come for him.

It was almost there.

Soon the Beast of Fang Rock's hunger would be sated.

— CHAPTER ELEVEN —

Terror at West Crag

Lethbridge-Stewart looked back up at the tower, at Heggessey, who had remained out on the gallery to keep watch. Heggessey was peering through a pair of binoculars; his voice crackled over the short-range radio. 'Difficult to say which direction, Colonel, but my guess is its somewhere near West Crag.'

'Right then.' Lethbridge-Stewart checked his watch then looked up at the sun. 'West is that way,' he said and pointed. 'Corporal, I want you and Saunders to branch out in a south-westerly direction. Owain will accompany me on a north-westerly approach. Now remember, if it is another Rutan that has landed – and I think that highly likely, all things considered – then it will not be a ghost this time. If we're to believe the evidence we have, then a Rutan was responsible for many deaths almost seventy years ago. Seventy years is a long time, and you can be sure that it will be even deadlier now.' He removed his pistol out of the holster. 'Our own weapons have improved considerably since 1902; I'd be surprised if the Rutan's haven't as well. We're all armed, so don't be afraid to defend yourselves.'

Lethbridge-Stewart directed this final remark at Owain. He knew that George Vine had taken his sons clay-pigeon shooting in the past, so the young man knew how to use the rifle in his hands. But this was quite a different situation to firing at inanimate objects catapulted through the air, and Lethbridge-Stewart was pretty sure Owain had never fired a hi-powered Self-Loading Rifle before. Before they had left the lighthouse, Lethbridge-Stewart had made sure Bishop explained in detail what they had witnessed when they had come across the ghostly Rutan eviscerating Ben Travers' corpse, and as an added bonus he'd given Owain a crash-course on the SLR. Owain nodded grimly.

'Right then. Spread out. If you find a Rutan, call it in. Mr Heggessey is watching from above, so remember to use the flare gun to signal your location. Close up, one dratted rock looks like any other, so the flare signal is essential.'

Saunders patted the flare gun in his coat pocket and looked around. 'Even more so now,' he said, pointing out towards the Channel. The men looked to see a mist slowly rising.

'A rather inopportune fog,' Lethbridge-Stewart said. 'Does this rock have a history of sudden fog build-up?'

'You'd best ask Ivan,' Saunders said.

So Lethbridge-Stewart did. The answer was not encouraging. 'Not since the early 1900s.'

Bishop grinned. 'Naturally. Not a coincidence.'

'No,' Lethbridge-Stewart agreed. 'Perhaps a defence mechanism of the alien craft? Some kind of atmospheric manipulation.'

'We had fog last night,' Bishop pointed out. 'Although it didn't last long.'

Lethbridge-Stewart considered this. 'No, it didn't. About as long as the Rutan from the past. Ghostly fog?'

'Just what we need,' Owain said.

'Quite. Very well, you have your orders. Keep close, and don't take unnecessary risks. This is primarily reconnaissance. If we need reinforcements from the mainland, then it'll be useful to know the full extent of the danger.'

This said, Bishop and Saunders broke off from Lethbridge-Stewart and Owain. The young man hefted his rifle to a more comfortable position.

'Keep your eyes sharp,' Lethbridge-Stewart said as they moved into the fog.

'What was that?'

Anne looked back at Charlie Crane and suppressed a shudder. It had nothing to do with the cold night air biting against her face and through her tights – she had been loaned Scott's thick greatcoat to protect her against the elements – but rather it was the way the fear just poured out of Charlie. The man was giving her the jitters. And maybe with reason; after all there was no proof that she was to return to the future. 'Just the wind,' she said, more for herself than anything, and glanced at Archibald, who chuckled.

She wasn't quite sure what to make of her ancestor. He certainly wasn't what she had expected, although when she really thought about it, she supposed she couldn't pinpoint what she *had* expected. Just not the man who now walked the precarious rocks beside her. As they walked, the only decent source of light coming from the moon above and the precisely timed flash from the lamp room in the tower behind them, she watched him as closely as she could without being obvious, trying to see traces of her mother in him, or perhaps even her brother. How many generations of Goffs had there been since Archibald? If Rupert Slant was to be believed then right now Archibald had at least one son out there, a son who would father his own son in thirteen years' time. The earliest Goff Anne had ever heard mention of: John Goff, her great grandfather. So, if a generation was roughly twenty-five years, then there was almost six generations between Archibald and her. It was little wonder she saw so little of her maternal family in the man beside her.

'How do you fare?' Archibald asked, his eyes catching her looking at him.

'I fare well,' she said. 'What is your son's name?'

Archibald stopped. 'How come you by such knowledge?'

'I told you, I'm from your future.'

Still Archibald didn't look entirely convinced. He glanced at Charlie. 'Well, dash it, I do have a son!' He narrowed his eyes and peered at Anne through the dark. 'But how is it that you do not know his name?'

'One hundred and forty-six years is a long time, Archie,' she said, using the name she remembered from the letter, hoping the familiarity of it would serve to convince him. 'I only know of your grandson, John.' As soon as she said that, Anne realised her mistake. Revealing knowledge of future events could maybe change things, make you second guess your natural instincts; she knew this well from the past couple of days. But Archibald did not seem put out by this future knowledge; indeed he just looked at her and laughed. And it was a proper belly laugh, the kind that rumbled and erupted. Anne couldn't help but smile in return, for a moment reminded of her Uncle Sebastian, who also had the kind of laugh that could cure the world of its ills. Perhaps the Goff gene did carry on to future generations after all.

'A grandson! I will be a grandfather! Well, what say you to that, Charlie?'

Charlie said nothing, he just continued to look at them as if they were mad.

'So, you believe me, then?' Anne asked.

It took Archibald a few moments to compose himself, then he shrugged. 'Well, why not, eh? Why not indeed! You strike me as a woman unlike any other. A ghost from the future. And what a future!' He laughed again.

Anne waited patiently. 'We should get on,' she urged him, once his laughter had returned to a manageable level. 'We must find Jacob.'

'Yes, quite so.' Archibald looked at her for a moment, then with a smile he moved forward, holding out his lantern ahead of him. 'Just one thing makes me wonder, though. If you are from the future, and descended from me, then how come you to be a Travers?'

They were nearing the edge of West Crag, a slight cliff looking out over the English Channel. It didn't look much different to Bishop than the rest of the crags of Fang Rock. He supposed there *was* a difference, but to him it was just another clump of rocks. Of course, the isle looked better now the sun was out. Even in the fog he could see the jagged edge of the crag ahead, could imagine the damage it had caused unwary mariners over the years. The sloping rocks beneath his booted feet were drying out, as the fog continued to grow thicker the nearer to the water they got. He looked up at the blue sky. White clouds and not a hint of an oncoming storm. So why the fog? Could the colonel have been right? The Rutan's possessed some fierce technology if they could affect the local atmosphere in such a way.

Mindful of this, he shifted the grip on his pistol. He much preferred to carry his old rifle, but he had to remind himself that he was no longer part of the Black Mafia and as such would have to get used to smaller arms. Lance corporal now, after all, not a rifleman. Still, whatever armed service he worked for, he was a trained marksman and he would make every shot of his pistol count.

He glanced back at Jim and was about to speak, but the sound of movement nearby stopped him. He raised a hand and signalled Jim to stop. Both men listened for a moment. The sound was drawing closer, a strange slithering and squelching, as if something was climbing over the rocks themselves. He recognised the sound from 1902, and signalled caution. The two men moved forward, their guns at the ready.

They didn't need to move far. In the light of day, the Rutan looked even stranger. Although still partly obscured by the fog, it appeared to be almost translucent, with a strange glow emanating from its centre. The tendrils writhed around it, while it moved across the rocks like a slug across a paving slab in a garden. For a brief moment Bishop wondered what its tendrils were for, since they didn't appear to be used to propel the creature, but then he remembered the spectral image he had seen hours earlier when it was still dark.

Jim gasped beside him and tensed his arms, the gun held in both hands, aiming directly at the Rutan.

'Calm,' Bishop whispered. 'It doesn't seem to have noticed us yet.'

He gently pushed Jim's arms down.

'Sorry,' Jim said, and swallowed. 'It's my first alien.'

Bishop thought back to Bledoe and the Yeti. 'Wish it was mine,' he said.

'What's it doing?'

Bishop didn't have an answer. Other than moving slowly forward, the Rutan didn't appear to be doing anything of any interest. Looking at it, as it continued over the rocks, Bishop wondered how it could possibly be intelligent enough to fly a spaceship. It really did look like a giant green jellyfish. It had no discernible features that portrayed an intelligence; no eyes, mouth, ears, nothing. Just a green globous mass with writhing tentacles. Yet somehow it had to be intelligent.

It stopped its advance, and seemed to turn to face them. Bishop raised his pistol and aimed. Beside him Jim did the same. 'Hold your fire,' Bishop said, and retrieved the bulky short range radio from his shoulder. 'Colonel, come in, over.'

There was a crackle of static, behind which, just barely, Bishop could hear Lethbridge-Stewart's voice. 'Go ahead, Bishop, over.'

'Sir, we've located the…' Bishop let out a gasp of shock and dropped the radio. He looked at his hand and saw the reddened skin, burned from an unexpected electrical surge.

The sound of crackling energy drew his attention back to the Rutan, which was now rearing up on its tendrils, away from the surface of the rocks. Although still a few feet away, standing on its tentacles like some slimy spider, the Rutan towered over both men. Electrical charges ran across its body, the deadly blue-white energy lashing out towards them. A charge struck Jim's gun, and the cameraman jumped back in surprise.

'Humans,' came a strange voice, sounding like it was being transmitted across a weak radio bandwidth. 'You have contravened galactic law, and as a level five civilisation you cannot hope to stand against the Rutan Host. You will release us.'

'What? Release—?' Bishop didn't get to finish. Beside him Jim aimed the flare gun into the air and fired. Their eyes followed the flare, but were torn from it as the Rutan rushed forward, electric charges crackling across its body.

Bishop fired his pistol, but the bullets were useless. They hit the body of the Rutan, erupting in little sparks, burned up in the electrical field that seemed to protect the creature.

He continued to fire regardless, pushing Jim away. 'Fall back!' he shouted, and the two men turned and ran.

Archibald couldn't believe it, even though Anne – as she insisted on being called – had seemed so sincere as she'd told him. She didn't go into much detail, because, she said, it wasn't too clever to know too much about your own future, but he understood enough by her tone that the Goffs and the Travers were destined to be entwined for a very long time. And not always in good ways. One good way, though, to his reckoning, was Anne. If she was the culmination of such entwining then he was glad. He couldn't pretend to understand what kind of future she lived in, but he looked at her and saw… Potential. A woman so very far removed from the women of today, one who knew her own mind and didn't need a man to help her. And to think it all began when he had happened upon Jacob at Bethlem.

Incredible!

'Where are we?' Anne stopped and looked around. The rain had begun again and visibility was becoming an issue. She lifted her hand to cover her eyes. 'The lighthouse is over there, and it's about quarter past one on the morning of Friday 26th September, so...' She looked up at the moon. 'We're somewhere near West Crag, right?'

Charlie was amazed. 'You can work that out so easily?'

'Well, of course,' Anne said, as if the difficulty of such an act had not occurred to her. 'All you need do is take into account the date, the time and the lunar cycle. Fairly basic orienteering, really.'

'For a sailor, yes, but you're...' Charlie struggled for words.

'A woman, I believe is Charlie's meaning,' Archibald explained helpfully. 'I myself have little understanding of such calculations, but understand that sailors have navigated this world just by the celestial bodies. But for a woman to understand such things, and to divine the answer with such ease...'

Charlie nodded. 'It is amazing.'

Anne shrugged. 'Of course, that's a give-away, too,' she said, point at the crag's edge overlooking the Channel in the near distance. She enjoyed the look of humour that passed over Charlie's face. A nice change. 'Now,' she continued, 'the Rutan landed near East Crag in 1902, and the UFO was seen to head that way the other day, so...' She stopped and smiled. 'Sorry, I mean in my time, not the other day here.'

'To which other day do you refer?' Archibald asked.

'It's a turn of phrase, in this case it means two nights ago.'

'And what is a you-eff-oh?'

'It's a...' Anne stopped. 'A shooting star,' she tried. 'Probably the best way to explain it.'

'A star falling from the heavens. A bad omen,' Charlie said.

'Well, it certainly didn't work out well for those on Fang Rock in 1902, that's for sure. But my point is, why do the Rutans always fall near East Crag? It must be their trajectory and angle of entry based on the Earth's rotation. Both times at night, probably around the same hour too.'

Now Archibald was truly lost. And he could see Charlie was too. So he tried for the one piece of information he had understood. 'You mentioned the *Rhoo Tun* before. This is the name of the Beast?'

Anne nodded. 'I believe so, yes.'

'And it is like the *Moddey Dhoo* on the Isle of Man?' It was clear Anne had not heard that name, so Archibald explained what he knew of the *Moddey Dhoo*.

'No, it's nothing like that. The Rutan is no myth, nothing supernatural. It is an alien, a... Well, an intelligence from another planet.'

'Another...?' Archibald could just about believe that Anne could have come from the future – there was enough about her to convince him of that – but the idea that there was life on other planets. It just wouldn't do! 'Forgive me, my dear, but all rational men know that there are no living beings on any world other than ours. We are the centre of God's creation, after all. The pinnacle of all He achieved.'

'Don't be silly, Archie. Are you saying that men like William Herschel were not rational? I may not know a great deal about your time, but I know that the idea of extra-terrestrial life is pretty widespread among the scientific men of the early 19th Century.' Anne considered him a moment, and Archibald was not sure he cared for the intensity of the consideration. 'I'm surprised at you. For a believer in the supernatural, I would have thought your mind to be more open than that.'

'Well,' Archibald said gruffly, glancing at Charlie, 'of course I'm not a deeply religious man, but my work has shown me that there is more to this world than is commonly believed. It has shown me the diversity of creation, and there is no doubt in my mind that man is the pinnacle of that. Only man is capable of rational and intelligent thought. Why would God create other beings of equal, or of a more vast, intelligence on other worlds?'

'I'm talking about science, not religious belief.'

'I am not a man of science.'

'Obviously.'

At that Archibald wasn't sure what to say. Of course, he had crossed words with women before, but other than in affairs of the heart, no woman had ever made him feel so inferior with so few words. He drew himself up to his full height, so as to save face in front of Charlie, but before he could say anything that would redeem him, Anne pointed.

'Look! What's that?'

Archibald and Charlie looked. In the distance, seemingly coming from the rocks submerged beneath the water, was a pulsating green glow.

Owain spotted it first. 'It's a cave.'

'A littoral cave,' Lethbridge-Stewart said.

'A what?'

'Also known as a sea cave. Made by the corrosive effects

181

of salt water on the igneous rock that forms this land mass.' Lethbridge-Stewart smiled at his nephew. 'You really should read more, Owain.'

'So I keep getting told.'

They drew closer to the sea cave. It wasn't very big, and sat a short distance from West Crag, which overlooked the English Channel before them. Around the mouth of the cave, and littered over the wet rock, were many tiny crystals shining against the blackness. He brushed his hand against the crystals that lined the cave mouth. They were jagged, newly broken. He looked around him. The remains of some kind of wall blocking off the cave? Judging by the scatter pattern of the crystals on the rocks, he felt certain. But if so, what had shattered the crystal wall? And why? Lethbridge-Stewart wondered how deep the cave went. It had to have been formed a very long time ago. He nodded. 'It's probably submerged when the water is high. Perfect for hiding an amphibious life form, wouldn't you say?'

'Why amphibious?'

Again Lethbridge-Stewart was surprised at Owain. He was usually such a sharp young man, but then, Lethbridge-Stewart reflected, he hadn't gone much further than Liskeard for most of his life and was only now venturing out in the real world. Experience would be his best teacher. Experience and a few good books.

'Each time a Rutan ship has been seen it has landed in the Channel; twice in the last few days, and probably in 1902, too. Now, I don't see any evidence of a submersible on the rocks, which means the Rutans must be amphibious.'

'Giant jellyfish,' Owain remembered.

'Exactly. Make sure your rifle is—' Lethbridge-Stewart

182

was cut off by the crackle of his radio.

'Colonel, come in, over.'

He unshouldered the radio and clicked to send his message. 'Go ahead, Bishop, over.'

'Sir, we've located the…'

A loud crackle and white noise. Lethbridge-Stewart shook the radio and tried to call Bishop. Nothing.

'Perhaps we need to…' Owain trailed off, looking up. Through the fog they could see the red trail of a flare rising up from a point over the edge of the crag.

'Trouble,' Lethbridge-Stewart said. 'Let's go!' He set off in the direction of the flare. A squeal of pain stopped him and he looked back. Owain was on the ground, wincing as he held his ankle. Lethbridge-Stewart doubled back and crouched down next to his nephew. 'What happened?'

'I slipped,' Owain said ruefully. He winced. 'Think I've sprained my ankle. Not doing very well on this rock, am I?'

Lethbridge-Stewart patted him on the shoulder. 'That's the spirit. Keep your rifle ready, just in case there's more than one Rutan.' He stood up. 'Will you be okay on your own?'

'Yeah, copasetic. Go on, they wouldn't have fired the flare if they didn't need help.'

Lethbridge-Stewart nodded sharply and readied his pistol. As he scrambled away, careful not to lose his own footing, he called Heggessey on the radio. Bishop and Saunders weren't far away, but the fog was getting denser. He'd need help triangulating their position, and Heggessey had the best view for that.

It was a littoral cave. Some of it was still underwater, but

183

Anne wasn't too bothered by that; after all they were all quite wet from the rain and wind already. She advanced, but Archibald pulled her back.

'Do they not advise caution in the future?'

'Sometimes. But I must find out the source of the glow.'

'It ain't natural,' Charlie offered, still some feet behind them, hugging himself fearfully.

'No, it's not,' Anne said as firmly as she could. 'But I'd make a bet that it isn't *super*natural either,' she added, looking up at Archibald. 'Simply advanced technology.'

The green glow was coming from inside the small cave, its reflection cast in the water that was, by Anne's estimate, at least up to her knees. The glow reminded her of something, but she couldn't quite place what. It was artificially produced, of that she was sure. And in the decade where the arc lamp had barely made it past Humphry Davy's lab, she knew it had to be something to do with the Rutan. Perhaps this was where it hid. And if it hid within, then it was possible Jacob was inside too. Prisoner or victim of the 'Beast'?

Archibald removed an antiquated pistol from his coat. Antiquated from her point of view, of course; no doubt the small gun was a new model to Archibald. Much good it would do, Anne thought, unless he was a crack shot. He'd only get one go with that thing. But it seemed to reassure him and he nodded his readiness. They looked back at Charlie, who shook his head and took another step back. Anne glanced up at Archibald.

'Ready, *Grandfather*?' she asked with a slight smile, conveying a confidence she didn't really feel.

Archibald looked at her as if she were mad, then he

smiled too. 'You are queer in the head,' he said. 'Most certainly a Goff.'

'On my mother's side,' Anne added cheerfully and set off into the sea cave.

Archibald handed her his lantern, which she held aloft, while he stayed close by her side. As they went deeper into the cave, the water level rose. Anne had been right: it went no higher than her knees. She looked around. The walls of the cave were still wet; they seemed to be covered in the green luminescence, but she doubted it was due to any natural phosphorescence in the rock. Like the water around her legs, the wet walls were simply reflecting the emanation that came from deeper in the cave.

'This reminds me of—' Archibald was cut off by a voice. 'Retire from here… *Please*.'

They looked at each other, but did not stop. Archibald raised his voice slightly. 'Jacob, is that you?'

'It's here. The Beast. Leave, please, I cannot stop it.'

Anne paused at the sound of terror in the voice. It felt wrong, as if the voice belonged to a kind soul tormented beyond reason. The voice of her paternal three-time-great grandfather. For a moment she was frozen by the absurdity of the situation. A few weeks ago she had heard of neither Archibald Goff nor Jacob Travers, and now here she was stuck one hundred and forty-six years in her past with both men. Men who were the source of her paternal and maternal ancestry.

'Step forward, Jacob,' Archibald said. 'We can get you away from here. We can face the Beast together.'

For a moment there was only the sound of the wind outside, and then Jacob said gently, 'Very well.'

Movement, someone wading through the water. A figure approached. As he came into the light, Anne got her first look at Jacob Travers. Even in the low light cast by the lantern she saw a man familiar to her. It took her a moment to realise why. The hair was much the same, but the mutton chops were a far cry from the handlebar moustache she had previously seen on that face. A face that was the spit of Ben Travers.

Jacob stopped and looked at Anne curiously. He reached out a hand, then pulled back and shook his head. 'No, for a moment I thought... But no, you are not Vina.'

That name rang a bell. It had to be Jacob's wife, which meant... 'Of course!' Anne said, louder than she intended. 'Vina, the woman from Alun's research, the source of the bad blood between...' She trailed off and lowered her head. Too much information again. She went to meet Jacob's gaze, apologise, but her eyes lingered on his hands. She stared.

With a horrible sound of bones popping out of their joints, Jacob's fingers seemed to stretch, thick coarse hair grew out of the back of the hands. Anne wanted to pull her eyes away, but she couldn't. She watched as the hands distended, growing unnaturally long, more like claws.

A horrible sound echoed around them. It was enough to break the spell. Anne looked up, immediately realising that the sound was Jacob screaming. The scream changed pitch, from pain to... Anger! A roar. A feral cry.

The lantern was still held before her, and in the low light an inhuman shadow was cast onto the walls. Anne looked into Jacob's face. Only it was no longer Jacob's face. His nose had bulged into a snout, while his jaw jutted forward to make room for the sharp teeth that were snarling at them. All that was bad enough, but it was the eyes that startled Anne the most. They weren't human, but yellow, vulpine...

'It was Jacob all along,' Archibald said, as he slowly backed away, pulling Anne with him, their eyes never leaving the feral werewolf before them. 'He's the Beast!'

For the first time it hit Anne; perhaps the colonel was right. She *would* die in the past.

The first thing Lethbridge-Stewart found was the flare gun. It was abandoned on the rock, charred and broken. He picked it up and looked around, trying to locate his missing men in the fog.

'Sir!'

Bishop's head appeared from behind a nearby rock. He climbed over and jumped down, scrambling across to Lethbridge-Stewart.

'Where's Saunders?' Lethbridge-Stewart asked.

'We got separated. It was a Rutan, sir, as we thought. It chased us, but...' Bishop finally noticed the useless flare gun in Lethbridge-Stewart's hand. 'Did it get Jim?'

'Let's hope not.' Lethbridge-Stewart tossed the gun aside. 'Where did you see the Rutan?'

'This way.' Bishop stepped forward and pointed, then rubbed the back of his neck. 'I think.'

'Let's find out. But keep them peeled for any sign of the Rutan, or Jim.'

They proceeded in the direction Bishop had indicated. While they walked, careful to tread slowly as the rocky path sloped upwards, Bishop gave his report. The Rutan was as dangerous as they had expected, with the ability to use electricity as a weapon. Although where it got its electricity from was anybody's guess. Bishop was sure the Rutan generated its own electrical field. Lethbridge-Stewart didn't see how it was possible, but then he was no scientist. He'd ask Miss Travers when…

He changed his train of thought with regret. Miss Travers was gone, lost to them forever.

'Here, sir. It was coming from this direction.'

Lethbridge-Stewart carried on past where Bishop was indicating and stopped at the edge of the crag. He looked over the edge and saw in the distance to the north, the littoral cave. It was a little too far to see clearly in the fog, but he couldn't make out any sign of Owain. 'We need to get back to… Hello!' Something underneath the water had caught his eye. He knelt down carefully to get a closer look. For a moment he thought it was a reflection, but peering closer… He looked towards the sea cave, then at Bishop. 'Corporal, what do you make of this?'

Bishop knelt next to him. Some ten feet below them, beneath the water, was a shape; it was hard to make out, but it was large and possibly ovoid, easily big enough to hold three people, its surface twinkling beneath the water. Like crystals catching the sunlight. Lethbridge-Stewart was reminded of Miss Travers' machine, the one that had gone missing with her.

'Is that what I think it is?' Bishop asked.

'I do believe so. We've found the Rutan's space craft.'

— CHAPTER TWELVE —

Lost & Found

The wind batted the rain into Charlie Crane's face as he ran. His heart pounded against his chest. First ghosts, then a woman from the future and now... A man who looked like a wolf! He wanted to pretend he had imagined it, but he knew he hadn't. He had seen it, approaching Archibald and Anne near the mouth of the cave, and had he not heard Archibald call it a name moments before he fired his iron?

Jacob! Archibald had called it Jacob. But that was impossible! Jacob was... But then he had heard the stories on the mainland, of the keeper driven insane by the things he had witnessed on Fang Rock. Of the Beast he had seen, the Beast he came to believe himself to be.

It was true. Jacob *was* that wolf-man.

Charlie wasn't paying attention to where he was going; he just knew he had to get away. He was a coward, of course he was. He didn't want to die. He wanted off the rock. So he continued to run, his booted feet slipping on the wet rocks. He crashed down hard and felt at least one finger give way. He rolled over and for a moment lay there, looking up at the dark sky, feeling the rain on his face.

A distant howl made him scramble to his feet. Was it the wind or the Beast? Charlie didn't wait to find out. It may have sounded distant, but how far was truly far on Fang Rock?

He continued running, heading towards the one source of light he knew he could trust. The lighthouse. He reached for the handle, made to turn it, and yelled in pain as his broken finger met the cold metal. He gasped, silently chastising himself for using his cack-hand. It had been drummed into him since he was a kid to not use his left hand, even if that was his natural instinct. Only stupid people used their left hand, and he would never amount to anything should he do so. He opened the door with his right hand and ran across the generator room, laughing. Even as he fled, scared for his life, his mind turned to such a foolish thing. As if being cack-handed mattered when the wolf-man was hunting him!

'Mr Scott!' he yelled as he scrambled up the stairs, his wet boots constantly slipping. He checked in the library, but it was empty. He continued up, checking the bunk rooms, but still no sign of Scott. He called out again. No response, just the sound of his voice echoing up and down the spiral stair. Charlie couldn't understand it. Scott always had such good hearing; there was no chance of him failing to hear Charlie's call.

Finally he reached the lamp room. There was someone on the gallery. From behind it could have been either Wishart or Scott, although Scott had said he'd send Wishart out after them. Charlie rushed over to the hatch and crouched his way through it. 'Mr Scott, I…' His voice trailed off as the figure turned around.

It was Edgar Wishart.

'What are you doing here?' Charlie asked stupidly.

'Keeping watch, what do you think, boy? My job. Why aren't you sleeping? It's not your watch for another two hours.'

'My...?' Charlie shook his head. 'You don't know, do you?'

'Know what, boy?'

'It's back. The Beast. I seen it, and...' He swallowed, his broken finger throbbing with pain. He looked out towards West Crag. 'It's Jacob. The Beast is Jacob.'

Wishart's expression said it all. 'Calm down, boy,' he said, laughing. 'You are ailed by bad dreams. It'll be that Goff man, I'll wager, telling you ghost stories.'

'It's not a story. I seen him, I tell you. At West Crag. We went out there to look for him; me, Archibald and Anne. Scott told us to...'

'Anne? Who the blazes is Anne?'

'She...'

'A woman on Fang Rock?' Wishart bellowed another laugh. 'Oh, you have been dreaming. Did she come out of the water? Half fish, was she?'

Charlie was used to being mocked by Wishart; the old buffer never had any respect for him, always treating him like a child, but this time... 'Listen to me!' he shouted, putting every bit of his frustration into the words. 'I am not telling tall stories. Why hasn't Scott come up to relieve you? He said he would.'

'I haven't seen Alfred since I took over from him. I ain't seen no one.' Wishart glanced at Charlie's mangled finger, and his expression changed. 'What has been going on?'

Charlie didn't know where to begin. So much had happened in the last few hours. As he began to explain, a sense of their seclusion hit him. They were out here alone, cut off from civilisation. With no help coming. Just them and the Beast.

Lethbridge-Stewart and Bishop returned to the lighthouse, secured the door behind them and, on the way to the crew room, found Heggessey in the kitchen. He was busy making a brew and explained that Owain and Jim were upstairs. Jim, it transpired, had found Owain a short distance from West Crag and helped him back.

'Corporal, go and check on them. I'll be up shortly.' Once Bishop had gone, Lethbridge-Stewart helped Heggessey with the tea-making. 'How are you holding up?' he asked the keeper.

Heggessey took a moment to answer, and when he did, he laughed with more than a hint of incredulity. 'Can't say I was expecting this when Trinity House asked me to take up a position here. I was quite happy at *Les Casquets*,' he said, the French wording sounding rather mangled by his Hampshire accent. 'I'd heard all about the ghost stories, of course, and I'm not without some superstitious beliefs of my own, but now we're dealing with aliens? Well. What can you say?'

Lethbridge-Stewart nodded, and poured water from the kettle. 'I quite understand, Mr Heggessey. I was much the same only a few months ago.'

'Now you're a believer?'

'Well, I wouldn't say that, but facts do not require belief. I can't deny the evidence of my eyes.'

'*Faith is the substance of things hoped for, the evidence of things not seen,*' Heggessey said. 'Not sure I'm ready for the idea of aliens. How do they fit into things? Did God make them, too?'

'Well, I suppose he must have.' Lethbridge-Stewart cleared his throat. Theological discussions were not really his strong suit. He lifted the tray. 'Shall we see how the men are?'

'After you, Colonel,' Heggessey said, stepping back to let Lethbridge-Stewart pass.

The lighthouse was still some distance away and, Anne was certain, the werewolf was between it and them.

She wanted to laugh. Werewolf indeed! But, like in London, she had to accept what her eyes told her. She had seen Jacob transform!

She was hiding with Archibald behind a large outcrop of rock, sheltered from the wolf but not from the rain. She glanced up at Archibald, who stood there, his face ashen, the shock maintaining its hold on him. For her own part she was crouching as close to the rock as she could, peering around the edge at irregular intervals. She couldn't see Jacob, but she could hear him. Prowling, growling, stopping occasionally to sniff the air. She just hoped the wind and rain was enough to hide their scent.

'*Lest the madly ravenous werewolf too savagely tear or devour too much from a godly flock,*' she muttered softly.

'What?' Archibald said, his first word since his single shot had failed to affect Jacob in any way.

'King Canute. The first mention of a "werewolf" in written form.'

Archibald knelt beside her, the shock beaten down by his academic interest. 'I do not know this word, although evidently it refers to Jacob.'

'Old English, from the Germanic *wer*, meaning man. Literally, man-wolf.'

'You know much about this.'

'I wish I did.' Anne wiped the rain from her eyes. 'I only know what I've read, which isn't much, and it certainly didn't prepare me for this.' She looked up. 'It's not even a full moon, which kind of disproves whatever I do know.'

'How do we kill it?'

Anne stared blankly at Archibald for a few moments, then asked, 'What?'

'We must kill him. Whatever it is, it's supernatural, and I have never come across a man-wolf before. Demons, ghosts... possessions, all kinds of phantasmagoria I have experience of. I have heard stories, of course, of men who become wolves, but this... I believe I have heard that a "werewolf" can be cured of its ailment by striking it on the forehead with a knife, or piercing its hands with nails.'

'Don't be so stupid, that's as much use as calling him three times by his name. Superstitious nonsense.'

'Then we must kill it.'

'Do you have any silver bullets?'

Archibald shook his head. 'Of course not. What possible use can they...?'

Anne shushed him. 'We cannot kill Jacob. If we do, then my entire family will cease to be. Without him, there will be no union between your family and his. I will never be born.'

'And if it comes down to him or us?'

Anne knew it was a very real possibility, but nonetheless... 'He's still family.'

Archibald was silent, digesting this. Anne peered around the rock again and listened, trying to ignore the noise of the rain and wind. There was no sound of Jacob. Perhaps he had returned to the cave.

'Your future is safe,' Archibald said, when she looked back at him. 'Jacob already has children, including a son.'

That was good to know at least. She narrowed her eyes, fixing him with the look that brokered no argument. 'Nonetheless, Jacob is not going to be killed. We have to save him.'

'How do you propose we do that? He has already killed once. Either we kill him, or he kills us. There is no other outcome.'

They arrived at the crew room to find Owain limping his way down the stone steps. Heggessey helped him across the room to the sofa while Lethbridge-Stewart placed the tray on the small table.

'How's the ankle?' Lethbridge-Stewart asked.

Owain rubbed it, wincing. 'It started swelling, but it should be okay,' he said, lifting the trouser leg to show the damp cloth wrapped around it. 'No ice bags, unfortunately.'

Bishop returned first, followed by Jim. Both men, it seemed, had popped up to the bunk rooms to secure the windows. Once everybody was there, warming their hands around the hot cups, Lethbridge-Stewart began.

'Okay, we've secured the lighthouse as best we can. We should be okay, as long as the Rutan can't get in here, at least for now. But we need to remember that one of these creatures killed seven people in 1902, and while I'd like to say we're more capable than those people, so far our weapons have proven quite useless.'

'Are you sure there's only one of them?' Jim asked.

'Only one has been sighted, by you and Bishop, but we found the Rutan's spaceship. Granted, it was beneath the water, and several feet away, but to me it looked at least big enough for three people. So it's entirely possible there is more than one Rutan out there.'

'And we still have no idea what it wants,' Bishop said.

'To kill, surely,' Heggessey said, looking around at the other men. 'Like it did in 1902 and in the 1820s.'

'What makes you think the Rutan was responsible for all those deaths?' Owain asked.

Heggessey looked at Owain like he was stupid. 'Well, it's obviously the Beast of legend. I thought it was agreed that this Rutan has been on Fang Rock before.'

Bishop nodded. 'He's right. According to Anne's grandfather there was a falling star in 1823, too. But we still don't know *why* it wants to kill us.'

Jim leaned forward and handed out cigarettes to all the men except Lethbridge-Stewart. 'Does it matter?' he asked, lighting the cigarette. 'Surely the point is we're in danger here. After all, even in 1902, they must have thought to secure the lighthouse. It didn't stop the Rutan then; why should it do so now?'

'I should think the locks of today are slightly more secure than they were almost seventy years ago,' Lethbridge-Stewart pointed out.

Heggessey laughed and shook his head. 'Colonel, we're talking about an alien here. From a different world! We can't even make it to the moon; how can we possibly think our locks are a deterrent for a creature than can do all that and more?'

Lethbridge-Stewart kept his tone calm but firm. 'Okay, Mr Heggessey, I think you need to calm down. We all do.' He couldn't have the men getting worked up. He had dealt with cabin fever before, and although they had all managed to get some air, they were still all essentially trapped in the middle of nowhere with a violent alien apparently impervious to their weapons. 'Let us deal with this rationally.' Lethbridge-Stewart waited until all the men nodded, then he looked back at Heggessey. 'I want you to man the gallery and keep a lookout for the Rutan. Jim, you'll assist him. Bishop, Owain, I want you two to go down to the generator room and find whatever you can to fortify the door. Meanwhile, I will get a message to the mainland and call in reinforcements. Perhaps our pistols have no effect on the Rutan, but we have weapons now that weren't invented in 1902, and I wouldn't mind testing the SLR. The Rutan has picked the wrong time to come to Earth.'

At last they made it back to the lighthouse. Archibald was still trying to convince her of the sense behind killing Jacob, but she refused to accept that as an option. If Lethbridge-Stewart had been the one to go back in time, as he had suggested, then there was no doubt in her mind that he would be working with Archibald on a plan of attack. But he hadn't come back. She had, and she was not a killer. She had never taken a life, and she didn't intend to start now.

'Unless I'm mistaken, you're the one who brought him back here!' Anne snapped at Archibald's back as the two of them quickly ascended the stone steps of the lighthouse. 'So, this is all your fault.'

Archibald stopped and turned to face her. He was a few steps higher than she, and looking down at her from his vantage point, he seemed to assume a greater size, his voice a greater force. 'My dear woman, I brought him here to confront the Beast! I never entertained the notion that he and the Beast were one in the same. Not ever!'

'You told me you found him in Bedlam,' Anne said. 'He was no danger to anybody there.'

'You would have your own blood condemned to the wing of the criminally insane?'

'I... Well, of course not. But it has to be better than this.' She shook her head. She knew enough of the medical practices of this time that she wouldn't wish them on her worst enemy. But what was the other option? To become a wolf and kill people? 'He spent almost a year there, you said, and not once did he transform into a wolf.'

Archibald took a deep breath and conceded the point. 'You are correct. Only on Fang Rock has such a metamorphosis taken place.' He lowered his head and turned away. 'Perhaps you are right. The fault is mine.'

Anne remained where she stood as Archibald continued his way up the staircase. Why was it men always did that to her? They stubbornly refused to accept blame when they made a mistake, and then when she proved they were to blame, their admission of culpability left her feeling guilty, as if she had betrayed a weakness they wished to keep secret. Her father was the same, and so was Alun. As for Lethbridge-Stewart... She resumed her climb, surprised to find that she missed Bill.

On the next floor, she bumped into Charlie and Archibald talking outside the provisions store. 'What's going on?' she asked.

'It would appear Mr Scott has gone missing,' Archibald said.

'And Wishart has not seen him since he took over the watch,' Charlie added, his voice oddly excited by the implication. Although Anne wasn't entirely sure what was being implied. She turned back to Archibald, but before he could explain, Charlie spoke again. 'Mr Scott sent us all out to find you, told us he would relieve Wishart, but he never did.'

'I'm not sure I—'

'He warned us off West Crag,' Archibald said. 'And he was rather insistent about it. Eager to see me go, eager that Charlie join me, too. Now why would he have wanted us out of the way?'

Anne racked her brain, certain that she was missing something. 'He was also pretty insistent that we took Charlie with us to look for Jacob, despite Charlie's obvious condition.'

'My condition?'

'Your fear, boy,' Archibald snapped, somewhat unkindly.

Charlie lowered his head and mumbled something, but Anne was no longer paying attention. An unwelcome thought had entered her mind.

'Was Scott here last year? When Jacob killed Williams?'

'No, when Scott returned with the Master of the Tender, they found Jacob quite out of his mind,' Archibald explained.

'Master of the Tender?' Anne asked.

Archibald looked to Charlie, but the youngster was still looking at the floor. He cleared his throat, and Charlie reluctantly peered up at them. 'Well?' Archibald snapped.

'Tell Anne. You're the keeper here.'

'I... Yes. The Master of the Tender is responsible for the delivery of stores and oils essential to the maintenance of the lantern, and the safe transport of keepers to and from the signal house at Hove. He's on call twenty-four hours of the day, ready to set sail at a moment's notice should an emergency arise. It is reasonable to say that Captain Leask is our lifeline!'

'Okay, and Scott has been here ever since he and the Master of the Tender found Jacob?'

'He never leaves. We're allowed two weeks on the mainland every six weeks, but Mr Scott only ever takes a few days. He says it is because his brother died building this place, believes it his duty to maintain and watch over the light.'

Archibald frowned at Anne. 'I do not follow your thoughts on this.'

She waved his comment away. 'So, he's basically lived here since...?'

'Since the lighthouse was built,' Charlie said. As he spoke, his voice became stronger. Anne smiled in encouragement, feeling a little sorry for unintentionally goading Archibald into his harsh comment a few moments ago. 'He took over work on the construction at only fourteen years, the youngest person to ever work on a lighthouse. He had no choice, as with his brother dead, there was nobody else to earn for his family.'

'And over the years Fang Rock has essentially become his home.' Anne nodded. 'So, it's reasonable to say he's explored every inch of Fang Rock. And, I'll lay money on him being left alone on this rock when Jacob was taken back to the mainland. Am I right?'

Charlie nodded. 'For many days – until Wishart arrived.'

'The only man left alone. The one man who knows Fang Rock better than anybody. Just why do you think he warned you away from West Crag?' Anne waited a moment, looking from one man to the other. 'He knows all about the littoral cave.'

Silence echoed through the lighthouse as the three of them let this sink in. If he had spent that much time on the rock, and knew about the cave, then his warning about West Crag had to mean...

'What is that sound?' Charlie asked.

A muffled humming could faintly be heard over the ambient noise of the lighthouse. It was strangely familiar. She turned to the door of the provisions store, exchanged a curious look with Archibald, and opened the door carefully.

'The glow!' Charlie said, the words barely a breath.

And he was right. At the far end of the stores was, however faintly, the same green glow they had seen at West Crag. Anne stepped forward once it was clear that neither Archibald nor Charlie were going to do so. A wooden box, its lid barely resting on top, was the source of the vague glow. Or rather, the thing inside it was.

Anne couldn't believe it, but she knew it had to be in the past somewhere. The machine inside the box was an exact copy of the one she had received from Rupert Slant. No, she realised, it wasn't a copy; it *was* the crystal machine. Which meant the Rutan had to be nearby.

'The cave,' she whispered. 'It has to be in the cave, and Alfred Scott is keeping it hidden.'

*

Lethbridge-Stewart looked from Jim to the radio equipment. Whoever had been at it had done a good job. Jim dropped the shattered mic on the table among the smashed insides of the radio, which now had a huge hole in it, the electronics hanging out in a tangled web of cables and transistors.

'Now what do we do?' Jim asked.

'Ask a more important question,' Lethbridge-Stewart said. 'Like, who did this? We've locked the doors, and we were the last inside. Did the Rutan get past us?'

'Surely we would have noticed an amorphous life form? There's not many places it can hide in here.'

Lethbridge-Stewart wasn't so sure about that. Neither he nor Bishop had checked the generator room when they had returned; the only rooms that had been checked were those the men had been in prior to their meeting in the crew room. But then, if the radio had been damaged before they returned, then surely Mr Heggessey would have noticed when he returned from the lamp room? Unless...

'Do you think you can do anything with this, Mr Saunders?' Lethbridge-Stewart asked, not wanting to voice his suspicions just yet. 'Perhaps patch up our short range radios?'

'Not really my area of expertise, I'm afraid. I just use electronic equipment, I don't fix it.'

'I find that hard to believe. What happens if your camera gets broken? Surely you must have some basic re—'

'Colonel! You better get up here!' Heggessey shouted from above.

A quick glance between them, and Lethbridge-Stewart and Jim clambered up the ladder into the lamp room. Heggessey was standing near the window, looking up. He must have been listening to their conversation, because he said, 'We have bigger problems. Look!'

The two men looked. Its distance was hard to make out due to the sheer size of the thing, but in the sky above the lighthouse was an object which appeared to be made up of many crystal-like blocks connected to a central sphere which looked like a giant crystal ball.

'That thing by West Crag was a scout pod,' Jim said.

Which had to mean... 'That's the Rutan mothership,' Lethbridge-Stewart said. 'We really are in trouble.'

CHAPTER THIRTEEN

The Enemy Within

Perhaps he should be in Bethlem himself, Archibald considered, as he continued to follow Anne along the rocks. But he couldn't help but be caught up in her wake; she had so much energy and direction. Even now it was nearing half two, and though he couldn't deny that Anne looked tired, she refused to let her tiredness get in the way. Archibald felt admiration for her, admiration and something more. Pride, perhaps? Which was foolish – after all she was almost a stranger to him, despite what she claimed. He believed her, of course – how could he not? But still, she *was* a stranger. He tried to see his family in her, and perhaps there were suggestions in her manner. But pride in a stranger... A puzzling notion.

They had left Crane behind, wisely he thought. Before they left Anne had administered to Charlie's broken finger, showing more care than the boy deserved. He was witless, and of no real use to them. He would be better off in the lighthouse with Wishart. And then there was Scott... Still Archibald could not quite grasp it.

'What reason would Scott have to lie?' he asked, drawing level with Anne.

'I'm not sure, but he clearly has been. Perhaps the Rutan has some hold over him?' She shook her head, her dark hair once again flattened by the rain.

Rhoo Tun. Again she used this word with such ease. Perhaps in her time the idea of creatures from beyond the stars was normal, but for him... 'What does this *Rhoo Tun* look like?'

'I haven't seen it, but I'm told it looks not unlike a giant jellyfish.'

'And that is the Beast?'

Anne stopped. 'I'm not sure. The Rutan or Jacob... There must be a connection. After all Jacob has only transformed on this island.' She fixed Archibald with that all-discerning look of hers. 'You said it landed last year.'

'Did I?' Archibald did not remember saying such a thing. 'I know of the shooting star, but that something landed? This is a new revelation to me.'

Anne sighed and continued on.

'What irks you?'

She glanced back. 'It's most difficult to remember that I know things that have yet to transpire for you. The letter you left for me. You haven't even written it yet.'

So, he was to write her a letter. Archibald would have to remember to do that. Although he did not know what he could say that she didn't already know. 'So,' he said, returning to something his mind could handle, 'there is a connection between the *Rhoo Tun* and Jacob? They were both here last year, and the *Rhoo Tun* landed before he lost his mind. Jacob must be the Beast – he killed Williams, did he not?'

'I thought so, yes, but now... I don't know. And there's another thing I don't get. I thought the Beast killed two people and drove one mad? That's what I have heard.'

'Two? I am glad to say not. Only Davy Williams was killed.'

Anne shook her head. 'I guess history can lie. Either way, the Rutan is hostile; in eighty years another will arrive on Fang Rock and kill seven people, including my great uncle. Why? We still don't know. And then there's the fact that Jacob has only transformed on this rock, where the Rutan is. They are clearly connected, although which is the Beast?'

They continued on in silence, with only the howling wind around them for company. Anne's great uncle – a descendant of his, or Jacob's? Archibald couldn't imagine a reason why any of his children would work on a lighthouse, so he reasoned it must be one of Jacob's offspring. It would explain Anne's focus. Losing one Travers to a Rutan on Fang Rock was bad enough, but two? If it was his own family he'd probably feel the same.

After more muted talk and further clambering over rocks, Anne and he descended to the lowest point of West Crag: the littoral cave. He placed a hand on Anne's shoulder. She glanced up at him.

'I still question the wisdom of this,' he said. 'By your own confession, the *Rhoo Tun* is hostile, and now we are about to enter its stronghold. And out there, somewhere, Jacob still roams. I fear you are being careless.'

'Am I?' Anne gently removed Archibald's hand. 'Perhaps I am; even if the future of my family line is secure, my *own* future may not be. I could still die here, over a hundred years before I was born. But I weigh up the risks, and I'm left with this; we need to know what's going on. It's why I was brought here, why you asked me here in the future.' She turned to look at him, although while she talked Archibald could not help but waver his eyes from her pretty face to the ethereal glow which continued to emanate from the cave mouth behind her. 'I understand how strange this is for you, to be confronted with the consequences of things you haven't done yet, but understand this is not usual for me either. Time travel is not common place in my time. Three weeks ago I hadn't even heard of you, and now here I am, one hundred and forty-six years in the past, with a man who I wouldn't even recognise if we passed in the streets. A man who is the direct ancestor of my mother.'

The madness of the situation was clear to both of them. But here they were. Two members of the same family brought together across time to solve a mystery that would see their family's come together as one. It was insanity. Complete insanity.

He removed his Derringer and pocketed the spare rounds. He would not be caught so short this time; just hoped Anne would be enough of a distraction should he need to reload. 'Then let us enter and face this *alien*.'

'And find some answers,' Anne added, leading the way.

Water sloshed around them as they walked deeper into the cave. The glow continued, stronger than the last time. Further down – for the cave was indeed going down – was the sound of movement. Something was in the cave with them.

'Jacob?' Archibald asked in a whisper.

Anne shook her head. 'I don't think so. Listen.'

He listened. At first he wasn't certain what he was listening for, but then he heard it. A kind of slithering, squelching sound. Whatever it was, it wasn't Jacob. He swallowed, but carried on until they entered a wider space.

He looked around in awe, unsure exactly what he was looking at. The walls of the cave were covered in strange crystalline shapes, connected by what, to Archibald's untrained eye, looked like strands of seaweed. The crystals gave off a green glow and pulsed rhythmically. The whole apparatus reminded him a little of the thing they'd found in the provisions store.

'What is this?' he asked.

'A genetics lab,' came the answer, although it was not Anne who answered. The voice sounded unreal, mechanical almost. Archibald turned his head to its source and stepped backwards involuntarily. The creature before him, standing above the water on spindly off-white legs that looked more like tentacles to Archibald, was the luminescent form of the *Rhoo Tun*. Anne had been right. He could see why someone would call it a giant jellyfish, but that hardly did it justice. He knew jellyfish from growing up on a coastal town, but this... Although similar, it was grotesque. It stood at least eight feet tall, the bell-head glowing green. Inside the bell, muscles and endocrine glands twitched and quivered, the gut pulsated. Hanging from beneath it, protected by the tentacles, were several willowy strands of oral arms throbbing with vicious lightning. The creature filled him with dread. It was *not* of this Earth, not a creation of God but of the Devil himself. The *Rhoo Tun* seemed to ignore him, turning its attention to Anne. 'Welcome, Miss Travers,' it said.

Anne was understandably confused. 'You...' She swallowed. 'You know me?'

'Of course. And you, too, Mr Goff,' it said in a disapproving tone Archibald found all too familiar. The green glow intensified and Archibald watched, his eyes disbelieving, as the creature changed, its shape reforming until standing before them was the rotund form of Alfred Scott. 'I did warn you to stay away from West Crag,' he said.

'It's just resting there. Why doesn't it do something?' Owain asked, looking through the window of the lamp room. He turned around, careful to manoeuvre his weight off his sprained ankle. 'I mean, good it's not doing anything, but why not?'

It was the question on Lethbridge-Stewart's mind, too. He removed the binoculars from his eyes. The ship was a lot higher than it appeared; he supposed, if anybody was looking out from Brighton, they'd barely even see it. The crystal pods seemed to bounce the sunlight off their surface, while the ball in the centre of the ship was smoother than any surface he'd seen. Looking through the binoculars he could see no sign of weapons, although something told him the ship carried them in abundance. If one Rutan managed to kill seven people so easily seventy years ago, then what damage could a ship that size do?

'Okay,' he said to those in the lamp room. 'The situation hasn't changed. We need to defend the lighthouse from the Rutan outside, and we need to get a signal to the mainland... Only now more urgently. Suggestions?'

'Short range radios. There has to be a way to adapt them,' Bishop said. He turned to Jim. 'I have some technical skill. Between us we could maybe knock up a stronger transmitter.'

Jim shook his head. 'Like I told the colonel, I don't fix

things, I just use them.'

Lethbridge-Stewart raised an eyebrow at this, but turned to Heggessey. 'Semaphore?' he asked.

The keeper mulled that over. 'Bit out of date, and it would take some time to set up – I doubt the Rutans would give us that time.' He pursed his lips together and patted the large glass lamp. 'Morse code, simple but effective. And the signal house on the mainland is always checking for the light.'

'Just the ticket.' Lethbridge-Stewart reached into the top pocket of his combat jacket and pulled out a small pad. On it, he scribbled a simple message: *Hobo level. Military assist.* To the unwary it would be gibberish, but Hamilton was waiting on the latest report, and the signal house at Hove knew this. Hamilton would understand the message well enough. He handed the note to Heggessey, who looked at it and nodded. 'We'll leave you to it. Send at regular intervals, but keep an eye on that ship up there. Let me know if there's any change.' Lethbridge-Stewart handed Heggessey one of the short range radios and turned to the others. 'You men, with me.'

He climbed to the service room below and waited for the men to join him. Owain was the last down, hopping on his good ankle from one rung on the ladder to the next.

'Okay, unless the Rutan left the lighthouse while we were up here,' Lethbridge-Stewart began, 'which we will know by the lack of bolt on the door, then we're trapped in here with it. Now, this is the unfortunate truth that I didn't wish to labour Heggessey with: either the Rutan is in here with us, or we have a saboteur.' He watched the reactions. Only Owain looked perturbed by this. Bishop kept his face straight, his eyes never wavering from Lethbridge-Stewart; you had to hand it to the Academy – he was certainly well-trained. Jim also didn't react, which was in Lethbridge-Stewart's view a little suspicious. But no doubt the man had done some National Service, so he was probably trained too, and Lethbridge-Stewart knew it was natural for him to have less trust in Jim than his nephew and adjutant. 'Given our predicament, I don't see any course of action but to continue as we would otherwise. It could be any of us, including Mr Heggessey. As it stands, I'm afraid I'm inclined to suspect either Mr Heggessey or you, Mr Saunders.'

'Now, see here, Colonel, if we're casting suspicions, then why should I trust any of you?'

Lethbridge-Stewart smiled. That was a more reasonable response. He ignored it. 'If Heggessey is the saboteur, then he does not know we suspect him. I want you to keep an eye on him, Owain. How good are you with Morse code?'

Owain shrugged slightly. 'I can get by, probably.'

'Good. I want you to make sure he's sending the right message. If he is, then it's a fair bet he's not the saboteur. Of course, he could just be a very good actor. Although what reason he'd have to keep us stranded, I have no idea.'

'And I *do* have a reason?'

Once again Lethbridge-Stewart ignored Jim's outburst. He was, of course, the other possibility, although again Lethbridge-Stewart couldn't see what Jim would have to gain by stranding them with a hostile alien. However, somebody had done so, and they were the only two suspects. 'Corporal Bishop, I want you and Mr Saunders to go and search the provisions store and generator room, every nook and cranny; if the Rutan is in the lighthouse I want it found. I'll search every room between here and the provisions store. Once we're all agreed we have no Rutan infestation, we shall have to weigh up our options.'

Bishop nodded and removed his pistol.

'You have to be pulling my leg, right?' Jim said. 'It wasn't me. When did I even have a chance?'

'Mr Saunders, when I returned to the lighthouse, all three of you returned to the crew room alone. Your bunk room is nearest this service room. You had the opportunity.'

'I did not come up here,' Jim said. 'If anybody had the opportunity, it's Ivan. He's the one who passed through here just before you got back.'

'Agreed. Which is why Owain will keep an eye on him.'

Jim shook his head. 'What makes you think it's not Owain?'

At this Lethbridge-Stewart raised his eyebrow. 'I would rather trust my nephew than a man I barely know. I'm sorry, Mr Saunders, but my choice is limited. We can all stand here accusing each other and wait for the Rutan to attack, or we can try and do something productive.'

'Productive? While Bill has his gun on me?'

'Very well.' Lethbridge-Stewart nodded at Bishop. 'Corporal, holster your side arm. But keep your wits about you.'

'Yes, sir.'

'And so will I, don't you worry,' Jim said.

Anne stood still, careful to not give away her fear, and turned to her safe harbour: scientific detachment. The crystal technology on the walls matched the inside of the

Rutan time machine, although the seaweed was a new touch. Clearly the Rutans evolved from the seas, so it made sense they would use such things in their technology. Even on Earth using natural resources to create electrical energy was not all that unusual; all one had to do was consider the use of citric electrolytes found in certain fruit. Even in this century it wasn't unknown; it was only thirty-three years since Alessandro Volta created the first electric battery using brine.

Another thing apparent was the smell; it was like standing in a fishmongers, although not quite as strong, which fit with the aquatic evolution. So, if confirmation was needed, the Rutan was intelligent. Of course, intelligence did not always equate virtue.

History was littered with intelligent people who had done a lot of evil things. And she knew from the history of Fang Rock the violence a Rutan could do. No doubt that would be enough to convince Lethbridge-Stewart, but she didn't see things in such black and white terms. It wouldn't be fair to judge all Rutans on the acts of one of their kind, no more than it would be fair to judge all of humanity by the actions of such people as Myra Hindley or Hitler. But then there was the case of Alfred Scott...

If he was the Rutan, then what happened to the real Alfred Scott? Surely there had to have been one? After all, he had been living on Fang Rock since the lighthouse was lit in 1790.

'I am not the enemy,' Scott said. 'Although I was once.'

She felt Archibald move beside her. 'No, Archie, wait,' she said softly, gently pressing his arm down. She took a breath, and looked back at Scott. 'Did you kill Scott?'

'I did. Mistakes were made, but things were different a year ago, much has changed since then.' Scott narrowed his eyes at Archibald, the subtle movement so normal, so *human*. 'We tried to keep you away from here. *I* kept Jacob at Bethlem Hospital, in an attempt to manage a serious mistake. But you, you brought him back!'

'You...?' Archibald raised his Derringer, shaking Anne's calming hand away. 'You did this to Jacob?'

Scott nodded. 'We... *I* told you, Goff, I told you that you should not meddle in things you do not understand.'

The Rutan mothership continued to hover a safe distance away, silently watching. At least, Owain assumed it was a safe distance. One thing he did know, though, was that Ivan wasn't a saboteur. He had sent the Morse message at regular intervals, just as the colonel had asked. Owain's ability to read Morse was far from great, although his dad had taught it to both Lewis and him, but he knew enough to get by. Alistair had whispered the message he had written down for Ivan, so that Owain would know if it was really being sent. Owain was confident that it had been. Which meant, to Owain's mind, that Ivan was not the saboteur. It would make no sense for him to dismantle the radio equipment and then send the message.

He looked up at the mothership, which glittered with reflected sunlight. Did the Rutans understand the message? If they did, why not act? Perhaps they were not bothered by the reinforcements that were, hopefully even now, on the way. Military hardware was not a speciality of his – he could fire a rifle, but that was about as far as it went. But he doubted whatever the army could send would be a match

214

for an alien spaceship of such unearthly design.

He lowered the binoculars and turned to Ivan, who had come to join him on the gallery. 'Do you think they've found anything?'

'If they had, I suspect the colonel would have let us know by now.' Ivan lifted his own binoculars and after a moment smiled. 'Good. The mainland received our signal,' he said, pointing at a distant light flashing due north. 'Here.' He handed Owain the short range radio. 'I'll go and see what's happening downstairs, let the colonel know that help is on the way. If there's any change in the mothership…'

Owain nodded. 'I'll send a signal of my own, don't worry.'

Jacob ran. It was all he could do. The Beast was there, wherever he turned. Behind every rock, under every crevice. He wanted to return to the cave, but even at the thought of that he sensed the Beast laughing at him.

It knew something he didn't.

The woman he'd seen with Archie seemed nice, so nice that his heart raced and the Beast howled. It wanted her. To tear out her throat. But Jacob could not allow that. Davy Williams had died because Jacob was not strong enough; he could not let another pay for his weakness. So he ran. He ran because he knew the Beast would follow him.

Even now, as he hid behind a rock, the rain crashing down on him, he could feel the breath of the Beast tickling the back of his neck. Which was odd, as he had his back to the rock.

He steeled himself for another run. As long as he kept moving the Beast would leave the others alone. The Beast howled and Jacob ran.

*

Ivan passed Lethbridge-Stewart on the stairs; he was stepping out of the kitchen, lowering the radio from his ear. He looked up as Ivan joined him.

'Colonel, the signal house has received our message, so help should be on the way soon.'

'Yes, Owain just told me. Seems you're in the clear, Mr Heggessey.'

'In the… Excuse me?'

Lethbridge-Stewart explained his suspicions, and Ivan realised how stupid he was for not anticipating them. Of course the saboteur could be any one of them. There was no reason to assume the Rutan was in the lighthouse. Judging by the stories of '02, Rutans were not the kind of creatures to hide for long. Now he thought about it, Ivan knew he should cast his own suspicions, but he couldn't think of any reason that anybody would wish them to be stranded. But then, how well did he know any of them? Lethbridge-Stewart was a decorated officer, and Bishop would certainly not be here if he couldn't be trusted. Owain was the colonel's nephew, which to Ivan suggested an element of trust. But Jim… He was only here because he had caught the first Rutan ship on his camera. But Ivan didn't believe Jim would betray them – what was in it for him?

Ivan shook his head. He should have stayed at the Casquets. 'You still suspect Jim?'

'Well, I can't see who else it could be.'

'But why would he do it? He's as stranded as we are.'

'That's the problem, isn't it? Someone destroyed the radio equipment, and as far as we know nobody has any motivation to do so, although all four of you had the opportunity.'

'You all got separated outside, too,' Ivan said. 'We've all been alone at some point.'

'Quite right, although I recall the radio equipment being operational before we went to look for the Rutan. And I'm the only one who hadn't been near the service room until we found the damaged equipment.'

'So, why not Owain?'

The colonel shook his head. 'I trust him, Mr Heggessey. But I have reason to not trust journalists.'

'Jim isn't a journalist.'

'Close enough.'

Ivan didn't want to believe Jim was a saboteur. But then, what did he know of Jim really? He shook his head. No, he wasn't having it. 'It has to be the Rutan.'

'If so, then where is it now? Come on, let's see how Bishop and Saunders are getting on in the generator room.'

They continued down the curved staircase, but just before they reached the generator room, Lethbridge-Stewart turned to Ivan. 'Actually, Mr Heggessey, there is something I would like you to do for me.'

Ivan listened. He didn't like it, but he understood the sense of it. One way or another they needed to know who the saboteur was, and at least it seemed like Lethbridge-Stewart trusted him, which meant he was off the suspect list. Unless Lethbridge-Stewart was trying to call his bluff?

Ivan followed the colonel into the generator room, where they found Jim and Bishop on their hands and knees checking under the generator itself. Ivan hadn't seen the Rutan, but from what he'd heard it was a great deal bigger than any jellyfish on Earth; he supposed if it was like its earthbound counterparts then it would be able to flatten itself quite sufficiently. But enough to hide under the generator? Ivan doubted it. He could only assume they had looked everywhere else.

Bishop looked up at the sound of their footsteps. 'Sir,' he said, quickly standing and saluting. 'The bolt was still secured when we arrived, so nothing has left the lighthouse since we returned.'

'And I take it there's no sign of the Rutan here?'

In lieu of a response, Bishop glanced at Jim; the look was slight, but pointed. Ivan wasn't keen on this development; despite what Lethbridge-Stewart had said on the stair, he still couldn't believe Jim was a saboteur. Clearly, though, Bishop was of the same mind as his commanding officer.

'No, sir. Not a dickie bird. We did a thorough check of the provisions store, bathroom and generator room. Unless it managed to pass us on the stairs...'

'And I checked all the other rooms.' Lethbridge-Stewart nodded. 'Then we are left with the same problem.' He looked at each man in turn. 'Suggestions?'

'I think we should barricade ourselves in here,' Ivan said. 'Wait until the reinforcements arrive.'

'I second that, sir,' Bishop said. 'It's our only defensible position.'

'Jim?' Lethbridge-Stewart asked, turning to the cameraman.

'Me? You're asking my opinion now? I thought I was suspect number one.'

'Well, as Mr Heggessey reminded me, we are all under suspicion. We've all had opportunity, although motive is another thing.' Ivan watched Lethbridge-Stewart closely. The man was lying; they were not all under suspicion at all. Lethbridge-Stewart had no doubt in his mind who was the saboteur. There was no evidence of deceit on his face, so Ivan said nothing; he could see what the colonel was doing. 'And, although the tower is the only position we have that could be defended, I don't think we'd do much good if that mothership opened fire on us. We have limited firearms here, nothing that could do any real damage, so I intend to visit that Rutan pod thing and see what we can find there.'

'Sir, that would expose you to the mothership. Not to mention the Rutan itself.'

'Yes, Bishop, I am aware of that. But until Hamilton can get reinforcements here, my duty is to protect this lighthouse and the people in it.' The colonel pulled out his pistol and checked the clip. 'Corporal, I want you to remain here. Work with Mr Heggessey to find anything we can use for defence. Look for flammable material, empty bottles, anything that can be used against the Rutan. Mr Saunders, you're with me.'

'I beg your pardon? I'm...' Jim shook his head. 'I don't think so.'

'This is not a democracy, Mr Saunders. I want you where I can see you, and I'm afraid I'd prefer you to be out there with me than left here to sabotage Bishop's efforts.'

'And what about Ivan? He's no longer a suspect, I take it.'

'He's either bluffing very well, or he's on our side. Either way, I'd rather he remain here with Bishop. One potential suspect is enough.'

Jim let out a sigh and glanced at the bolted door. 'Fine,

take me out there. But I demand a weapon.'

'Much good it did you last time,' Bishop said.

Lethbridge-Stewart nodded sharply. 'Mr Heggessey, remember what I told you. Make sure you and Owain get ready. Bishop; *Celer et Audax*.' With that, the colonel nudged Jim towards the door and the two men left the lighthouse. Bishop followed and bolted the door behind them.

'What did he say to you?' Ivan asked.

'It's the motto of my previous regiment. *Swift and Bold*. But why say that?'

Ivan knew. 'I think it's the colonel's way of telling you to trust me, and to listen to what I have to tell you.'

Anne couldn't explain it, but she trusted the Rutan Scott. Perhaps it was the sincerity of his voice; such things could be faked of course, but Anne was sure Scott's emotion was genuine. With some persuasion Archibald had left them alone; she had told him to return to the lighthouse, to make preparations. She had a plan, and whispered it to Archibald.

'We come from the same time as you,' Scott said, once Archibald had gone.

'You do?'

'Yes. We've been on this planet for a year; it didn't take us long to realise that we had arrived in the past. Human technology is far below level five; which is what we discovered when we first scanned this planet.'

'You keep saying *we*. There are more than one of you here?'

Scott smiled. 'Forgive me, it takes much effort to refer to myself in the singular. Even after a year of being cut off from the Rutan Host. Another reason I knew I had travelled back in time. I have not been able to sense the hive mind since I crashed here.'

Anne wanted to ask more, but she knew there were more important things to discover than Rutan culture. 'How did you get here?'

'I think the answer may lie in how you got here.'

'I... Well, I used your time machine,' Anne said. 'Identical to the one in the provisions store.'

'You have the osmic projector in your time?'

'Yes,' Anne said, and explained how she came to be on Fang Rock in the past. When she was finished the Rutan nodded.

'Then it was you who sent me back here. When you first activated the osmic projector – the same one that existed in my own pod. They became slave to each other, catapulting me back in time.'

'How?'

'Have you ever tried to place two like-poles of a magnet together?'

Anne smiled. 'Of course, the same time machine existing twice in one place, when activated, repels itself. That makes a certain sense. And once I used that rod...'

'It snapped you back to the origin point of the projector. I tried to repair it, but my means are limited. However, I have left it running ever since. In the vague hope of rescue. Using the direction rod linked the two projectors together once more, connecting the two time periods.'

'Which means...' Anne felt a shudder pass through her. 'This is all my fault. If I hadn't activated the projector then you would never have ended up in the past. None of this would have happened.' She looked around the cave. 'I need air.'

She walked back up the cave until she stood at the mouth, and took in a deep breath of sea air. She let out a shiver, the wind passing through her clothes despite the coat she wore. Scott came up behind her.

'You are not to blame. Who knows where all this began? After all, you only came into possession of the projector because of a letter, because of what happened here.'

'Which only happened because I sent you...'

Scott placed a hand on her shoulder. It was an oddly human gesture of comfort. 'Paradox, Miss Travers. A causal loop. The Rutan Host are all aware of the risk of such things. However you look at it, we all had a part to play. You, Archibald... me. But mine is perhaps the worst part.'

Anne turned to look at Scott. She found it hard to believe he was an alien. His expression, the grief in his voice, it was all so human. So normal. 'How?'

'I am responsible for what happened to Jacob,' the Rutan Scott said. 'I turned him into the Beast.'

Along the way Jim hit on the idea of visiting the cave. Lethbridge-Stewart listened to his reasoning: the crystals near the mouth suggested the Rutan had been there, since they were similar to the crystals of the osmic projector – Anne's machine. Lethbridge-Stewart wondered how Jim knew about the cave, since he had supposedly found Owain some distance away, a fact which only raised more suspicion in Lethbridge-Stewart's mind. But he was willing to allow Jim his head – after all, if he was in cahoots with the Rutan, for reasons unknown, then he needed to be routed out. Besides, Lethbridge-Stewart had his pistol on him, and he wagered that his reflexes were better than Jim's.

They reached the mouth of the cave. Jim looked back at him, noticed Lethbridge-Stewart's hand hovering over his holstered pistol. 'Come on, Colonel, I'm unarmed, what can I do?'

That was another thing Lethbridge-Stewart had noticed: the further they got from the lighthouse, the cockier Jim became. As if his façade was dropping. Whatever game he was playing, he was beginning to enjoy it now he was out in the open once more.

'That remains to be seen.' Lethbridge-Stewart glanced around him, spotted movement in the distance, and smiled to himself before looking back at Jim. 'Very well, Mr Saunders, now we're here, what do you suggest?'

'That we go inside. Find out what the Rutan's left here.'

'What makes you think it left anything?'

Jim indicated the crystals on the rock around the cave mouth. 'Looks to me like this cave used to be secured; recently not so much. Which suggests something was being kept safe inside. Weapons maybe?'

Lethbridge-Stewart kept his expression passive. Fine, he'd play along. 'Lead the way, Mr Saunders.'

The cave was deeper than Lethbridge-Stewart had expected. Soon they came to a wider area, and he took in the change in the crystals on the walls. They looked dirty, covered in algae, but they were still impressive. However that was not what gave him pause, but rather the skeleton laying on a rock at the far edge of the cave. He brushed past Jim and went to examine the skeleton. He was no expert, but it had clearly been hidden behind the crystal wall for many long years. He reached down and tugged at a piece of cloth that was wedged between a shard of crystal and the rock on which the skeleton lay; the cloth was dirty, but beneath the dirt he was certain he saw a dulled orange.

Miss Travers, I should never have let you go back. I'm sorry.

'We made the mistake of choosing an outsider,' Jim said behind him. 'But he was the first person we came across; Owain had already moved away from this cave, so be thankful. It could have been him.'

Lethbridge-Stewart lifted his eyes from the cloth in his hands. He would deal with Miss Travers' death later – if he made it off Fang Rock. He was about to question Jim, ask what the hell he was on about, when his eyes alighted on another form. This one was easily identifiable, despite the lacerations all over its body. Lethbridge-Stewart kept his eyes on the Jim that stood there, smiling, while he moved closer to the dead Jim that lay discarded on a rocky outcrop.

'Sorry, Jim,' Lethbridge-Stewart whispered to the dead man, feeling a little relief in the knowledge that whatever had happened, Jim had not betrayed them.

'Divide and conquer, basic military manoeuvre. We are sure you'll understand that.'

Lethbridge-Stewart's eyes boggled as a green glow surrounded Jim and his form began to blur and change. He swallowed. A few moments later another very familiar figure stood before him. Everything was recreated perfectly, including the uniform. He was looking at himself.

The copy looked down at itself and smiled. 'Splendid. Infiltrate by using the most-trusted of men. All we need now are your memories; unfortunately for you it's a process that kills.' The ersatz Colonel Lethbridge-Stewart advanced, its arms outstretched, electrical energy dancing across its hands.

— CHAPTER FOURTEEN —

The Mistake

'What happened?' Anne asked, sitting down on a rock, not caring that it was wet. She was tired now, tired and hungry.

Scott looked out to the sea, his expression distant. 'Okay,' he said, 'but you know how it began. One hundred and forty-six years from now I was a Rutan scout, especially trained in the new metamorphosis techniques. A brutal process, for the Rutan and for the subject that is copied. On the surface it looks painless, but for the Rutan it is excruciating. One day I'm certain it will improve, but for now the process is in its infancy. And for the victim, to successfully infiltrate we need the memories of the subject, and absorbing such memories, taking everything that makes individuals what they are – it kills them.' At this, Anne let out a gasp. Rutan Scott turned his head slightly. 'What is it?'

'Sorry, I was just thinking of Alfred Scott.'

'Yes,' the Rutan said, lowering his head. Anne wanted to stand and comfort him, but she had to keep in her mind that she was talking to an alien, a killer. Regardless of its grief now, it had killed before, and it could do so again.

'Please,' she said, a bitter taste in her mouth, 'continue.'

'The Rutan Host used to control the whole of the

Mutter's Spiral, but our enemies had driven us to the far fringes of the galaxy. The Rutan Queen called it a series of strategic withdrawals to selected strong points, but I now see the truth of it.

'Earth was obscure, but its strategic position was sound. The Rutan Host thought to use it as a launch point for the final assault on the enemy "rabble". We scanned your planet and determined that the inhabitants were primitive bipeds of no value; although they had a level five status, we knew they would present us with no threat. We had already scouted all the planets of this solar system, and only Earth suited our purpose. Once I had finished my reconnaissance, I was to return to the mothership. We would then inform the rest of the fleet...'

'Wait,' Anne interrupted. 'What about Earth in my time? If you don't respond will they send another scout? The mothership?' She took a deep breath. 'Worse?'

Rutan Scott considered this. 'A scout perhaps.' He shrugged. 'It is hard to say.'

Anne let that settle. She only hoped that if such a thing did occur, Lethbridge-Stewart and Bill would be able to handle it.

'As you now know,' the Rutan continued, 'we were catapulted back in time, although at first I did not realise. We have had time travel ability for many years, although it was still not tested in battle conditions. We, ah, procured it from our enemies.'

'Enemies?'

'Yes, a cloned race of warriors. Brutal.' The Rutan shook his head. 'But back to the story. Time travel was painful, confusing; it felt like I was being torn in two. Indeed I recall a specific feeling that for an instant there were two of me. The Rutan do not recognise individuals, we are all part of the Rutan Host, of the hive mind. But for an instant I felt alone, even though there seemed to be two of me. And then, next thing I knew, I had lost control of my pod and we crashed into your atmosphere. Our pod landed just off West Crag. Just over there.' He pointed. 'My pod was damaged. Flight was impossible, so I did what I was trained to do. I came to the land and observed the humans here. Decided to infiltrate, find out what I could, perhaps use the technology of Earth to send a distress call.

'I attempted to copy Jacob, but I made a mistake. I have since learned why. Years ago, before Jacob was born, his father picked up a disease in India, a very specific and rare mutation. He passed it on to Jacob. I did not know at the time, but Jacob carried in him a strand of morphic DNA, a redundant mutant gene. I could not copy him, but I did accidentally activate the gene. He became the Beast, this animal – I witnessed him kill Davy Williams.'

Jacob crouched atop East Crag, the deadliest point of Fang Rock. His eyes beheld the light as it turned, offering protection for those who dared to sail too close to the rock. It flashed his way, casting a red glow over him.

It was here that Davy Williams had died. It was here, at East Crag, that Jacob had watched, unable to stop the Beast. And he *had* tried. But the Beast was too strong for him. All he could do was watch as the claws ravaged Williams, tearing at his clothes, shredding them, cutting into the flesh beneath. Jacob felt it tear so easily, like pulling apart a cobweb. He felt the warm blood on his hands, the taste of it in his mouth as the Beast bit into Williams' throat.

Jacob shuddered at the memory, his stomach churning. But the Beast laughed, a deep, guttural sound. And Jacob knew that it would kill again. It would kill, and he would feel it as surely as if it was him doing the evil deed.

'I did not care, primitive humans were of no concern, but I became curious about him,' Rutan Scott explained. 'And so I watched Jacob, night after night, as he slowly descended into madness. He could remember what he did, but his mind refused to process it. I soon realised the metamorphosis only happened when he was in proximity to me – my own morphic field affected his mutated gene. Alfred Scott and Captain Christopher Leask returned to Fang Rock and found... Well, you know what they found. I watched, waited. It soon became clear that these were not the humans I had scanned. I checked my instruments and realised a temporal shift had occurred. I was not certain how many years I had travelled, but I knew I was stranded. For the first time ever I could not sense the hive mind. It was just me. No longer part of the Rutan Host. I was just a Rutan – one, an individual. But that was alien to me. How does one function without the voices and thoughts of the Host?'

The Rutan fell silent, and in the hush Anne considered the idea of being tapped into so many thoughts. It was bad enough when she argued with herself; she couldn't imagine being part of a hive mind. She shivered.

'For months I remained hidden, watching in secret. Until one day Alfred Scott happened across the cave and found my lab. In a fit of anger I killed him. But as soon as I had I realised that he was my salvation. I could not live as a solitary Rutan, but perhaps I could live as a human. So I absorbed his memories, and I returned to the lighthouse as Alfred Scott.

'I have been Scott ever since, learning to be human. I have visited his family, explored Hove a little. And I have found humans to be interesting. Their individuality is intoxicating. I made arrangements for Jacob to be put into Bedlam Hospital. It was best he be kept away, for he was a danger to himself as well as his family. I had done enough damage, and I could not let him one day return here. I could not risk that. I think,' Rutan Scott said, with a slight smile, 'I developed a conscience. An affinity for these *primitive bipeds*.

'My people have been at war for so long, I think we have forgotten what it is to feel anything but rage. A conscience is of little use when all you know is war.'

It was a lot to take in, but Anne was touched by the pain in his voice. She understood making mistakes; she was far from perfect herself. 'None of this explains 1902, or the ghosts.'

'Like the ghost of you?'

'Yes,' Anne said with a nod. 'I reasoned that they were echoes, bouncing back and forth in time because of the osmic projector.'

Scott smiled at her. 'Yes, that makes sense. Temporal echoes created by the time field generated by the projector's presence in the lighthouse.'

'Only there have been no echoes from 1823. Just 1902.' Anne stood and stretched. 'Another Rutan landed there, killed seven people.'

'That... is unlikely,' Scott said. 'There is no record of a

previous visit to Earth. If there was the hive mind would know.'

'It's a matter of fact. Lethbridge-Stewart saw the Rutan kill my great uncle after he hid the direction rod there for me to find.'

'That might explain it. The rod would focus those temporal echoes forward, trying to connect with the rest of itself which you had activated in the future.'

That at least confirmed Anne's earlier hypothesis about the correlation between the manifested ghosts and the presence of the osmic projector on Fang Rock in her time.

'But that is the future,' Rutan Scott said. 'For now we have a bigger problem.'

'Yes: Jacob. Is there nothing to be done to undo the damage?'

'Nothing. I have tried. It is why I called him back to the cave. Your arrival interrupted my attempt, but the inefficacy of my methods was already clear. Alas, I feel such genetic engineering is beyond my means. What technology I salvaged from the pod is not enough. On Ruta Three it would be child's play, but here? No.'

Anne thought for a moment. 'There has to be a way. He's my ancestor. I can't let him live with the madness such a state brings.'

'Then... perhaps. If we can get him off the rock. Away from me. He will not change again if he remains off Fang Rock.'

Anne agreed. 'Then we must capture him first,' she said. 'Which brings me to my plan.'

Lethbridge-Stewart had no other choice but to whip out his

pistol and fire. The result was encouraging. The Rutan copy of him staggered back. There was no sign of a wound, but putting the creature off balance was enough for Lethbridge-Stewart. He barged the Rutan with his shoulder, clean in the Rutan's midriff, and rushed past. Any hope that he had winded the creature was soon dashed though, as the Rutan made a sweep of its arm, catching Lethbridge-Stewart on the back of the neck.

He was falling before he even had a chance to register the blow. Instinct took over, and his left arm shot out, taking most of the weight of the fall, allowing him to twist around and re-aim his pistol. It was a strange sight, to see his own face baring down on him, blue-white fire dancing around his features. He pulled the trigger and the bullet impacted with the dead centre of his head. Well, not *his* own head, of course, but it felt like it.

The Rutan flopped back again, and Lethbridge-Stewart helped it with a push of his foot. He wasn't sure how the Rutan channelled the electrical energy, but he was glad that it did, otherwise as soon as the Rutan hit the water, he would have been electrocuted. As it was, all he felt was the water growing warm around him.

He sprung to his feet and made for the mouth of the cave, hoping that Bishop was in position.

A short distance from the cave, Bishop was ready. He'd tracked Lethbridge-Stewart and Jim just as he was ordered – via Ivan – and saw them both enter the cave. He wondered if he should follow, but trusted the colonel could handle himself. His orders were to hold back, to keep hidden, and be ready to shoot should the Rutan appear. To that end he was now pressed against a rock on the crag overlooking the cave, the rifle in position before him.

He didn't feel bad for admitting that this is how he preferred it. He hadn't joined the British Army to work in administration; if he had he wouldn't have enlisted with the Royal Green Jackets. He had been trained for combat and was a crack shot with a rifle. He was glad to finally be able to use the SLR himself; he'd briefly shown Owain how to use it, but Owain was far from the expert. Gas-operated with up to eight-hundred-meter range, the L1A1 Self-Loading Rifle was a powerful piece of equipment, with thirty rounds in the magazine clip. He couldn't miss.

However, it would have helped if he knew what he was supposed to be shooting at. He watched as in quick succession the colonel staggered out of the cave followed by... the colonel.

Archibald wasn't happy with Anne, that much was obvious. He kept casting cold looks at Scott. She had managed to prevent him opening his mouth a couple of times, but knew it was only a matter of time before he let something slip to either Charlie or Wishart. And so she'd insisted he join Scott and her outside, baiting the trap.

'Nervous?' she asked him.

Archibald buffed up his chest, as she'd expected. 'Of course not. I have my trusty iron.' He brandished his Derringer. 'What say you, *Scott*?'

Now he was no longer playing the part of Scott, the look the Rutan gave Archibald was enough to shut the other man up. 'I will do my part,' he said.

'Well, here we go.' Anne swallowed hard. The sound of

growling grew ever closer. She wasn't sure this was the best plan, but it was that the only one they had. They had no weapons that would work on Jacob, and besides killing him wasn't an option. Getting him off Fang Rock was.

He appeared from behind a rock. Anne wasn't sure what she had been expecting, but out in the moonlight, the light above rotating and throwing shadows on the rocks, Jacob looked even worse than when she'd last seen him in the cave. His keeper's uniform was filthy and torn, the coarse fur protruding from every gap. He walked upright, more like a man than a wolf, but he carried himself with the kind of strength that was, frankly, inhuman. Ancestor or not, she was not keen on feeling his embrace.

He could feel their fear. No, Jacob realised, only two of them were afraid. The woman and Archie. Scott didn't fear the Beast. Jacob felt the Beast smile, saliva dripping down its muzzle, and in his mind Jacob could see a green glow as a shape descended upon him.

Pain wracked his body, and his bones popped. It was like a herd of elephants was trampling over him. He remembered it all. And with the memory he lost control, a dark fugue shrouded his reasoning, and the Beast lurched forward.

'I'm here, Jacob!' Scott yelled, and darted towards the werewolf.

Anne yelled out to him. This was not the plan. She went to move forward herself, no doubt foolishly, but Archibald grabbed hold of her and kept her back. 'No,' he hissed. 'It's time the *Rhoo Tun* paid his price.'

All Anne could do was watch as Jacob viciously tore into

Scott. The alien keeper attempted to fight back, but the vulpine keeper was too strong for him. Claws slashed, teeth bit. It was over in moments. The wolf-man stood there, holding the limp form of Scott aloft with one arm looking square at Anne and Archibald.

'Run!' Archibald said, and pushed Anne towards the tower.

For a moment, Anne felt oddly proud of her ancestor's bravery. But she didn't get a chance to comment. Jacob threw Scott's body at Archibald with such force that Archibald flipped head over heels under the impact. Anne winced at the crack of his skull on the rock.

She stared at her grandfather's body. This wasn't right. He had to live. To send her the letter. If he died, then how could any of this happen? Without the letter she would never end up in the past. Was time changing around her – how long before the ripple hit 1969? What damage had she caused by coming back here? And where would it end; with her death?

The roar of Jacob pulled her out of her indecision. Her death was staring right at her! She darted into the lighthouse. She had barely crossed the generator room before Jacob was on her. His claws grabbed at her coat, but she pulled her arms out, kicked backwards, and carried on running. She heard the wolf tumble down a few steps. But she knew it was only a slight reprieve. Her lungs hurt, but she continued to run. Up, up, up...

She scrambled up the ladder and into the lamp room. 'Charlie!' she called. 'It's coming!'

She rushed across the lamp room, turning to look back before ducking out onto the gallery. From there she watched. Hidden either side of the lamp, over which a large trawling net hung, Charlie and Wishart waited. The wolf entered the lamp room. It tilted its head. Anne's heart jumped into her mouth. It was going to notice Charlie! She banged on the glass to get the wolf's attention, and Charlie and Wishart made their move. They pulled at the net, dragging it off the lamp, and threw it over the wolf. As hoped, the enraged instincts of the wolf forced it to react against captivity. It struggled, but only succeeded in tangling itself up even more. Wishart and Charlie stepped back, careful to avoid the frantically scrambling claws. Charlie looked over at Anne, opening his mouth to speak, but before any words could form, his face froze with surprise, as from behind her a tentacle lashed out over the guardrail and snaked into the lamp room. It wrapped itself around the edge of the net and yanked with tremendous power.

Net and wolf were torn through the small hatch, cracking the metal either side. In her shock, Anne barely registered the netted wolf flipping over the edge of the guardrail. She was dimly aware of Charlie calling out to her, but she didn't know what to say.

Charlie and Wishart joined her on the gallery and all three of them looked over the guardrail to the rocks below. Of the wolf there was no sign. But down below two prone forms remained. Scott and Archibald.

'What was that?' Charlie asked.

Anne knew, but how could she explain? In the distance though, she saw the answer. A green luminescent glow disappearing behind rocks, heading towards West Crag.

Bishop wavered, eyeing each man in turn through the sights.

He could try to disarm the Lethbridge-Stewart with the gun... or maybe a knee shot to both men would do the trick? He didn't much like the idea of wounding his commanding officer, especially not during his first week on the new job. And if he called out, he'd give away his position. Of course, none of this helped with the overriding question; how could there be two Lethbridge-Stewarts?

Was this like Finney's novel? Pod people? He'd only recently finished re-reading *The Midwich Cuckoos*, to commiserate John Wyndham's passing, and was well acquainted with the idea of duplicate humans. But, he reminded himself, this was real life. For a moment, he couldn't help but smile. Somehow he was living science fiction. He shook his head, hearing the voice of his sister: *Out of the clouds, Billy*.

He just needed to work out which was the real Lethbridge-Stewart, and then take the other one out. But how? There had to be some sign.

Lethbridge-Stewart stood his ground, gun aimed at his doppelgänger. He needed to give Bishop a signal. He knew the corporal was out there; he'd seen the sun reflect ever so briefly off the young soldier's rifle. Bishop would be watching them as they fought, switching his aim between targets.

'When will you learn that your primitive weapons will not harm us?'

'Harm you, perhaps not. But they hurt. Sometimes hurt is a good place to begin.' Lethbridge-Stewart fired and the doppelgänger dropped to the ground. Lethbridge-Stewart stepped forward, keeping his aim true. He still had a few shots left. He glanced towards Bishop's position, just briefly, not enough to allow the Rutan to make a move. *Come on, Corporal*, he thought, *pay attention.*

The Rutan looked up at him, hazel eyes appearing blue in the sun-light, just like his own eyes did. It was unnerving to see oneself reflected in such a way. He was reminded of Sally and her nickname for him: 'Sinatra'. She only ever said it because she knew it annoyed him.

'How many more shots do you wish to take?' he asked, dragging himself back to the present. It wouldn't do to be distracted now.

'How many have you got left? Or, maybe, you'd like a different target?'

Accompanied by the same glow as before, the Rutan's shape changed, much to Lethbridge-Stewart's relief. What now lay on the rock before him wasn't even remotely human. It was humanoid certainly, dressed in a soft armour, stocky and broad, its neck disappearing into a metal collar. The head looked to Lethbridge-Stewart much like a badly baked potato. What kind of alien was that supposed to be?

'We find this to be a great target,' the Rutan said, its voice having now taken on a gravelly texture.

'Yes, I imagine it will be,' Lethbridge-Stewart said, and stepped back. He waited until the Rutan stood, and then yelled, 'Now!' In unison he fired his remaining rounds as from his vantage point Bishop fired his SLR. The new stocky form of the Rutan dropped, its body shaking under the impact of the rifle rounds.

Lethbridge-Stewart knew it'd do no permanent damage, but it was enough for him to beat a retreat. He signalled Bishop, then haired off at his best speed.

Anne wasn't too sure she wanted to step back outside. The rain seemed to have abated with the disappearance of the Beast, but that didn't help convince her. Outside on the rocks, just on the other side of the door, was her dead great-great-great grandfather, the catalyst for everything that had happened to her in the last few weeks. With him dead, she had no idea what the future held. What damage his death would do to her future... Not only hers, but generations of her family not even born yet.

Charlie stood behind her, holding the torn coat that she had borrowed. She sighed heavily and leaned her forehead against the cool iron of the door. She wanted to just curl up and sleep. But she knew she had to face it, had to go and see the Rutan Scott. He was the only one who really knew how to work the osmic projector – yes, she had managed to bring herself *back* in time, but that was largely down to luck. No Om-Tsor to help her here.

Bracing herself, she stepped outside, and was amazed to find Archibald standing there looking at the dead body of Scott. He glanced up at the sound of the iron door opening, and offered her a weak smile. A gaping wound stood out on his head, and blood trickled down the side of his face.

'You're alive!' Before she even knew she was going to, Anne rushed over to him and threw her arms around him.

'Surprisingly,' he said into her shoulder. They released, and he nodded towards the dead body. 'Which is more than can be said for our *Rhoo Tun* friend.'

It wasn't a pleasant sight, and for a brief moment Anne didn't understand, but then her basic medical training kicked in. There was no way Archibald would know, but the rate of decomposition indicated that the body of Scott had been dead for a long time – at a guess she'd say at least nine months – when the Rutan had killed him. For it was the real Scott's body. She suppressed a smile. It would have been inappropriate, but she had to admire the neatness with which the Rutan operated. As far as Archibald was concerned, the Rutan had given his life to stop the Beast.

Anne explained what had happened in the lamp room. 'A freak gush of wind knocked him over,' she finished, lying to save more complicated explanations. 'We need to find Jacob.'

Archibald nodded. 'Yes, this whole gruesome affair needs an end.' He wiped the blood from his eye, noting the concern on Anne's face. 'I will live. I'm sure I've survived worse.'

They set off together, in the direction of West Crag.

The Beast rose to its full height and faced the thing before it. Jacob remembered; the green glow, the thrashing tentacles. They had dragged him into the cave before the Beast came. They had done something to him...

His heart beat faster, and he could feel the blood pumping through him. Everything became clear. In the cave he had watched himself, reflected in the surface of the crystals, as he changed, his arms stretching, nails turning into claws, and his teeth... Oh, what big teeth he had! He'd seen the Beast he had become, seen it through eyes that were yellow in their reflection.

It was him. Like a sack of coal it hit him. Perhaps deep down he had always known; perhaps that is why he had lost his mind. But now it made sense. He couldn't run from the

Beast because the Beast was always with him. *He* was the Beast.

Jacob growled. *You did this*, he thought, but all that came from his mouth was a howl of rage. Words no longer belonged to him. Only rage. Rage and hunger.

He had killed Davy Williams. *He* was the Beast of Fang Rock. But this creature before him had made him.

With a roar of hatred, Jacob launched himself at the green creature. Tendrils wrapped themselves around him, and pain surged throughout his body. But he would not be stopped. Jacob was the Beast, and the Beast's hunger would be sated this night.

It wasn't long before they came across Jacob. He was still tangled in the net, but no longer in wolf form. Anne had a feeling she knew what was going on, but had no way to be sure. Yet. She crouched down and reached out for his neck.

'He's alive,' she said.

'I am more relieved to see he looks normal.'

'Likewise.' Anne stood again. 'We need to get him safely inside the lighthouse, then send a signal to the mainland. The sooner Jacob is off Fang Rock, the safer it will be for everybody. Including him.'

Lethbridge-Stewart and Bishop ran, the Rutan in pursuit. It had given up its potato-headed form and nimbly skittered across the rocks on its tentacles. It was unusually agile, Lethbridge-Stewart noted with dismay. The lighthouse wasn't far away now, but it still wasn't close enough.

Lethbridge-Stewart raised his hand and they both stopped. 'Enough of this,' he said, and turned to face the

Rutan. It slowed, probably curious as to what the humans would do next. 'One final attempt, Corporal?'

Bishop readied his rifle. 'By all means, sir.'

'Splendid. Those tentacles there; five rounds rapid should do the trick.'

Bishop fired, aiming for one of the tentacles at the front of the creature. The result was as Lethbridge-Stewart had hoped. The hi-powered velocity of the bullets was enough to sever the tentacle. The Rutan staggered to a stop, maintaining its balance with its remaining tendrils.

'Fire at...'

'Sir,' Bishop said, his tone uncertain. 'What's got its attention?'

The Rutan had tilted its face towards the sky. Curious, Lethbridge-Stewart followed the direction, just in time to witness the mothership vanish in much the same way as Anne had.

'Well, that's one problem we don't need to concern ourselves with,' Lethbridge-Stewart said.

A split second later an unearthly shriek sent a shockwave through the air. It was the Rutan. Electricity arched around it, and its tinny voice screamed, 'You did this!'

A tendril lashed out and wrapped itself around Bishop. He convulsed as the blue-white electrical charges wrapped around his body. He was tossed aside, and lay motionless on the rock, leaving Lethbridge-Stewart alone to face the enraged Rutan.

— CHAPTER FIFTEEN—

End of the Horror

Archibald winced as Wishart continued to clean the wound on his head. He was still trying to work out just what had happened, and why the *Rhoo Tun* would give its life for them. It made no sense. The creature had taken the blame for Jacob's condition, although Anne claimed that Jacob had inherited it from his father. He was more prone to believe Anne, but there was some doubt in his mind. She and the *Rhoo Tun* had worked together to trap Jacob, after all, which did suggest some goodness in the creature.

Archibald had never been a God fearing man, but he had never denied the existence of God either. The *Rhoo Tun* looked to be the work of Satan, and yet the good it had done… *Greater love hath no man than this, that a man lay down his life for his friends.* That's what the Bible said.

Archibald closed his eyes. When he'd arrived at Fang Rock he was so sure of himself and his path in life, but now… Things no longer made the sense they once did.

Ye are my friends, if ye do whatsoever I command you.

At least Jacob was safe now. Quiet, haunted probably, but whole once again. If nothing else Jacob had faced the Beast and survived. At least in that Archibald had succeeded.

'History will remember this night, mark my words,' Wishart said.

'Yes,' Archibald agreed, thinking of Anne. 'Yes. It will.'

It was no surprise for Anne to learn that Jacob, now secured in the highest bunk room of the lighthouse, was in fact the Rutan. Things had quietened down in the lighthouse; Archibald was being attended by Wishart, and Charlie was sending a semaphore signal to the mainland requesting the return of Captain Leask.

'What about the real Jacob?' Anne asked closing the door of the bunk room behind her.

'He's dead.'

Anne slumped on the wooden stool. She opened her mouth to speak, but the words wouldn't come. The Rutan sat on the bunk, maintaining the form of Jacob, as if to mock her.

'There was no other option. How could we hope to return him to the mainland?' the Rutan asked. 'He would have been the Beast, not able to metamorphose back into humanity until off Fang Rock. How would that be explained?'

Anne shook her head. 'But he was my...' She placed her head in her hands. 'What will happen now?'

'I will go back to the mainland as Jacob, and I will find a way to undo the damage I caused. My recompense.'

'But...' No, Anne realised, it did make sense. If Jacob lived, he would have been forever haunted by memories of the Beast, believing himself cursed. Destined to remain in Bethlem Hospital. She sighed. 'What did you do with Jacob's body?'

'It's in the cave. Don't worry, it'll never be found, I've made sure that nobody will enter the cave again.' The Rutan leaned forward and reached out a hand. 'Your jersey is damaged,' he said.

Anne looked down. 'Must have got caught on the crystals in the cave,' she reasoned, 'or somewhere else on the rocks. It's possible. I have had a very trying night.'

'Yes. I'm sorry.'

'Why? You didn't cause this. I did.'

'Anne, I thought we discussed this. Nobody is to blame. We are caught in a paradox.'

Anne wanted to accept that, but to do so would mean that none of them had any say in what had happened. Their actions subject to the whim of... fate? Destiny? She refused to believe that. If it was true, then who was accountable? 'Help them,' she said. 'My family. The Travers, the Goffs. They have to remain connected until my father and mother marry. Promise me.'

Rutan Jacob nodded. 'I promise. I will do everything I can.'

'Good. But do more than that. If you're going to become human, then embrace humanity.'

'I will.'

She nodded. 'Good,' she said again, and stood. 'Now, I need you to show me how to use this properly.' Anne lifted the osmic projector off the floor and placed it on the table. 'I can't stay here, like you did.'

'Of course not. You don't belong here, but I did. First because I didn't know how far I had travelled and then...' Rutan Jacob held out his hands in a gesture that Anne found so endearingly human, and she nodded her understanding. He walked over to the table. 'Of course, this projector still exists in the future, three time periods connected by the same machine. Using it once sent me here, using it a second time brought you here, too. Using it a third time...'

'Could also bring something else back?' Anne thought about this. What was left in the future that belonged to the Rutan? 'I suppose we better hope that another scout wasn't sent to find you, or worse.'

Rutan Jacob smiled. 'Perhaps it's better if they did send another. Better the Rutan be in the past than be able to make use of a level five planet.'

Rutan Jacob, looking glum and haunted, sat in the small boat, the osmic projector covered and safe beside him. It was a convincing act; neither Archibald nor Charlie had any inclination of the truth. The three of them stood on the rocks, saying their goodbyes. Wishart, naturally, remained at the lighthouse keeping watch. In the distance was a ship belonging to Captain Leask, to which Archibald was about to row. Enquiries would be made, of course, once Scott's body was returned to the mainland.

'Of course,' Anne said. 'The second dead keeper.'

Archibald looked away from his goodbye to Charlie. 'What say you?'

'Remember I told you that by my time the story is that two keepers were killed and one driven mad? Well, the second is Scott. Over time, the events of tonight and last year must merge into one.'

'Yes, that would seem reasonable.'

For a moment they stood looking at each other. Anne wished she had got to know Archibald better, for she felt there had to be more to him than what she had seen in the last few hours. Already he had surprised her; he was not the man she had first met. He seemed burdened now, no longer assured and arrogant. 'What troubles you?' she asked.

'The truth,' he replied, and gave a slight smile. 'I came here to increase my fame. In my pomposity I believed I could cure Jacob, but instead... I have seen the truth of our place in the universe. God's hand I have felt on me this night.'

Anne wasn't sure about that. What he had seen was science at work. Time travel, alien life, and technological advancement way beyond his time... His mind simply couldn't comprehend the rationality of it all. Too steeped in superstition, despite his protestations to the contrary. Unfortunately there was nothing she could do about that.

'Remember, you must write that letter to me,' she said. 'Date it for May 2nd, 1969, and be sure to get that machine to *Morecombe & Slant Solicitors* in London.'

'I know of no such establishment.'

'Perhaps they do not exist yet, but they will. Give it another seven years, then find them.' Anne took his hands in hers. 'Promise me.'

Archibald searched her face. 'This is all extraordinary, but I have seen too much this night... Of course, I promise.'

She leaned forward and pecked him on the cheek, and laughed at the look of surprise on his face. They said their final farewells, and as the boat sailed out to meet the ship. Anne remained, watching first her three-times-great grandfather disappear into the inky distance. Once he was gone she looked back, and was surprised to find that Charlie, too, had stayed to watch.

'You should go, see how Wishart is doing.'

'What of you?'

Anne shrugged. She could feel the pull already. The Rutan said it would take a while, but eventually she would simply fade away and reappear in her own time. 'I won't be here much longer.'

'You're going back to the future?'

'I am.'

Charlie shook his head, laughing nervously. 'As long as I live, I do not think I will ever believe any of this night happened.'

'It's probably for the best,' Anne said, patting him on the shoulder, and walked away.

As she made her way across the rocks, the sky grew brighter, which only served to make her more tired. It was worse than jet lag; she had already lived through 5am, less than five hours ago, and now here she was living through it again, only one hundred and forty-six years beforehand. Time lag, temporal lag? She wasn't sure what to call it, but she would be glad once she was back in '69 and, more importantly, in her own bed. She felt like she could sleep for days.

She finally made it to the cave and realised what the Rutan had meant. She pressed her hand against the wall of crystal that now blocked the cave mouth. Even if anybody came upon the cave, she doubted they'd be able to break through. She leaned against it. On the other side was not only the genetics lab the Rutan had set up, but Jacob. Dead. This was now his tomb. After all that had happened to him on Fang Rock, he would never leave it again. The curse began and ended here.

She supposed there was some kind of symmetry in that.

*

Anne opened her eyes to sound of gunfire. She blinked, lifting her hand to block out the bright sun above. She was on the rocky ground outside the cave. She sat up, noticed the crystal fragments around her. She was home, back in '69. And she was alive!

Anne scrambled to her feet and ran across the rocks until she finally came upon the source of the noise. Lethbridge-Stewart stood there, a rifle in his arms, firing wildly at a Rutan. The creature was barely upright; tendrils scattered on the ground around, only four left to keep it off the ground. A willowy filament twitched beneath the bell of the Rutan, what for a terrestrial jellyfish would have been the oral arm containing the stinging cells, but which in the Rutan contained something else entirely. Bolts of electricity shot out of the oral arm, striking the rock around Lethbridge-Stewart, scorching black gashes into the stone. The colonel was dodging the bolts for now, but she could see he was growing tired. Nonetheless he continued to fire, bullets ripping into the remaining tentacles.

Anne's scanned the surrounding area, looking for something that she could use to help. Two ammo clips lay on the ground near Lethbridge-Stewart, and a short distance away... Her hand flew to her mouth at the sight of the figure lying on the ground. It was Bill!

She had to help, but what could she do? Before she had a chance to think, the whirring of helicopter rotor blades filled the air. She looked up and saw several military choppers flying overhead. Two of them slowed above her, their hold hatches opening. Men leaned out, and more rifle fire joined that of Lethbridge-Stewart. She watched, almost feeling sorry for the Rutan, as it caved under the continual onslaught of high velocity bullets. The remaining tentacles were shredded from it and the creature collapsed onto the rocky ground, squashing its oral arm. Threads of electricity sparked from its body, sputtering weakly into the air. Lethbridge-Stewart raised a hand and waved at the helicopters. The soldiers stopped firing but the choppers continued to hover above.

Atop a small outcrop above the Rutan, another figure appeared. It was Owain. He stood awkwardly, wincing in pain, and lifted a bucket into the air. From the bucket poured a slick, dark substance, covering the creature below. Oil, Anne was sure. The creature shrieked. Electricity crackled around it. Ivan ran from behind another rock carrying in his hand a flaming torch. He yelled and struck the Rutan. The flame touched the oil and the Rutan went up in a ball of flame. Ivan jumped back, his arms covering his face.

Not unlike the jellyfish of Earth, the Rutan was susceptible to the intense heat. It died screaming, every drop of moisture scorched from its body. The flames subsided, leaving a desiccated, grey residue on the rock. Looking at this Anne wondered if it was the same Rutan she had only recently – no, over a century ago, she realised – said goodbye to. But it couldn't have been; it must have been another scout. She smiled. Earth would be safe from the Rutan Host after all. At least for now. How long before they decided to renew their interest in the strategically favoured planet?

As the choppers floated off to find a safe landing zone, Anne walked over to the men. But as she neared she felt her legs give way. She wasn't sure if it was from tiredness, or the sight of Bill's badly burned form lying on the rock. Either way, if it wasn't for Lethbridge-Stewart's quick reactions she would probably have landed flat on her face.

'Miss Travers, nice of you to join us,' he said, with a slight smile.

'Glad to be back,' she said, offering her own tired smile, surprised by the relief in the colonel's eyes. 'What about Bill? Is he...?'

Owain looked up from where he knelt, checking Bill's pulse. 'He's alive.'

Miss Travers insisted she remain with Bishop, and so it was that Lethbridge-Stewart returned to the lighthouse with Owain and Mr Heggessey. En route they came across a squad of troops heading their way. The man leading the squad was known to Lethbridge-Stewart.

He offered a salute. 'Colonel Douglas!'

Lieutenant Colonel Walter Douglas of the Prince of Wales' Own Regiment of Yorkshire returned the salute. 'Colonel Lethbridge-Stewart.' The two old friends shook hands and Douglas looked around. 'Where's your wounded man?'

'Heggessey will show you.'

Colonel Douglas turned to his squad. 'Captain Norton, if you would be so kind.'

'Aye, sir,' the captain said, in a South African accent. 'Lead on, Mr Heggessey.'

Lethbridge-Stewart watched them jog back towards West Crag. 'Royal Hampshire Regiment? Got bored of County Down, Dougie?'

'Luckily I was visiting the wife when I got the call from Hamilton.'

'Ah.' Lethbridge-Stewart nodded at the departing troops.

'That Captain Norton, isn't he the chap who got awarded the Victoria Cross for his actions in Montegridolfo in '44?'

'The very same. Only the best to help you out. Although looks like you took care of things without me.'

'Can't be helped, Dougie.' Lethbridge-Stewart turned to Owain. 'You remember my nephew, of course?'

'Of course.' Douglas shook Owain's hand and nodded at his limp. 'War wound?'

Owain grinned. 'Something like that.'

'Not to worry, my men will soon have you patched up. This way.'

They fell out and continued on towards the lighthouse.

'Back to deal with the Irish trouble next week,' Douglas said as they walked. 'But had a bit of leave and thought I'd make use of it. Which reminds me, Penny insists you and Sally join us for dinner on Friday.'

'Well, I have a date at Hyde Park tomorrow, so I shall let Sally know.'

'Good, now that's sorted... I suspect we have some cleaning up to do?'

'Don't we always,' Lethbridge-Stewart replied sardonically.

Sometime later Anne stood outside the cave entrance, next to Lethbridge-Stewart. Covered in a sheet beside them was the body of Jim Saunders. So many dead...

'I think the mothership ended up in 1902,' Anne was explaining. 'Remember the stories of the explosive light over the lighthouse? It had to be the mothership. It's the only thing that makes sense.'

Lethbridge-Stewart nodded. 'I can live with that

explanation. What do you think happened? Self-destruct?'

'Maybe. Maybe we'll never know.'

'Or perhaps we will,' Lethbridge-Stewart said with a knowing smile. 'Seems before he returned from 1902, Owain swore he saw a police box on Fang Rock.'

'I'm not surprised.'

'You're not?'

'No. Had a suspicion he was involved.'

'So, Miss Travers, your return here helped save the day.'

Anne wasn't so sure about this. She still felt all of this was her fault. Somebody had to take responsibility, and that was down to her. Her and her family. Jacob, Scott, all those who had died in 1902, and now Jim – all that had gone wrong on Fang Rock was down to the Travers and the Goffs.

Captain Norton and Owain emerged from the cave carrying between them a sheet, within which were the skeletal remains of Jacob. Anne walked over to them and placed a hand on the sheet.

'I'm sorry, Jacob. But it's time to finally go home.'

She would make sure his bones got buried in the Travers' plot in Kensal Green Cemetery. He had spent more than enough time on Fang Rock.

Two helicopters remained. Jim and Jacob had already been lifted off the rock, back to the mainland where they could be put to rest. Soon the rest of them would be back at RAF Odiham, and then onto London and, Anne suspected, a long period of debriefing. In the meantime Douglas and his team would remain on Fang Rock until decisions were made regarding the Rutan technology left behind. It'd probably end up in the Vault, just like the alien tech left over from London a few months ago. Fortunately, such decisions were not her problem.

She found Ivan sitting on the porch step outside the lighthouse, watching the soldiers buzz around him, a cigarette in his mouth. He looked up at her. 'I think this is the end of Fang Rock,' he said. 'Trinity House will shut it down.'

'Back to Casquets for you, then?'

He shrugged. 'Probably, although considering the things I've seen today, I imagine I'll be slapped with the Official Secrets Act.'

'At least you're alive to read into it,' Anne said, thinking of Jim.

'There is that.' He offered her a weak smile. Ivan reached into his pocket and removed a packet of Embassy. 'Want one?' he asked, stumping one out and taking out another.

'No thanks.' Anne nodded at Lethbridge-Stewart as he approached. 'Anyway, here comes some good news.'

Ivan stood up and offered the colonel a lazy salute. Lethbridge-Stewart didn't seem to mind. 'Mr Heggessey, I've arranged a meeting with Trinity House for Wednesday.'

'You have?'

'Of course.' Anne took over from the colonel, with a grin. 'Didn't I tell you? We're going to put in a good word. The ghosts won't come back now that all the Rutan technology is going. No more osmic projector linking the time periods.'

'Good. It would be a shame to see the last of Fang Rock.'

Anne was pleased by the smile on Ivan's face, but she wasn't sure she agreed with that sentiment.

Lethbridge-Stewart turned to Anne. 'Speaking of ghosts

from the past, Miss Travers, when we get back to Odiham, I think you and I need a private discussion about dead soldiers and capsules from other worlds.' He nodded at Ivan. 'See you Wednesday, Mr Heggessey. And I'll meet you in the chopper, Miss Travers.'

Anne watched him go, biting her lip thoughtfully.

'What was all that about?' Ivan asked.

'My fault,' Owain said as he limped out of the generator room. 'Couldn't help but overhear.'

Ivan looked from Owain to Anne. 'I'll leave you two to it,' he said, and with a cheery wave he ambled off towards the chopper.

'Well?' Anne asked.

'I, er, kind of let slip about you working on the same case that led to Alistair's disappearance last month.' Owain held up his hands. 'Sorry, didn't mean to. Was having a bit of an honest moment, and he seemed so disturbed by whatever it was he experienced.'

Anne didn't need to wonder how Owain knew; she knew Bill and Owain had spent a lot of time together since arriving on Fang Rock. Boys will talk, she guessed. To her surprise she found she wasn't that bothered. After everything that had occurred overnight, she didn't really care about keeping secrets from people who deserved to know the truth. If Hamilton had a problem with it, then he could rap her knuckles later. Until then she'd tell Lethbridge-Stewart whatever he wanted to know.

But at least Owain could *try* and look apologetic, not just stand there smirking. Perhaps he was embarrassed; he was avoiding her eyes, looking pointedly over her shoulder. She was about to pass comment, but before she could, he clapped her chummily on the arm, nodded in the direction he was looking, and moved away.

'What's he smiling about?' she heard from behind her.

She turned. Bill stood there, a little pale perhaps, but his eyes were bright. 'Who knows?' she said, and for a moment let the silence sit between them, before reaching out for his bandaged hands. 'Are you okay?'

He smiled at her. 'I'll be fine – better, now you're back.'

Anne couldn't help but smile in return. *That* was a conversation she didn't really want to have right now. So instead she asked, 'Do you think Rutan Scott held to his promise?'

'I do.'

'You do? Why?'

'Because we're all still here.'

Anne rested her head on Bill's left arm, and the two of them walked towards the waiting chopper.

— EPILOGUE—

He was becoming quite the regular visitor at Strategic Command, but regardless Lethbridge-Stewart liked to maintain a sense of decorum about his visits. This time, though, it was different. After Fang Rock, for him, things had changed. Especially since Miss Travers had phoned him before leaving London.

Lethbridge-Stewart waited while Hamilton finished reading the report that had been sent to him in advance of the meeting. He closed the manila folder and sat back, steepling his fingers. 'Well,' he began, 'I guess that pretty much says it all. Threat from an intergalactic war...' He shook his head and looked down at the closed report. 'Perhaps this will be the evidence we needed.'

Lethbridge-Stewart raised an eyebrow. 'One would think so. But there is more, stuff that I wasn't at liberty to include in my report. Something Miss Travers said to me, about you...'

Hamilton's response was guarded. Eventually he nodded his head slowly. 'Very well. What has she told you, exactly?'

Lethbridge-Stewart told him everything Miss Travers had said about her work in the Vault, but he did not tell Hamilton about the rest of it. About the way Hamilton had enlisted Miss Travers and her father to look into Lethbridge-

Stewart's disappearance. That bit would keep, for now.

Hamilton didn't confirm or deny anything. He just listened. 'You put her in the Vault for a reason,' Lethbridge-Stewart said when he'd finished. He was probably overstepping his bounds, but he was tired of being treated like a fool. Hamilton was playing a long game, one Lethbridge-Stewart had become a part of. And he was damned if he was going to continue walking around blind. 'And I have a feeling it's connected to what's been going on since Bledoe.'

'No one puts anybody in the Vault, Colonel, for one thing, and all this has been going on for a lot longer than Bledoe. But, yes, I recommended her for a position at the Vault for a reason. Because I need to know what's going on there, what exactly they have access to. And since Department C19 doesn't appear to want to share their intelligence, Doctor Travers has been reporting to me ever since she was insinuated into the Vault.'

'Department C19? I thought the Vault came under the Ministry of…'

'It does, but the Ministry is just one small part of a much larger government organisation. Don't ever think that Mr Wilson knows even half of what's really going on.' Hamilton held a hand up. 'Colonel, that is all I can tell you at this time; indeed, it's probably more than I should. But I trust your silence on this. We're going to need Miss Travers, and so she needs to be ready. Her experiences in the Vault will prepare her for us.'

'So, two birds with one stone?'

'Quite so.' Hamilton tapped the report. 'There is enough in here for me to approach… certain people. Two men in particular who will be very helpful to us in the long-term. In the meantime, I want you to contact this man.' He scribbled on a piece of paper and handed it to Lethbridge-Stewart. 'Tell him I sent you. He will tell you everything you need to know.'

Lethbridge-Stewart looked down at the note. There was a number, accompanied by a single name: Gilmore. 'Who is this?'

'An ally, Colonel. He can tell you more than I can at this time.'

'Very well.' Lethbridge-Stewart stood up and placed his cap on his head. He offered Hamilton a salute and turned to leave. Then reconsidered. 'Just one more thing, General. Why did you feel it necessary to divulge to Miss Travers information regarding previous visits by the Cosmic Hobo, and yet neglected to inform me?'

'Miss Travers has a loose tongue.'

'Perhaps, but she thought it pertinent to tell me. As do I.'

Hamilton sipped his whisky. 'Colonel, I'm not sure questioning the decisions of a senior officer becomes you, but be that as it may, Air-Marshal Gilmore and I agreed that sharing said information with Miss Travers was *pertinent*, and you did not need to know. Gilmore will reveal all we know of the Cosmic Hobo. And more besides. Dismissed.'

Lethbridge-Stewart saluted again. He had learned all he could for now.

'Just one more thing, Colonel.'

Lethbridge-Stewart looked back. 'Sir?'

'You need to tell Gilmore this message from me, and you will get full disclosure. Just one phrase, Colonel. *Let slip the dogs of war.'*

Earlier that day, Anne stepped into the small café in Soho and looked around. True to his word, Rupert Slant sat at a small table in the far corner, wrapped in warm clothes and sporting a hat despite the sun outside. She took a seat and ordered a strong coffee before saying hello.

'And now you know,' Rupert said.

'Yes,' she said, 'now I know.' She peered closely at the old man. 'Somehow I have a feeling you knew all about it.'

Rupert smiled at this. He sipped his tea and nodded. 'Well of course, how else could I have been friends with your grandfather?' He leaned forward and whispered. 'I promised you I would help your family, and I did.'

'You promised?' For a moment Anne was confused, then realisation dawned. 'You're... Rutan Scott. That was you?'

'The very same. Rupert the Rutan; has a nice ring to it, doesn't it?'

'But how—?'

She was interrupted by the arrival of her coffee. She took the mug and helped herself to some sugar from the glass bowl in the centre of the table, careful to brush aside the hardened sugar-clumps that had already been touched by who knew how many dirty spoons.

Anne took a short sip, and hissed at the burning taste. Cheap coffee, of course. While she sipped she considered what Rupert had said. The same Rutan that she had left one hundred and forty-six years in the past... 'How *old* are you?'

Rupert, who had been humming along to Fleetwood Mac's *Man of the World*, which was playing softly in the background, looked at her with a smile. 'Who is to say? The lifespan of the Rutan Host is unknown. All are killed in the war at some point, but I suspect I have lived longer than most. Perhaps even longer than the current Rutan Queen.'

Anne sat back. It all made a sort of sense, she decided; it certainly explained all those feelings she'd had about him when they had first met. All those hints about his incredible age, his connection to her family. 'What happened when you returned to the mainland?'

'It was so very long ago, although for you it's been only a couple of days. One hundred and forty-six years for me, Anne, and I have lived every day since as a human. First as Jacob, until one night he went for a walk in the snow and never returned. But not before he healed the pain of his family, before he set his son on the correct path. Not before I had paid my debt, made recompense for the damage I caused in 1822. Or, at least, most of it. Unfortunately after Jacob went missing his wife, Vina, blamed Archibald. 1829, that was.'

'The start of the bad blood between my families.'

'Yes,' Rupert said, with a nod. 'I'm afraid so. It was always meant to happen this way, Anne. Anyway, I shifted my form once more. Although I have gradually aged my appearance,' he added with a slight smile. 'With John Morecombe I set up the solicitors that would protect the financial future of Archibald's family, and kept safe the osmic projector until it was time for you to have it. When the time was right I passed the direction rod on to Ben's father with express instructions, showing him a letter written by Jacob in 1829 shortly before he died.' He stopped there, and gave her what she could only describe as a mischievous smile.

'Just like you did with... Wait.' Anne blinked, as everything fell into place. 'Archibald didn't write that letter, did he?'

'In such good English?' Rupert chuckled. 'Have you ever read anything written in the 1830s? It's not the easiest form of English to understand.'

Anne had not considered that before, but... 'I had no trouble understanding. It was oddly phrased at times, but...'

Rupert nodded with a soft smile. 'Centuries ago, more perhaps, the Rutan gene pool was manipulated to enable us to process and translate any spoken language we're exposed to. It makes us better at infiltration. I, ah, doctored the paper on which the letter was written. When you touched it, a genetic sample from me, containing the translation matrix, entered your system. Which means you will now be able to understand any language you're exposed to, although it does take a little exposure to take proper effect.'

'You mean...?' Anne shook her head. That was amazing. To be fluent in every tongue on the planet. The practical uses of that were... endless.

'Archie was going to write to you, of course. We spoke a lot over the years, first as Jacob, and later as his solicitor. But his experiences on Fang Rock changed him; he became obsessed with the idea of finding the truth behind life. He never did find out, of course. Anyway, he never got around to the letter, and so I did so on his behalf. After all, I knew it had to happen. If you didn't receive the letter in '69, then the events of 1823 would have gone very differently.'

'So you made all this happen.'

'Only because you told me it *would* happen. We've both been stuck in something of a causal loop, I'm afraid. Things only happened in the past because of events in the future. And the events of the future only happened because of what happened in the past.'

Anne digested this for a moment. 'But what of the osmic projector that took me back? It had its origins in the 1820s, but it didn't materialise with me in the past.'

'Well, that is a mystery. One that has always puzzled me.'

The scientist in her wanted to explore that further, but she supposed she had enough to think about as it was. So instead she latched onto something a little easier to absorb. 'What did happen in 1902? Did you ever find out? The accounts are so unclear, despite what we've managed to piece together in the last few days. But you lived through that, too. You said the Rutan Host has a hive mind, so you must have been able to sense the thoughts of that Rutan, right?'

'Yes, but the answer was not as expected. You remember I told you I felt like I had been split in two when I travelled back in time?' Anne nodded. 'The Rutan procreate with binary fission,' Rupert explained. 'Two identical Rutan are produced. The temporal malfunction did something similar. One of me arrived in 1822, another in 1902. The other me's pod was damaged, and so it did not know it had travelled back in time. Thus, as per its training, it did what any Rutan would do. It killed and replaced a local and sought a way to secure the planet for the glorious Rutan Queen. The distress signal of course got picked up in the future, a result of the temporal displacement caused by the osmic projector existing in both 1823 and 1969, with a duplicate of the projector existing in the crashed pod of 1902. Three time travel devices emitting the same signal on a quantum level. The signal got mixed up and brought the mothership to Earth, but when the mothership tried to respond to the signal directly it got caught up in the quantum slipstream caused by the duplicated time machine, and it shifted back to 1902 when we sent you forward. And there it was destroyed by... Well, a friend of yours.'

Anne smiled. 'The colonel was right about that at least. But what of yourself?'

'I have embraced humanity, as you told me to. It has not always been easy, but most days I forget I was born a Rutan. I live as a human, I think as a human. I do not even miss the presence of the hive mind. But this is not why I called you.'

'It isn't?'

'No. Before you return to the Vault—'

'How do you know about that?'

Rupert held out his feeble-looking hands. 'Anne, look at me. I have lived a *very* long time on this planet, I know about a lot of things I shouldn't.' Anne conceded the point and took another sip of her coffee. 'You must speak to Colonel Lethbridge-Stewart,' Rupert continued. 'Tell him that Earth is in danger, and make sure the pod from Fang Rock, the technology I left behind, does not fall into the hands of your paymasters. Consider it a gift for Lethbridge-Stewart.' He looked up towards the ceiling, but with an expression which suggested his gaze penetrated through to something greater. 'Out there the war rages on. Two machines of war, evenly matched.' He laughed. 'They don't even remember what they're fighting over, they've been fighting for so long. It's only a matter of time before the war finds its way to Earth,

263

especially now that both militia are aware of Earth's current level of technology. Level five. It should be protected by galactic law,' he said with a bitter laugh. 'It won't be.'

'And how do you suppose I tell Lethbridge-Stewart about this?' Anne asked. 'It's not that I don't believe you, but I can hardly tell him about you.'

'Of course not. I am harmless... mostly. But the threat of war is not. Tell him that you forgot in all the confusion, that I told you in 1823.'

Anne nodded slowly. 'Yes, that might work. I don't think he's made his report to Hamilton yet, and this information might ease things for him a little, help him get what he wants. Okay, I'll do it.'

'That is all I ask. I like this planet, the people on it. I suppose I've grown quite attached to it.' With a smile, Rupert finished his tea and stood. He held out a hand. 'Goodbye, Anne. I daresay we'll meet again, but when we do, I won't look like this.'

Anne stood. Beneath his hat, she could see his features subtly shifting. 'Why change now?'

'I am a long way from death. Perhaps I will never die. Either way, Rupert Slant can't live forever. It's time for the other partner to take over. Erica has been going on to me about handing over my share for a long time.' He turned and moved away from the table, but glanced back once more. 'Until next time, Doctor Travers.'

She watched him go, her mind still struggling with all that she had learned. Not just in the last half hour, but from all of the events that had surrounded her for the last few weeks, ever since Rupert had called her back to London. She shook her head. She felt terribly sad – bereaved almost.

This was silly. He was an alien, not an old friend saying goodbye for the last time. But that's what it felt like; as if she was watching a friend leave her life.

She couldn't allow it.

Anne rushed out of the café, calling 'wait' as she went. She stepped out onto Ganton Street and looked around. She couldn't see Rupert, and as she nearly tripped over a pile of clothing on the pavement, she realised why he had dressed in such heavy clothes and hat. To hide what he was really wearing. She reached down and picked up the coat and hat. Around her young people continued about their daily lives. Rupert could have been any of them. He could even have been that blonde-haired young woman turning into Carnaby Street. Well, she could have been if Rupert knew a sailor with fair hair, since as Anne watched one came over and after a brief exchange of words and smiles linked arms with the woman. Anne watched them walk out of sight and sighed. Rupert said they'd meet again. She had to hold onto that. One thing she would never do, however, was tell Lethbridge-Stewart that she was friends with an alien – a Rutan, to boot. The enemy. Her friend.

It was a new dawn, and the lighthouse of Fang Rock remained as it always had. Watching, guarding the rocks, protecting those who dared to tread its shores.

> *Far in the bosom of the deep*
> *O'er these wild shelves my watch I keep,*
> *A ruddy gem of changeful light*
> *Bound on the dusky brow of night.*
> 'Pharos Loquitor' by Walter Scott, 1814.

Working with Nicholas Courtney

Although I had the good fortune to appear in other *Doctor Who* stories with other Doctors, I only worked once with Nicholas Courtney. This in itself must constitute some kind of record considering his long and distinguished contribution to the series over several decades! It turned out that his debut as Colonel Lethbridge-Stewart in *The Web of Fear* was to presage an entire 'military' and actor's career devoted to the role.

There are stories that he was originally meant to be cast as Captain Knight, the role I played. No one ever mentioned this to me at the time – not even Nick – but if it was so then (director) Douglas Camfield must have realised very quickly that, unlike myself, Nick Courtney's whole demeanour gave off the subtle aroma of the 'gently-born' – the naturally posh. He had, and this is a great compliment, a PG Wodehouse way with him. An air that suggested, despite an impeccable work-ethic, that he should be elsewhere, in a Pall Mall club perhaps, or shooting grouse, drinking chota-pegs, falling in love farcically with the wrong gal, entertaining formidable aunts, playing polo, etc.

In *The Web of Fear* I had, as plotted, to regard him with suspicion; a bogus officer, especially wearing that silly Glengarry cap, but it was obvious, despite the storyline, that here was the genuine article, born with a field marshal's baton in his play-pen.

One of the underlying tensions which animate the scenes in *The Web of Fear* leading to Captain Knight's death is surely that between our characters and leadership of the men; between the period's up and coming Grammar School, hard-working, 'own bootstraps' new officer class and the Public School educated, doing what comes naturally 'my family have always been soldiers' type. Today's Army list demonstrates the success of the former; most officers interviewed on radio and TV in recent conflicts demonstrate their class origins without any self-consciousness – parading a variety of regional accents in reply to questions. How right Douglas Camfield was all those years ago! Lethbridge-Stewart was a good personification of the fair minded, 'cares for his men', tactically ruthless and super-efficient officer of the Old-School (think Monty!) – it says much about Nick that he was able to sustain this character for forty years.

As I've said, I never worked with him again after this, his initial appearance in *Doctor Who*. We met afterwards, of course, in places like the BBC Bar and canteens of various kinds in BBC Television Centre, or the newly built East Acton Hilton, as the new BBC rehearsal studios became to be known, and particularly in Equity meetings. His work for Equity – a council member – is documented elsewhere and though we were at different ends of the political spectrum he was never less than charmingly courteous – as his name truthfully suggested – and fair-minded even when we disagreed.

So here's to him, Nicholas Courtney – Lethbridge-Stewart, an officer and a gentleman.

Working on Horror of Fang Rock

Paddy Russell directed *Horror of Fang Rock*; she was one of the TV directors created by television. Initially an actress she moved into 'stage-management' in the television sense of the job description – eventually becoming one of the first women Floor Managers – that is the director's executive in the studio whilst they are working in the gallery with the screen technicians away from the actual set. In this capacity she worked with possibly the greatest TV director of the times, Rudolph Cartier. She then became one of the first two women directors in television which at that time was a male dominated profession – and so apart from directing, unlike the men, had to continually prove her 'worthiness' in the job.

By the time *Horror of Fang Rock* came around she had a huge amount of experience over a wide range of TV drama including directing *Doctor Who* with William Hartnell, Jon Pertwee and the new to the role Tom Baker. I had first met her in the *Z-Cars* series where I had been an amateur house-painter villain! I'd enjoyed working with her and so looked forward to playing Ben Travers in what turned out to be a popular and fascinating *Doctor Who* tale.

I soon became aware that shooting it wasn't so straightforward as the script suggested. The script was erratic, although the storyline was strong some transitional scenes were sketchy and didn't bear too much examination. The sudden presence of a party of shipwrecked upper-class persons seemed a bit extra and really unexplained. The Rutans without the aid of modern technology and special effects were the rudimentary 'green blob' of early sci-fi. The episodes were to be shot in Birmingham at Pebble Mill, this meant removing Tom from his familiar London watering holes and the Soho scene. It's a matter of record that he and Louise hadn't as yet sorted out their acting relationship – indeed she records on the DVD that it was in this story that they both resolved the snags in their respective roles. So there was a tension in the air.

John Abbot, new to the medium of TV found himself having to cope with acting as a young lighthouse keeper with no visible set, no sea, acting against blue screens whilst twelve feet up in the air – with Tom teasing him by acting in eight different styles in rehearsal and then quite differently on the takes. The Pebble Mill TV team had never shot *Doctor Who*-type drama before – and yet rose wonderfully to the occasion – nothing was too much trouble or effort and they generated a keenness and excitement that was beginning to be lacking in BBC TV Centre. Thank goodness Paddy's stature was such that she was able to weed all this discourse into a solid structural drama full of notable parts, Colin Douglas, Alan Rowe, Louise (outwardly a Victorian Miss, inwardly a warrior), Sean Caffrey all gave memorable characterisations.

One of the most enjoyable aspects for me working on *Horror of Fang Rock* was acting with Colin Douglas. He was a stalwart of TV in those days, about nine hundred parts in a wide range of roles – not least the patriarch in *Family at War*.

To me he was a very special friend and colleague. Perhaps the first of the 'Drama Docs' as they were then called was *Close the Coalhouse Door*. This was a series of episodes spun out of the Golden Wedding celebrations of a retired Geordie miner and his family. Based on stories by Syd Chaplin it spanned the whole history of mining for coal, the miners' struggle for wages, formation of unions, lockouts and strikes, etc – all taking place with songs, a thirty-two-piece silverband, words and music by Alex Glasgow, script by Alan Parker, directed by BBC TV director Bill Hayes. In it Colin played the old miner and I played his grandson – the one who had escaped mining via university. Both of us Geordies, both of us with mining connections in our families.

We had played and sung together on stage, TV, on tour round Britain and in the West End for over two years. I mention all this because it meant that when we came to act together on *Horror of Fang Rock* – from first rehearsal onwards we were able to establish a really strong and prior relationship between our characters from the word go.

The tension between us – the old lighthouse ways and the 'modern' electric system which underlies our sparring with each other in *Horror of Fang Rock*, unknown to the *Doctor Who* TV audience, mirrored the struggle between old and new mining techniques our characters had played in *Close the Coalhouse Door* for years.

I think this explains the depth and rapport and ease in our few short scenes together, and it gives viewers a memorable character which makes for a real situation on

which the rest of the tale is built. The pleasure of working
together again was an added joy.

Ralph Watson, October 2015

Mutually Assured Domination

As they neared it, the scale of the installation became apparent. It loomed like a leviathan out of the fog. A central block-like building was ringed by a number of smaller structures, all windowless, with bright searchlights at each corner shining out into the mist. Other smaller huts and outbuildings were scattered around the central structures, and the whole thing was surrounded by a high wire fence topped with barbed wire. More lights sat atop the posts supporting the fence, casting blue-white beams through the whiteness. A distant humming and a sharp, minty chemical tang laced the misty air.

Keith racked his brains, as they walked up to the fence, as to what it could be. Some government installation, or something to do with the military? Could be – it was lit up like a Christmas tree; whoever owned it clearly didn't care who knew it was there. It had to be pretty new, as it wasn't on the map, or in the guide book.

Whatever it was, it represented civilisation.

The two hikers stood staring up at the fence.

'Looks deserted,' muttered Marie, some of her good humour deflated by the sight of the seemingly impregnable industrial fortress.

'Come on, let's find the main gate.'

They set off alongside the chain-link fence, but they walked the entire length of it without finding sign of an entrance. They did find, however, a sign with big white lettering on a red background, bearing the legend:

DOMINEX INDUSTRIES
KEEP OUT!
TRESPASSERS WILL BE DESTROYED

Keith snorted. 'Destroyed! Ridiculous. Someone's having a laugh.'

But Marie looked scared. 'Come on, Keith, let's get away from this place – I don't like it.'

The sign annoyed Keith and he felt personally insulted by the over-the-top threat. He walked up to the fence, kicked it. 'Hey, there's a loose bit here!'

At the base of one of the fence posts, the concrete had crumbled away from the pins supporting the wire. Keith pulled the chain-link back and the resulting gap was easily big enough to admit them.

'Keith, no… Let's try your other idea; find the road back to Buckfastleigh.'

'Nuts to that,' grunted Keith, who was already forcing his way through the gap. 'I want to meet these idiots and tell them where to shove their sign.'

With a final tug at the wire he was through, and he stared back at Marie through the wire-diamonds of the fence. 'Well, come on!'

With great reluctance she followed him through and soon they stood on the fresh tarmac, in the glare of the lights. In front of them the grey corrugated wall of an outbuilding rose like a cliff face. Bright white searchlights blazed down at them.

Keith felt rebellious excitement well up within him. 'Right!' he said and strode off towards the outbuilding.

'Keith...' Marie trailed in his wake, hugging her bare arms to herself. 'This is stupid. I don't wanna be destroyed!'

'We won't be destroyed!' Keith scoffed. 'This is England, they can't shoot us just for trespassing.'

An enormous voice, seeming to come from all around them, bellowed, 'Stop!'

Keith and Marie froze, caught like rabbits in the headlights.

'Do not move!' The voice was male and sounded psychotically angry.

Keith found Marie's hand and gripped it tightly. 'Look, we're sorry! We'll just turn around and go away.'

'Please don't destroy us!' Marie wailed.

'Shut up!' Keith hissed. 'We got lost in the mist,' he called out once Marie was quiet. 'We hoped you'd help us...'

His voice trailed off as, with a smooth action and a mechanical whining noise, a hatch in the corrugated grey wall opened, and two figures emerged. Two things.

Their bodies were robust grey blocks of what looked like lead, their heads spherical, split into textured octants, with crystalline spikes protruding from each side, fore and aft, and on top. They walked on shuffling shoebox feet, and, from the front of their bodies, rudimentary, oblong arms extended, deadly-looking apertures gaping at the ends. They were about five feet tall. The things, whatever they were, made constant burbling, chirping noises. They looked like oversized, demonic children's toys, or robots from a science fiction play on the telly.

'What the hell are they?' Keith cried, surprised at how loud and stupid his voice sounded.

The two improbable objects paused in their advance, and stood a few metres away, their blocky arms waving back and forth as if to swat flies away. They looked ridiculous – but also somehow sinister. One of them – or perhaps both of them, Keith could see no mouths in those spherical heads – spoke, in high, piercing, almost childlike voices which made his ears hurt.

'Shall we destroy? Shall we destroy?'

'Affirmative!' the giant voice bellowed again, making Keith and Marie jump. 'Quarks – deploy and destroy! Destroy! Destroy!'

Keith and Marie watched as the Quarks changed. Their box-like bodies split open and they rose up on mechanical cantilever legs. A profusion of lethal looking protrusions bristled forth from their unfolding bodies.

The Quarks towered ten feet tall. They stepped forward in unison.

Keith unshouldered the rucksack and hurled it at the nearest Quark. It bounced off its gunmetal grey armature and fell away uselessly to one side. The thing didn't even seem to notice.

The bristling machines stepped closer, stooping over their prey. There was a cold, calculated, smooth and deadly precision to their movements. Keith found himself staring right down the barrel of what was unmistakably some sort of weapon.

No way. No way. No way was this it, no way was this

the end of his life! What about his degree, what about his parents, what about Marie, what about the kids he suddenly realised he wanted to have?

Keith looked desperately at Marie, who was sobbing and trembling with fear like a cornered animal. He tried to find words of reassurance but all he could do was shout. 'Sorry! I'm sorry!'

Though the Quarks' forms had grown, their voices remained that of gleeful, cruel children. 'Destroy! Destroy!' they trilled.

Keith turned to run, yanking the shrieking Marie after him, but it was too late, far too late. Keith heard a colossal roar of energy, and felt an intense, burning fire engulfing him. He felt Marie's hand slip from his, heard her scream in mortal agony. He howled in helpless rage and searing pain as shuddering pulses of heat slammed through him, and died. His last thought was of Marie's face, laughing in the sunshine.

Thanks

Much like the TV story on which it is based, *Beast of Fang Rock* was a replacement story after another fell through. It was always intended to be in the Lethbridge-Stewart line-up, but not until 2017. Was never my intention to write more than one book every couple of years. Alas, things change, and we have to adapt to make them work. As such, *Beast of Fang Rock* was written during the upheaval surrounding the production of the previous book, and it couldn't have succeeded without the help of the following. Thanks especially go to (in no particular order):

Shaun, Hayley, and Will and all the guys at Candy Jar Books for their continued hard work. Terrance Dicks for giving me such a wonderful set of toys to play with. Paul Leonard for allowing me to use elements of his novel, *The Revolution Man*. Chris Williams at Nash Point Lighthouse for his insights into the keeper life and the history of Trinity House. Kevin Nolan for all things military. RM Ballatyne (and his diary from 1865) for the wonderful insight into the past lives of light keepers. Colin Howard for the frankly awesome cover. Tina Packer for being so brilliant as Anne Travers (hope you love your star billing on the cover). Louise Jameson for the fantastic foreword. Hannah Haisman for continued support and trust. James Rudge for allowing me to turn him into a female hippie. Adam & Garry for continued support at the Big Blue Box podcast, and Glenn, Keith & Shaun at Travelling the Vortex. Sam Hunt, Alexandra & Kevan Looseley-Saul, Owen Luckhurst and all the gang at The Who Shop. Ralph Watson for support and allowing me to turn him into a werewolf on the cover, and for being so brilliant as Ben in *Horror of Fang Rock* (special thanks to his son, Alex, for liaising). Gareth Starling, for always being a good and honest (and not at all insulting) friend. Gary Russell for the Vault and, as ever, starting me on this ride. Adrian Rigelsford for endless waffle and help.

And last, but by no means least, to all of my followers on Facebook and Twitter. For the support, humour and inspiration, and for reminding me how much you were all waiting to read this book: Yes, it's a sequel to one of the best *Doctor Who* stories – what pressure?

Andy Frankham-Allen, Cardiff, October 2015

Available from Candy Jar Books

LETHBRIDGE-STEWART: THE FORGOTTEN SON
by Andy Frankham-Allen

For Colonel Alistair Lethbridge-Stewart his life in the Scots Guards was straightforward enough; rising in the ranks through nineteen years of military service. But then his regiment was assigned to help combat the Yeti incursion in London, the robotic soldiers of an alien entity known as the Great Intelligence. For Lethbridge-Stewart, life would never be the same again.

Meanwhile in the small Cornish village of Bledoe a man is haunted by the memory of an accident thirty years old. The Hollow Man of Remington Manor seems to have woken once more. And in Coleshill, Buckinghamshire, Mary Gore is plagued by the voice of a small boy, calling her home.

What connects these strange events to the recent Yeti incursion, and just what has it all to do with Lethbridge-Stewart?

"A solid start to the series. The Brigadier is such an integral part of Doctor Who mythos, it seems right and proper he now has his own series." – Doctor Who Magazine

ISBN: 978-0-9931191-5-6